THE CORPSE ON
THE COURT

THE CORPSE ON THE COURT

SIMON BRETT

W🌐RLDWIDE₍ᵣ₎

TORONTO • NEW YORK • LONDON
AMSTERDAM • PARIS • SYDNEY • HAMBURG
STOCKHOLM • ATHENS • TOKYO • MILAN
MADRID • WARSAW • BUDAPEST • AUCKLAND

Recycling programs
for this product may
not exist in your area.

The Corpse on the Court

A Worldwide Mystery/March 2018

First published by Crème de la Crime, an imprint of
Severn House Publishers Ltd.

ISBN-13: 978-1-335-50650-4

Printed in U.S.A.

To
David and Sinead

ONE

'FORTY-FIFTEEN! Chase more than a yard worse!' called out the young marker, and the pairs of white-clad players changed ends.

To Jude his words made about as much sense as if she'd stumbled into a science fiction alternative universe. She knew the game they were playing was called 'real tennis' and that 'real' in this context meant 'royal'. She even knew, because Piers had told her, that in America the game was called 'court tennis'. But though he had spent painstaking hours spelling them out to her, she still hadn't a clue what thse rules were.

To be fair, it was the first time she'd been inside a real tennis court. Up until that moment her knowledge of the game had been entirely theoretical. 'It'll all make sense when you actually see the place,' Piers kept telling her airily. So far his optimistic view was not being borne out. Maybe if he were sitting beside her in what she had been assured was called the 'dedans', he might have been able to provide a running commentary on what was going on. But Piers Targett was one of the four players on court, clearly engrossed in this incomprehensible contest.

Jude had had lovers before who'd been interested in sport—not many, it was true, more had come from the artistic community—but this was the first time she had encountered one who was into real tennis.

She looked around the court, trying to make sense of it. When he'd first mentioned the game—on their first date at Arbutus—Piers had said, 'You know, like at Hampton Court. Everyone's seen the one at Hampton Court...where King Henry VIII played...saggy net...you *kn*ow,' he had concluded airily. 'Airy', Jude had soon discovered was Piers Targett's conversational default setting.

Jude had been taken to Hampton Court as a small girl, but her main recollection of the occasion had been of crying when she got lost in the maze. Maybe King Henry's tennis court had been pointed out to her, but it had not proved memorable to her childish preoccupations.

The court she surveyed that Sunday morning had been constructed in the late nineteenth century by the family who built the adjacent Lockleigh House on the foothills of the South Downs, about midway between Clincham and Fedborough. The Wardocks had made a lot of money in that period's boom in lawn tennis—or 'lawners', as Piers always referred to the upstart—but they had retained an interest in the much older version of the game.

Members of the Wardock family had continued to live in Lockleigh House until the end of the Second World War when declining business and increasing costs had forced them to sell up. Since that time the mansion had had various incarnations...as a hotel, a boy's prep school, and for the last twenty years as the Lockleigh House Nursing Home for the Elderly. The tennis court was owned by the care home company, who leased it out to the Lockleigh House Tennis Club. Some four hundred members kept the court fairly busy from the first hour-and-a-quarter booking at seven forty-five in the morning to the last at eight fifteen p.m.

The 'dedans' in which Jude had been told she was sitting was at one end of the rectangular court. Benches were arranged in rows behind a large slot in the wall, the shape of a giant letterbox. The purpose of this was clearly not just so that the spectators could see the action. Every time a ball thundered into the dedans it prompted clapping, so clearly a point had been scored. And given the speed at which the hard balls arrived, there was comfort in the fact that stout netting stopped them from hitting the spectators.

The atmosphere among those watching was distinctly benign. Though clearly absorbed in the game, they had an air of levity about them. Applause was accorded to what Jude assumed was good play, but there were also a lot of cheery insults called out between points. Though Piers was the only person in the court who Jude knew, she felt very welcome there.

The young man who was marking the game sat at the far end of the front bench in the dedans, calling out ever more obscure—to Jude—incantations, like 'better than the door', 'hazard chase the line' and 'more than a yard worse'. He had been introduced to her as 'Ned Jackson, our junior pro' and his was one of the few names she had retained from the list that Piers had reeled out to her on their arrival.

She had also taken on board the information that the event being contested that Sunday morning was the Secretary's Cup, known rather waggishly to all members of the Club as 'The Sec's Cup'. During their drive down from Bayswater in his E-Type Jaguar (Carmen red with black leather upholstery) Piers had explained to her that this was 'a doubles competition with random pairings'. His allocated partner was a teenage girl called Tonya Grace. Piers and Tonya had won through the preliminary rounds on the Saturday to earn a place in the finals.

He had also once again tried to describe the court to her, and once again assured her airily that it'd all make sense when she saw the thing.

It didn't, though. The area was probably about the same size as a lawn tennis court, but it was walled in. The floor was mostly painted in oxblood red, though a section at the far end was green. Different coloured lines, parallel to the net, were marked on the surface. On the walls, presumably to identify these lines, large numerals were painted.

Maybe twenty feet above the ground the side walls became large windows, leading up to a pitched glass roof. Although this transparent ceiling shed quite a lot of daylight on the court, between the rafters hung large silver-shaded lamps to illuminate the playing area. Along either side at the level of the windows were wooden walkways, presumably to give access for cleaning and maintenance.

On the wall to her left and the one facing her, Jude could see sloping roofs about ten feet off the ground. And the sound of balls bouncing on the wood above her head suggested that the dedans was covered by a similar penthouse. They looked like covered walkways and indeed under the long one was the passageway through which she had been escorted to her spectating position. The walls beneath this long roof only rose to about three feet; above that wooden support posts divided the space into window-like sections. Like the dedans, these recesses were backed by strong netting, presumably for the same reasons of safety.

On the right-hand wall at the far end was another strange feature, a rectangular recess that looked like a blocked-off window.

Just when Jude was reckoning that her survey had found enough architectural eccentricities, she noticed that towards the end of the long right-hand wall a section jutted out from floor to ceiling. For no apparent reason. Or no more reason than was offered by the other oddities she'd observed. But she did notice that any ball hitting this angled feature was likely to fly off all over the place.

And of course there was the saggy net that Piers had promised. Maybe as high as five feet at the sides, going down in an inverted arc to about three in the middle.

Another oddity to puzzle anyone who had only previously watched lawn tennis was the proliferation of balls on the court. Fifty, maybe sixty, accumulated at the foot of the net or in a wooden runnel in the dedans. The balls were covered in yellow felt and about the size of their lawn tennis cousins. But their minimal bouncing capacity and the sound they made when they hit the wooden parts of the court suggested they were a lot harder.

There was something odd about the rackets too. For a start, their frames were made of wood, which should perhaps have raised memories of long summer afternoon duels between Bjorn Borg and John McEnroe. But the shape was wrong for such comparisons. Bizarrely, the real tennis rackets were not symmetrical.

The head came out at a slight angle from the handle, giving the impression of a bent spoon. The alternative reality that Jude had felt herself a part of was now veering into Alice in Wonderland territory.

Her confused scrutiny was interrupted by the sound of a bell ringing and an eruption of applause from the benches in the dedans.

Time to seek help. She turned to the woman next to her and asked pitifully, 'What happened then?'

'Winning gallery,' came the reply.

'Ah.'

The blankness on Jude's face prompted the woman to ask, 'Don't you know the game?'

'First time I've seen a real tennis court.'

The woman smiled knowingly. 'Welcome to a world of obsession and eccentricity. My name, by the way, is Oenone Playfair.'

'Jude.'

A thin hand reached out to grasp her plump one. 'Sorry about the Oenone. My father had a classical education.' Jude must have looked blank again, because the woman immediately provided a gloss for her. 'Oenone was Paris' first wife. The one he dumped when he went off after Helen of Troy.' She spoke very quickly, her words tumbling together in the manner of an enthusiastic academic.

'Ah,' said Jude.

'Well, I suppose if you're going to be dumped for anyone, Helen of Troy at least has class. Better than your husband going off with his secretary...or the checkout girl at Tesco.'

'I suppose so. Anyway, sorry, you just said something about a winning gallery...?'

'Right. Yes, of course you're new to all this. Don't worry, it only takes about ten years to understand the rudiments of the game.'

'Thanks very much. Do you play?'

Oenone Playfair grimaced. 'Oh yes. Haven't been on the court since I had my hip replaced, though. First operation didn't work, dammit…so it'll soon be a few months before I'm back playing.'

Jude was surprised. Her question had only been a polite enquiry. It hadn't occurred to her that Oenone, who had to be well into her seventies, might really still play the game.

'Anyway, the winning gallery…' her new friend twittered on and pointed down the left-hand side of the court. 'Last gallery down the hazard end…any ball that goes in there is an outright winner. And there's a bell hung on the netting, which should ring…' Jude understood that bit. 'Though sometimes if the ball goes in for a chase in hazard second, that can make it ring too.' And once again Jude was lost.

'So that player—' she indicated a grey-haired, red-faced man whose portly belly raised the bottom of his shirt sufficiently to reveal a half-moon of flesh above the top of his shorts— 'has just scored a point by hitting the ball into the winning gallery?'

'Exactly.' Oenone nodded vigorously. 'Yes, a shot in the winning gallery is the Holy Grail for real tennis players…and I can guarantee I'll never hear the end of it.' Jude raised an interrogative eyebrow. 'He's my husband. Reggie.'

'Ah, so that's why you're here?'

'I'd have come even if Reggie hadn't made it to the finals. The Sec's Cup's always good fun.' Oenone

Playfair looked at Jude shrewdly. 'Any particular reason why you're here?'

Jude gestured to the court. 'I'm with him.'

The older woman nodded, as if some small mystery had just been explained to her. 'Ah, you're Piers' latest.'

Jude wasn't quite sure that she relished that definition, but she didn't comment, and further conversation was interrupted by a tap on Oenone's shoulder from a tall, grey-haired man in pebble glasses. He was dressed in ordinary clothes rather than tennis whites, a large-checked sports jacket and mulberry-coloured corduroy trousers. His thinly knotted tie featured crossed gold rackets under the emblem of a fish on a background of purple and green stripes. Other men in the dedans were wearing the same, so presumably it was the Lockleigh House club tie. And in fact Jude noticed the same logo in the blocked window feature at the other end of the court.

The man shook his head. 'Sitting there without a drink I see, Oenone—tut, tut. Can I get you one?' His voice sounded as if it had been marinated in superior claret.

Oenone Playfair declared that she wouldn't say no to a Sauvignon Blanc, then continued, 'Wally, may I introduce Jude?'

He reached forward to take the newcomer's hand. 'Enchanted,' he said, and he clearly was. Over the years Jude had got used to the appreciative eyes of men, even now that she was fatter and in her fifties. 'My name's Wally Edgington-Bewley.'

'Today's Jude's first time inside a real tennis court.'

'Is it really, Oenone? Well, Jude, we must celebrate

that fact by my buying you a drink. Would Sauvignon Blanc fit the bill for you too?'

Jude looked around. Though it was not yet eleven o'clock in the morning, many of the spectators—even some dressed in white and presumably soon to go on court—were nursing wine glasses. Be churlish not to join them.

So she replied, 'That'd be fine, thank you…unless there's a bottle of Chardonnay open.'

'Of course. Chardonnay it is.'

An elegant woman in a beautifully-cut tweed suit took a seat a little way away from them in the dedans. Probably in her sixties, she must once have been absolutely stunning and still looked pretty good. Bright blue eyes and hair so skilfully coloured that its blondness could actually have been natural. Wally turned to her with his customary charm. 'Just going on a drinks run, Felicity. Get you a snifter?'

She smiled, revealing perfectly maintained teeth and replied in a perfectly modulated voice, 'Bit early in the day for me, Wally.'

'Right you are. Oh, Felicity, can I introduce Jude? She's here with Piers. First time she's seen a real tennis court.'

'Ah.' The woman's blue eyes politely appraised the newcomer. She reached out a slender hand for Jude to shake. 'I'm Felicity Budgen.'

'Wife of our esteemed chairman,' said Wally. 'Right, off on my drinks run. One Sauvignon Blanc, one Chardonnay. And when I return, Jude, I will tell you all about the game of real tennis.'

'Oh, I'd like that.'

'Be careful what you wish for,' murmured Oenone as soon as Wally Edgington-Bewley was out of earshot.

'What do you mean?'

'Wally is a kind of historian of the game. Knows more about it than probably anyone on the planet. Even written a book on the subject. If he's going to tell you "all about the game of real tennis", I'd make sure you've got a couple of weeks free.'

'Oh, right. Well, thanks for the warning.'

'And would you be able to have a couple of weeks free?'

'Sorry?'

'It's my rather contrived and roundabout way of asking what you do.'

'Ah. Well, I'm a kind of alternative therapist.'

'Healer?'

'That kind of thing, yes.'

'Maybe I should get you to take a look at Reggie.'

'Oh?'

'Well, look at him.' Oenone Playfair gestured towards the court as if pointing out a particularly uncontrollable puppy. 'He doesn't take care of himself at all. He's seventy-four next year, and he's had a couple of heart scares. I keep trying to get him to make some changes in his lifestyle, but will he? Will he hell.'

And as Jude saw Reggie Playfair puff his way to miss another ball, she could see what his wife meant. His face was redder than ever and sweat dripped off nose and chin. Individual damp patches on his white shirt were starting to join together.

Oenone raised her eyes to heaven, expressing the hopelessness of trying to make her husband change in any particular, then asked, 'So do you do your heal-ing work at home?'

'Yes.'

'And where is home?'

'Fethering. Do you know it?'

'Of course. Just down from Fedborough. Where the River Fether reaches the sea.'

'Exactly.'

'And you're kept busy, are you…you know, with the healing?'

'It varies.' And with a feeling that was uncharacter-istically close to guilt, Jude realized that she hadn't ac-tually treated any clients for a couple of weeks. Hadn't actually been to her home, Woodside Cottage, for a couple of weeks. Since Piers Targett had come into her life. Or since she had moved into Piers Targett's life.

Something happened on the court that prompted raucous applause and cheering. 'Game, set and match!' called out Ned Jackson, for the first time that morn-ing saying something that Jude could understand. She watched the four players exchange handshakes over the low scoop of the net.

'Reggie will be insufferable now,' Oenone Play-fair observed.

'I'm sorry? Why?'

'Well, they won—didn't you notice? Means they'll go through to the semis.'

'Ah.'

'And Reggie will be particularly pleased to have beaten your Piers. There's always been quite a lot of rivalry between those two.'

'Friendly rivalry, I hope.'

'Oh, yes, friendly…not that that means it doesn't go deep.'

They looked up at the arrival of the four players in the dedans. Reggie immediately found a bottle of red wine and poured a glass, which he quaffed with relish. Piers, crossing towards Jude, ruffled his hand ruefully through her bird's nest of blonde hair. 'Not my brilliant best this morning, I'm afraid.' He grinned at Oenone. 'See you two've met. What've you been putting in the old man's cocoa? He was on fire.'

'Who'll they be playing in the semi?'

'Whoever wins the next one.'

Jude looked with pleasure at Piers Targett. Though in his sixties, he didn't have the kind of metabolism that put on weight and looked surprisingly trim. His hair was white but abundant and he wore it almost foppishly long with a centre parting. Eyes of a surprisingly deep blue. The recent exertions on the tennis court had not raised a sweat on his pristine polo shirt. His long white trousers were neatly creased, with a knotted striped old school tie doing service as a belt.

He turned at the approach of his young doubles partner, who had just been chatting with Felicity Budgen. The girl was pretty with black hair and ice-blue eyes. She moved coltishly as if she hadn't quite got used to her long limbs. 'Sorry, Tonya,' said Piers with mock humility. 'If the way I was playing this morning doesn't give you the message to steer clear of old men, then nothing will.'

The girl smiled nervously. On the court she had looked secure; she had been well taught, moving effortlessly into the right positions and returning the ball with a strength that was surprising in one so slender.

Outside the game, however, she was awkward, aware of her juvenile status amongst so many older people.

'Bad luck, Tonya,' Oenone Playfair commiserated and was rewarded by another edgy grin. 'How are Roman and Natalya?'

'Oh, you know. Grandpa's lost it a bit, really.'

'Yes, so I'd heard. Oh, sorry, this is Jude.'

'Nice to meet you,' said the girl politely.

'Anyway, Tonya,' said Piers, 'let me get you a drink by way of apology for my appalling tennis. What would you like?

'Oh, just a Coke, please, thank you.'

'Sure. And what about you ladies? Oenone...?'

'Wally's getting drinks for us.'

'What a gentleman that Wally is.' Piers grinned ruefully at an approaching young man in a smart blue tracksuit. 'Sorry, George, my volleying was all over the shop this morning. Forgot everything you told me in that last lesson.'

The man grinned back. 'Can't win 'em all.'

'No, winning some would be nice, though. George, must introduce you to a friend of mine. Jude, this is George Hazlitt, the club's senior pro.'

'Nice to meet you.'

'You too.' The professional smiled the smile of a man who had never doubted his attractiveness to women.

'George used to be top five in the world,' said Piers.

'A while ago, mind.' This was said with a self-depreciating grin. Close to, George Hazlitt was older than he had first appeared, probably well into his forties. It was his extreme fitness that made him look young.

He moved away. 'I'll take over the marking for this one, Ned,' he said. 'You go and get a cup of coffee.'

'Thanks, George.' The younger pro slid off his bench. As he moved through the crowd, he came face to face with Tonya Grace. Jude noticed the two of them exchange a private grin. Then the girl blushed and turned away.

A new pair of doubles was now knocking up on court, so George Hazlitt's marking skills were not yet required. To Jude's amazement she saw him pick up a bag from beside the bench where he was sitting and start sewing. Yes, no question about it. He had some pieces of yellow felt which he was sewing together with a large needle. His movements were practised, automatic; he hardly looked at what he was doing.

Jude nudged Oenone Playfair and nodded her head towards the Pro. 'Does he have a side line in embroidery?' she whispered.

The older woman grinned. 'No, he's making balls.' Seeing Jude's puzzlement, she went on, 'Real tennis balls are handmade—and they don't last long. It's part of the professional's job to keep up the supply.'

'Ladies, your drinks,' announced the marinated voice of Wally Edgington-Bewley. 'Now, Jude, move along a bit, make room for me...and I will regale you with the complete history of the ancient game of real tennis...'

It MUST HAVE been about half past twelve. Jude was on her third glass of Chardonnay and feeling no pain. From the club room area behind the dedans wafted intriguingly spicy smells. Piers had promised her that 'the lunches are always very good for the Sec's Cup—

there's an Indian member who does these amazing curries on the Sunday.' The smells made her realize that she was very hungry. She'd only snatched a slice of toast by way of breakfast at Piers' Bayswater flat. And that had been before seven o'clock.

Still, Jude was quite content. Though Wally Edgington-Bewley had continued to ply her with dates and statistics, she hadn't taken any of it in. She had remained sitting with Oenone Playfair, but their circle had widened as Piers introduced her to more of the real tennis fraternity. She was struck by how nice they all were. And a little surprised by how mixed. Though she heard a good few hyphenated names and cut-glass vowels, there were plenty of members whose voices suggested much humbler origins.

But the main thing that impressed Jude was how much they all seemed to like Piers Targett. The whirlwind of their romance over the previous few weeks had not involved much socializing with other people. But Piers had been committed to participating in the Secretary's Cup before they'd met, so this was really the first time he had introduced Jude to any of his friends. And she enjoyed seeing him in a context where he so clearly felt at ease.

On the court Reggie Playfair and his partner were playing their semi-final match. And they were finding the going tougher than they had in the previous round. Their opponents were both fit men in their thirties and though, according to Piers, they were 'giving away a lot in the handicap' (whatever that meant), they were making few mistakes and slowly grinding down the older pair. His partner was coping with the pressure better, but there was now an air of desperation about the way Reggie hurled his ageing body around the court.

In spite of everything Piers had told her and the information overload supplied by Wally Edgington-Bewley, Jude still hadn't grasped the basic rules of real tennis. During the rallies, she could vaguely understand what was going on, but the scoring and the reasons why the players kept changing ends left her completely baffled. She didn't mind, though. Calmed by Chardonnay, she settled into cheerful incomprehension and let her mind wander.

Suddenly there was a commotion at the far end of the court. Jude missed the first impact, but it looked as though Reggie Playfair had slipped and crashed into the side wall. The consternation among the spectators, however, suggested something more serious. Oenone seemed frozen in shock. George Hazlitt was instantly up from his bench and in charge of the situation. 'Henry, you're a doctor. Go and check him out. I'll get the defibrillator.' And the professional was suddenly running up the passageway alongside the court.

At the far end, on the painted floor, Reggie Playfair lay very still.

TWO

As it turned out, the defibrillator wasn't needed. After a couple of moments of agonizing stillness, life returned to Reggie Playfair. He sat up, propping himself against the wall, and looked with some befuddlement at the ministering George Hazlitt and the doctor called Henry. Oenone had also rushed on to the court, her paralysis of shock dissipating when she saw her husband move.

The doctor gave Reggie a fairly detailed examination, though from the dedans Jude couldn't hear what he was saying. There was still tension in the spectators muttering around her, but they had relaxed a bit when they realized there wasn't a corpse on the court.

Reggie Playfair's rising to his feet was a cue for a round of applause. He shook himself, waved and bowed towards the dedans, as if to indicate that the crisis was over. Then he picked up his racket from the floor and called out, 'Sorry about that little hiatus. Now what was the score?'

There ensued quite an argument between Reggie, the doctor and George Hazlitt. The player was insisting that he was fine to carry on, that he didn't want to let down 'his old mate' of a playing partner and that next time he'd 'remember where the bloody walls are'.

It was George Hazlitt who finally dissuaded him from continuing. As the court's professional, he was

responsible for the players' safety. And since quite a
few of the members were in their seventies and even
eighties, it was a responsibility that he took very seriously.

So Reggie and his partners' opponents were declared the winners of the game, and the little group
filed off the court towards the dedans. Oenone was
holding her husband's arm, but he shook free of her,
not wishing to look as if he needed support. 'God, I
need a drink after that,' he announced.

'I'm not sure that that would be a good idea,' said
Henry the doctor.

'What the hell do you mean?'

'I think that might be what caused the problem in
the first place.'

'Sorry?'

'I think the wine you'd already drunk might have
made you unsteady, which is why you lost your foot-
ing and fell against the wall.'

This was a moment that could have erupted into
something unpleasant. Reggie Playfair was not the
kind of man who took kindly to being told what to
do, least of all by doctors half his age. He was about
to come back with some scorching riposte, but the
gentle pressure of Oenone's hand on his arm made
him think better of it.

'Oh, well,' he said grumpily. 'Not sure I can manage
watching the rest of the day's play without a drink.'

'I don't think you should watch the rest of the day's
play,' said Henry bravely. 'You've got mild concus-
sion. The best thing you can do is go back home and
spend the rest of the day in bed.'

'Look, I'm not ill. I just had a fall.'

'Reggie,' said Henry, 'you should take things carefully. You're not as young as you were.'

'Oh, now you're telling me I'm about to pop my clogs, are you?'

'No, I'm just saying—'

'Well, if I've booked a one-way ticket to the crem, there are a good few things I want to do before I get there.' Reggie Playfair's voice was getting quite loud now and attracting uneasy attention from other people in the dedans. Jude saw the pained expression on the face of Felicity Budgen, a woman in whose presence, she got the feeling, everything had to be 'nice'.

'I'm not the kind of person,' Reggie went on vociferously, 'who believes in the idea of carrying secrets to the grave. No, my instinct has always been to come clean and confront people with—'

'I think you should go home and spend the rest of the day in bed,' Henry the doctor repeated firmly.

Reggie Playfair swung round to face him, as if about to burst into another tirade.

'Better do as the doctor says.' Oenone Playfair's voice was soft but forceful and it had the desired effect. Miserably, her husband let himself be led away to collect his clothes and sports bag from the changing room. When, a few minutes later, he and Oenone left the court, he was given a rousing round of applause from the dedans.

Meanwhile the doubles pair who had profited from Reggie Playfair's default kept saying how guilty they felt about it, and how that wasn't the way they would have wished to reach the final (though the way the game was going before Reggie had his accident, they would probably have won anyway). Jude was once

again struck by how nice and well mannered everyone in real tennis seemed to be.

Just before the second semi-final started Piers took
Jude through for lunch in the club room. This was a
large space with tall mullioned windows looking out
on to the well-kept Lockleigh House gardens. At one
end sagging leather sofas were gathered round a fire
that burned away merrily, though more for comfort
than because it was needed, the weather being mild
for early October. Doors to either side of the fireplace
led off to the men's and women's changing rooms.

At the other end the space was dominated by a large
refectory table surrounded by chairs. It was loaded
with bread and cheese, salads, chutneys and poppa-
doms. And a great many bottles of wine. From the
adjacent kitchen the smells of curry were almost un-
bearably tantalizing.

In glass cases along the walls were displayed discoloured, cracked rackets from earlier centuries, along
with other real tennis memorabilia. There were also
rows of honours boards, recording in gold leaf the
names of the champions in the club's various competi-
tions. Piers couldn't prevent himself from pointing out
to Jude the date, some thirty years previously, when
the Sec's Cup had been won by 'R.A.G. Playfair and
P.H. Targett'. Round the same time a board recorded
that he'd won another doubles title, partnered by Wally
Edgington-Bewley.

Members came and went at the lunch, drifting in
and out from watching the tennis. As places at the
table became empty, they were quickly and informally
filled. Nobody gave any sign of minding who they sat
next to and all of them seemed to know each other.

Jude and Piers had their plates loaded with craters of sharp yellow rice into which the curry was generously ladled. Then they took their places at the table and the cheery banter continued around them. A lot of the talk, being of course on the subject of real tennis, was incomprehensible to Jude, but she didn't feel in any way excluded. The curry was just as good as it had been puffed up to be, and meanwhile the Chardonnay flowed unstintingly.

She was feeling extremely mellow when Piers led her back to the dedans to watch the closing stages of the second semi-final, which was won by two women of about Jude's age. According to Piers, they had only just taken up real tennis, but both of them had once been 'county standard at lawners'. As a result, they were 'rather bandits in the handicap'. Once again Jude hadn't a clue what he was talking about.

But the women's banditry in the handicap stood them in good stead. Though the pair they were up against in the ensuing final were much better players, some incomprehensible system of taking points from one pairing and giving them to the other meant that the two men couldn't afford to make any mistakes. Unfortunately for them, they did make a few, just enough to tip the balance in the women's favour. The female pairing were declared the winners, and then came the presentation of the Secretary's Cup.

This took place on court. First the club chairman spoke. His name, according to Jude's ever-helpful guide, Piers Targett, was Sir Donald Budgen and he had retired a few years back after a long career in the Foreign Office which had ended up with his achieving the status of one of Her Majesty's ambassadors.

A tall thin man with greying hair, he wore a suit and tie that gave the impression he never 'dressed down'. The existence of a pair of jeans in Sir Donald Budgen's wardrobe somehow seemed an impossible incongruity.

The chairman said what a jolly occasion the weekend tournament had been, and how much the thanks for that were due to George Hazlitt and his junior pro, Ned Jackson. He then added thanks to all the people who had helped with the catering and other organization, finishing up with an accolade to all of the players who had ensured that 'the occasion lived up to the fine traditions of good sportsmanship which is so much part of the ethos of real tennis'.

After that he handed over to his wife to make the presentation. With a perfectly judged couple of sentences Felicity Budgen congratulated the winners and handed across the Sec's Cup. The successful pair were loudly applauded from the dedans, and after the clapping had died down, their male opponents were subjected to a good deal of raucous ribbing and congratulation. The voices calling out were interestingly mixed. Jude heard a good few her next-door neighbour Carole Seddon would have described as 'common'.

Jude, full of Chardonnay and delicious curry, had enjoyed her first encounter with real tennis. Still clueless for most of the time about what the hell was going on, she had liked the company.

And she had liked being with Piers.

IN THE FLAT that evening their love-making was as beautiful as ever. No rush, just slow, continuing appreciation of each other's bodies. Not for the first time,

Jude reckoned that there was a lot to be said for post-menopausal sex.

As they lay, infinitely relaxed in each other's arms, she murmured to Piers, 'You still haven't explained why it is that the players change ends.'

'Oh, it's very simple,' he said. 'It's all done by laying chases, and when two chases have been laid then you change ends. Unless one player's got to forty—in other words, game point—and then you change if there's only one chase. Now I did tell you about chases, didn't I? The chase is laid where the ball bounces for the second time, so if that second bounce is on, let's say, second gallery…'

Never failed. Within two minutes Jude was asleep.

SHE WAS WOKEN in the middle of the night. Probably a taxi door slamming. Bayswater was noisy after the rural quiet of Fethering. Light from a street lamp slivered through a gap in the curtains and illuminated Piers Targett's face. Even in sleep he looked very handsome. Within Jude there was a helpless stirring that she hadn't felt for a long time. Almost definitely love.

She thought back to how they had met, only a couple of weeks before. Jude had been attending a weekend conference of healers and other alternative therapists and staying with a kinesiologist friend in Notting Hill Gate. (The reason that a kinesiologist could afford such an address was that her husband worked as a banker in the City.)

On the Saturday night Jude's hosts had given a dinner party, at which Piers Targett had been one of the guests. Sensing the immediate mutual attraction, Jude and he had exchanged phone numbers and Piers had been quick off the mark, phoning her on the Sunday morning and inviting her to delay her return home to Fethering and have dinner with him. They'd had a wonderful meal at Joe Allen in Exeter Street (though neither of them could remember what they'd eaten) and ended the evening in Piers Targett's flat. From that moment they had hardly been out of each other's sight, and Jude's return to Fethering continued to be delayed.

She knew—of course she knew—that their romance couldn't continue for ever in this one-on-one exclusivity. Today had been a step, her becoming involved with his tennis-playing friends at Lockleigh House. If they were going to stay together, though, normal life had to continue at some level. At some point—and quite soon—Jude would have to get back to Fethering and Woodside Cottage.

Preoccupied with Piers Targett, she had been neglecting other areas of her life, her clients, her friends. She knew she had been neglecting one friend in particular. A friend who didn't take kindly to neglect. Carole Seddon.

THREE

HIGH TOR WAS looking cleaner than ever. Gulliver, its owner's Labrador, was groomed to within an inch of his life, his biscuit-coloured coat sullenly glowing. Carole Seddon's bad moods frequently found expression in manic bursts of tidiness.

She wouldn't admit to herself the cause of her disquiet. In fact she wouldn't admit there was any disquiet. Carole had been brought up to believe that introspection was mere self-indulgence, that there was only one way to treat the inconvenience of gloom, and that was to 'snap out of it'. She had no mental problems. On the contrary, she had an obsessive belief in her own normality.

The furthest she would go would be to admit to feeling slightly 'grumpy'. And there was nothing wrong with that—she had plenty to be grumpy about. She was in her fifties, retired from the Home Office, divorced and stuck in the Sussex backwater of Fethering with only Gulliver for company. If that lot didn't justify feeling grumpy, then what did?

And she didn't even have access at that time to the one person who could still bring an unfailing smile to her wan lips, her granddaughter, Lily. Carole's son Stephen and his wife Gaby, claiming that 'we should do these things before we get caught up in schools and term times', had taken their daughter off for a month's

holiday in California. Orange County to be precise.
Anaheim in Orange County to be even more precise
(and if there was one thing Carole Seddon liked, it
was precision). Apparently, according to Stephen and
Gaby, the appeal of that destination was its proximity
to various theme parks, most of which seemed to be
prefaced by the word 'Disney'.

Now Carole couldn't help herself, but she thought
anything to do with Disney was vulgar. The preju-
dice came from her parents who had assured her that
comics were vulgar and only existed for children who
couldn't handle 'proper books'. Animated films came
under the same blanket condemnation. Cartoons were
for common people. The idea of whole theme parks
dedicated to the propagation of the Disney *oeuvre* Carole's parents would have found appalling. And their
daughter shared that view.

Apart from anything else, Lily was far too young
to enjoy a theme park. Though her own had been relatively miserable, Carole Seddon wanted her granddaughter to have what she thought of as a 'proper
childhood'… In other words, one without excessive
entertainment…or electronic toys…or computer
games…or theme parks.

But Stephen and Gaby had not asked for her views
on the subject. They had simply announced that they
were taking Lily away for a month in Anaheim, Orange County, California, USA. That, thought Carole,
was an entirely legitimate reason for her to feel a little grumpy.

She would never have admitted the real cause for
her unease. The fact that she was missing her next-
door neighbour, Jude, who had announced a couple

of weeks before that she was going to some healers' conference (or, as Carole would have called it, 'some kind of mystical mumbo-jumbo') in London and not been heard from since.

Carole was bored, though again that was something she wouldn't admit to herself. In her lexicon the only people who got bored were those who 'lacked resources' and Carole Seddon wasn't the kind of woman to lack resources. When resources ran low, people like her just went out and found some more of them.

There was such a profusion of things that could be done by a healthy retiree in her fifties. Carole knew of a great many women locally who volunteered for charity work and got a great charge out of patronizing those less privileged than themselves. Then Fethering had no lack of clubs and societies for the 'active senior' to join. Perhaps she should offer her services as a prompter to the FADS (the Fethering Amateur Dramatic Society)? A monthly Book Group meeting was held in the local library—might she enjoy that? Or the Fethering Flower Club met on the afternoon of the second Wednesday each month, 'sometimes with guest speakers shedding light on hitherto hidden nooks and crannies of flower arranging'.

Or perhaps she should take on something that would 'improve' her by learning a new skill? Carole had heard about Fethering women of her age who'd enrolled in part-time courses at the University of Clincham, studying such diverse subjects as Fine Art, Creative Writing and Animal Management.

Then again, if she didn't want to make such a major commitment, The Edward James Foundation at West Dean offered short courses in skills like Woodworking

and Furniture Making, Metalwork…or even Basket-
making, Chair Seating and Willow Work.

Closer to home, the glass-fronted notice board outside the local supermarket, Allinstore, displayed cards
offering further variety of short courses. Maybe Carole would like to learn how to dance the salsa? Or
improve her fitness with Zumba classes? Then there
was a lady glorying in the name of Heliotrope Smith
who offered bridge lessons, quoting the line that 'it is
a brave person who enters into old age unable to play
bridge'. Or might she enjoy 'sharing Spanish conversation over tapas with Carmelita Jones'?

The possibilities were truly infinite. Given such
multiplicity of choice, how could a retired person in
the Fethering area ever find time to fit in the basics
of life like eating and sleeping?

Carole Seddon didn't want to do any of them. *The
Times* crossword provided her with all the mental
stimulus she required. She'd never had a problem,
she told herself, with enjoying her own company. Besides, she had Gulliver. If she were to go for a walk
on Fethering Beach on her own…well, people might
think she was a lonely, embittered divorcee. Nobody
would think that about someone with a dog.

In fact, Carole hoped they wouldn't think anything about her. She courted anonymity, choosing her
clothes, almost always from Marks & Spencer, so as
not to draw attention to herself. She was thin and in
her fifties. Her grey hair was cut into the shape of a
helmet with very straight edges. Pale blue eyes peered
beadily through rimless glasses. She didn't try to look
discouraging, but she wasn't the kind of person with

whom strangers would naturally initiate conversations. Which suited her very well.

When Carole Seddon did set out that Monday morning for her walk with Gulliver, she studiously didn't look at the house next door, Woodside Cottage.

ABOUT THE SAME TIME, in Bayswater, Jude announced, 'I must get back to Fethering.'

They were sitting in the bay window of Piers Targett's second-floor flat, looking through the trees of the central square to the matching terrace of tall, white-painted Victorian villas opposite. The room they sat in ran the whole width of the building, had a kitchen area at the back, separated by a free-standing work surface from an apparently artless collection of armchairs and sofas and the dining table in the window. It had undergone the careful attention of an expensive interior designer and, thanks to the daily ministrations of Piers' Lithuanian cleaner, every surface was immaculately dust-free.

The flat had an air of anonymity about it, particularly to the eyes of someone like Jude, whose front room at Woodside Cottage was a messy assemblage of furniture, each item draped with a rug or throw, and shelves cluttered with an apparently random collection of bric-a-brac from many countries. And yet every item there held a memory for Jude.

In Piers' flat every prompt to recollection seemed to have been hygienically removed. His kitchen looked as if it had never undergone the indignity of having food cooked in it. He ate out all the time, and his fridge played host only to bottles of champagne and white wine. A floor-to-ceiling rack next to it offered a comparable selection of reds.

And though the walls in the living room and bedroom featured some very well-chosen paintings, Jude got the impression that they reflected the taste of the interior designer rather than the flat's tenant. If Piers Targett were to move out the next day, the incoming resident would find no clue to the fact that he had ever lived there.

It struck Jude yet again that she knew very little about her lover's past and background, but this did not cause her any anxiety. She recognized in Piers a kindred spirit. Nobody knew much about *her* past or background either. That gave them both a sense of freedom. If their relationship developed in the long term, then some filling in of their backstories would inevitably be required, but that could wait. For the moment they were both enjoying the present too much to care about the past. Or indeed the future.

'What, today?' asked Piers. He looked up from texting on his beloved iPhone. 'You want to go back to Fethering today?'

'I think I'd better.'

'Well, that's fine…so long as you promise you'll be back here pretty damned quick.'

'I promise…though I will have to keep going back to Fethering.'

'To enjoy the pleasures of—' Piers shuddered— '*country life.*'

'Not that so much. Just to catch up with my clients… and friends,' said Jude, again thinking of one friend in particular. She had kept meaning to ring Carole over the last two weeks, but the more time went on, the more difficult she knew the eventual conversation would be. So, uncharacteristically, she shirked it. And of course she had been very preoccupied by falling in love with Piers.

'Anyway, as I say, no problem,' said Piers. 'In fact, I've got some meetings today.'

'Work?'

He nodded, but didn't volunteer anything else. Piers Targett hadn't actually been evasive about what he did for a living. He had talked—'airily' again—about being 'semi-retired' and having 'fingers in lots of pies', but he hadn't specified what fillings those pies might have. Wherever his money came from, he didn't seem to lack for it. Decades had passed since Jude had been to as many expensive restaurants as she had in the previous fortnight.

'Well, look, Piers, I think I should certainly stay down in Fethering tonight...'

'OK. But give me a call this evening. Let me know your plans.' He abandoned his iPhone as his reassuringly large hand encompassed her chubby one. 'I don't think I'll react well to being apart from you.'

'Don't worry, I'll call.'

'I hope you haven't regarded your time as being wasted...'

Jude leant across impulsively and kissed Piers' deliciously fleshy lips. 'Far from it,' she murmured.

'Apart from anything else, you have been introduced to the arcane mysteries of real tennis...'

'True.'

'...of which you now have a complete and total understanding.'

'Rather less true, I'm afraid.'

'Only a matter of time.'

'Look, I'm an overweight woman in my fifties...'

'Nonsense! You are a perfectly rounded, wonderfully sensual woman whose age is entirely irrelevant. You, as the French would put it, "fit your skin".'

'You silver-tongued devil.'

'I only speak as I find. Anyway, you do have to try real tennis. Anyone who is in a relationship with me has to try real tennis.' An idea came to him. He grinned. 'I know what. I'll get on to the professionals and book a court for later this week. No point in hanging about, you can have your introduction then.'

'Well, I—'

'Don't argue with me, Jude. There is no escape. You are going to have the experience of playing on a real tennis court.'

She grinned. 'Well, I'll give it a go.'

'You won't regret it. Soon you'll be laying chases with the best of them.'

'Sorry. Haven't a clue what you're talking about.'

'But I thought I explained the rules to you last night.'

Jude grimaced wryly. 'I think it's that word "chase". The minute I hear it, I feel as if I've just been given an overdose of Mogadon.'

'Ah.' Piers grinned boyishly. 'My mistake for trying to explain the rules when you're sleepy. But now of course you're wide awake! Well, the thing about laying a chase is that those parallel lines on the court—'

'No!' Jude put her hands over her ears in mock-protest. 'No! No! No!'

At which they both collapsed in giggles. When

those had died down, Jude said, 'On the subject of real tennis…'

'Hm?'

'One thing struck me…'

'What?'

'Why do you play at Lockleigh House?'

'Because I love the game. Surely you must've noticed that by now?'

'Yes, I had noticed it—and I think your love for the game hovers very near the edge of obsession.'

Piers conceded her point with a spread of his hands. 'Guilty as charged.'

'But that wasn't my question. I was asking, given the fact that you live in Bayswater, why do you go all the way down to the south coast to play tennis? You've told me there are courts in London…at Queen's Club…at Lord's. Hampton Court's not that far away.'

'Oh, it takes ages to get membership at Lord's.'

There was a note in his voice that Jude hadn't heard before in their two-week's acquaintanceship. A note of evasiveness. She pounced on it immediately. 'What do you really mean?'

Piers didn't attempt to deny or bluster his way out. He just grinned and said ruefully, 'Not much gets past you, does it, Jude?'

'I like to think not.'

'I used to live near Clincham,' he said. 'Little village called Goffham. That's when I joined the Lockleigh House Club. Only a quarter of an hour away then. I used to play a lot. Three, four times a week, matches against other clubs, even trips to foreign courts. Don't do it so much now. I'm not down there so often.'

Again Jude was acute to the nuance. 'Not "so often"? You mean you do still go down there sometimes?'

'Yes. Occasionally.' He could tell from her quizzical brown eyes that she wanted more information. 'I've still got a house down there. Where I used to live when I was married.'

Though she knew he must have been married, his words still gave her a little shock, perhaps in anticipation of all the other information they'd have to process through at some point. 'Are you divorced?' she asked.

'No. We just don't see each other.'

'Right.'

Jude might have come in with a follow-up question, but Piers didn't give her time. 'Since we've got to this confessional moment, I suppose I should check out your marital status too. Are you married?'

'Not currently.'

'Suggesting that you have been…?'

'Twice. Two marriages and two neat, matching divorces.'

'Ah.' Piers Targett nodded. 'Good. Well, that's cleared the air a bit.'

But as she travelled on the train from Victoria to Fethering, Jude wondered whether it had. She didn't love Piers any the less, she didn't regret a second of the past fortnight's love and love-making. It was just that their relationship had moved up to a different level. A level that was no less serious, but perhaps more grown-up. After two weeks of intense one-on-one, they now had to find out whether their relationship could survive in the wider world, a world of other people and other responsibilities.

And baggage. Nobody could get to the age that she and Piers Targett had reached without accumulating quite a lot of baggage.

WHEN CAROLE SEDDON returned from her walk on Fethering Beach that morning, it was with a new sense of purpose. Though still hurt by what she could only think of as Jude's defection, she'd decided that the only way out of her present doldrums was by being more proactive. She must get something going for herself to fill the days.

And it wasn't going to be salsa classes or Spanish conversation. There was no point in trying to get herself enthused about something in which she had no interest.

But a subject that did intrigue her was the solving of crimes. It was an undertaking on which she had in the past collaborated with Jude. But since that was no longer an option, she would have to proceed on her own. And indeed solving a crime on her own would give her quite a charge, a secret snub to her uncaring neighbour.

Carole Seddon's training in the Home Office had encouraged in her a natural tendency for the efficient organization of information. Her filing systems had always been immaculate, and when she became converted to the wonders of computers that offered even more opportunities for the management of directories and subdirectories.

On the shelves of the spare room where she kept the laptop (still perversely unwilling to acknowledge the machine's portability), Carole also had box-files of neatly catalogued newspaper clippings. Anything to do with murder in the West Sussex area. Occasional extracts from her daily *Times*, more frequent cuttings from the *Fethering Observer* and *West Sussex Gazette*.

Carole knew exactly which file to take down from the shelf and which folder to take out and open on the spare bedroom's table.

It was the dossier she had compiled on the unsolved crime known locally as 'The Fedborough Lady in the Lake Murder'.

FOUR

THE BODY HAD been found seven years previously. That summer was an exceptionally dry one, prompting dark mutterings from Fethering locals about global warming. The arid conditions had nearly dried up some of West Sussex's smaller streams. Even the strong tidal flow of the River Fether had been considerably diminished. There were panics about receding reservoirs and many village ponds shrank, exposing their muddy margins.

This had also been the fate of Fedborough Lake. On the outskirts of the town, a large expanse of water only separated from the river by a road, it was popular with tourists and dog walkers. A complete circuit of the lake made a pleasant twenty-minute stroll. Rowing boats and pedalos could be hired from the lakeside café which normally throughout the summer did a roaring trade in ice creams, crisps and Sussex cream teas.

But that year trade had been slack. As Fedborough Lake dried up, weedy mud banks were exposed and, quite frankly, stank.

The human remains that had been found were too degraded to add to the general stink, but they too were revealed by the receding water.

For once it wasn't a dog-walker who found them. That was the local cliché. Whenever a body was found, the report in the *West Sussex Gazette* would always begin: 'A woman out walking her dog made an unpleasant discovery…'

But no, on this occasion it had been one of the men who looked after the Fedborough Lake boats. Business was slack because no one wanted to venture out on to the noisome water, so he used his enforced idleness to clear some of the debris exposed on the muddy banks. He loaded his wheelbarrow with a predictable selection of bottles, polystyrene burger boxes, punctured footballs, slimy plastic toys…and then he found what was unmistakably a human femur.

At the time the discovery had caused a huge media furore, which had subsequently died away from lack of information. According to Carole's archive, the identity of the Lady in the Lake had never been established. Which made finding out what had happened to her an almost impossible task.

And Carole Seddon couldn't think of anything better to shake her out of her current torpor than an impossible task.

She also realized that she had collected her clippings on the case back in the now-unimaginable days when she hadn't had a laptop. She had never even Googled the Fedborough Lady in the Lake. How times had changed. Carole, for many years having pooh-poohed the very idea of computers, had now become addicted to the new technology. There was in her personality an obsessive strand—some people who knew her might even have described it as obsessive-compulsive. Along with her paranoia about dirt and untidiness, she suffered from a meticulous attention to detail…except of course, being Carole Seddon, she wouldn't have seen it as suffering.

She had entered the words 'Fedborough Lady in the Lake' into the search engine without much optimism. The trail must long have gone cold. She anticipated finding a few references to old newspaper reports, the clippings she already had in hard copy form, but not a lot else.

She had, however, underestimated the tenacity of the curious. It soon became apparent that, to a lot of people, the Lady in the Lake case was still very much alive. And if she herself had obsessive tendencies, they paled into insignificance when compared to some of the people out in the blogosphere.

It took some time before Carole got to the personal stuff. As she had expected, the first few hundred entries in Google were just newspaper reportage of the case. But eventually she reached the postings of un-qualified individuals, and it soon became clear that some of the more extreme views had to be discounted. Venting their opinions online offered a wonderful new platform to the kind of letter-writers who used to use green ink with a lot of capital letters and exclamation marks. But once Carole had weeded out the seriously unhinged, she found some ideas that were worthy of consideration.

A lot of the postings were very sad. As she read them, Carole became aware of how dreadful it must be when a family member or friend simply vanishes without a trace. In some of the online writers there was a desperation. The hope of seeing the missing person alive again was long gone, all the bereaved asked for was a kind of closure, the confirmation of their worst fears. A surprising number of people wanted to claim the Lady in the Lake as their own.

Carole had opened up a Word file and was starting to make some notes on her findings when she heard the front doorbell ring. She consulted her watch and was surprised to see that nearly three hours had passed since she first sat down in front of the laptop. And that meant three hours during which she had avoided self-pity and recrimination.

Those two emotions, however, returned forcibly when Carole Seddon opened the front door of High Tor. Because standing in front of it was Jude.

'OH, I HADN'T really noticed you'd been away,' said Carole with studied insouciance.

They were sitting in the bar of the Crown and Anchor. In one of the alcoves, each facing a large glass of Chilean Chardonnay. At first Carole had demurred at the suggestion of going for a late lunch at the pub, but Jude had been at her persuasive best and, besides, Carole was desperately curious to know where her neighbour had been for the previous two weeks.

As she was travelling down on the train from Victoria, Jude had decided that her approach would be very simple. It wasn't in her nature to play games. She would tell Carole straight away about her new relationship, and resign herself to whatever fence-mending and bridge-building efforts then became necessary.

But actually being with Carole didn't make it easy to carry out that plan. Jude felt an uncharacteristic upsurge of guilt. Now she was away from Piers Targett, it seemed inconceivable that during the last two weeks she hadn't found a moment to pick up her mobile and call her neighbour. Where had the time gone?

'And you've been all right, have you, Carole?' she asked. 'You know, since I last saw you?'

'Oh yes, never anything wrong with me,' came the brisk, lying reply. 'You know how it is. I've been busy, busy, busy.'

Someone else might have asked what she'd been busy doing, but Jude was too sensitive to do that. She knew about the deep-frozen loneliness that lay at the centre of her neighbour's heart. 'Have you seen Stephen and family?'

'No, I told you,' Carole replied sharply. 'They're in California.'

'Oh yes, sorry, I forgot.'

'Taking Lily to various Disney theme parks.' She couldn't keep the disapproval out of her voice. Nor could she prevent herself from adding, 'For which I'm sure she'll be far too young. But then, of course, children aren't allowed to have a proper childhood any more, are they?'

There were some pronouncements from Carole with which, Jude had learned over the years of their friendship, it was just not worth taking issue. So she just said, 'No.'

A silence was suspended between them. Which was unusual. Though Carole could be spiky at times, they rarely had a problem finding things to talk about.

Eventually Jude said, 'I was introduced to real tennis on Sunday.'

'I beg your pardon?'

'Real tennis. The game. Precursor of lawn tennis. Been around for centuries. You know, Hampton Court…saggy net…King Henry VIII…'

'Oh yes, I've heard of it. How on earth did you get involved?' Carole looked beadily at her neighbour. 'Was it because of some man?'

There was never going to be a better cue than that and Jude was about to explain everything when she was interrupted by the arrival of the Crown and Anchor's landlord, Ted Crisp, bearing the piled-up plates of their lunch. Both had ordered the dish of the day, smoked haddock with bubble and squeak and a poached egg on top.

Unkempt as ever, bearded, haystack-haired, Ted put the plates down in front of them. 'You'll like this,' he said. 'Chef's best. Haven't seen you two for a while.'

'Jude's been away,' Carole responded tartly. 'Some-where.'

'Oh yes?'

'Well, I…' Jude found herself blushing. And she never blushed.

'Never mind, your secret's safe with me. Anyway, just heard this new joke…'

'Oh dear,' said Carole.

'What's E.T. short for?'

'I don't know,' Jude came back at him in music hall style. 'What is E.T. short for?'

'Because he's got little legs!' Ted Crisp replied with a loud guffaw, and then went off to serve at the bar.

Jude laughed and then explained the joke to Carole, who didn't find it funny even when she understood it.

Then they got involved in eating their lunch, which was excellent. Ed Pollack, the Crown and Anchor's chef, really was going from strength to strength.

The two women ate in silence, which was not un-usual but was uncomfortable for Jude. She normally felt so serene, so secure in her own skin, that she wasn't used to the sensations of a simpering school-girl. She found herself wishing that when their conver-sation did finally resume, Carole would have forgotten the point where it had broken off.

It was, however, evident as her neighbour finished the last scrapings of her lunch, laid knife and fork strictly parallel on her plate, dabbed at her mouth with her paper napkin and asked pointedly, 'So who was it who introduced you to real tennis?'

'Well, it was—'

At that moment Jude's mobile rang. She snatched it out of her pocket and saw that the call came from Piers Targett. 'I must just get this,' she said, abruptly standing up and moving towards the pub door.

'There's a perfectly good signal in here,' Carole called after her, and as Jude moved outside she could feel her neighbour's reproachful eyes boring into her back.

FIVE

'HELLO, JUDE LOVE. I've missed you,' said Piers' voice. 'We've been apart now for…what? Getting on for four hours, got to be. Don't you ever leave me for so long again.'

'You are such a smoothie, Piers. And your chat-up lines are cheesier than a month-old Gorgonzola.'

'I know. Amazing that they still work, isn't it?'

'Amazing.' Jude giggled. 'I've missed you too.'

'Well, don't worry. I have arranged our next encounter.'

'Oh, really?'

'Yes. We will meet next on Wednesday morning.'

'Will we?' Jude was quite relieved. She would have liked to see him sooner, but she really needed the next day to get some kind of normality back into her life. Though the cleaning regime she imposed on Woodside Cottage was minimal—certainly compared to the scouring to which Carole subjected High Tor on a daily basis—it still had to be done. And there were messages on her answering machine that needed responses. Clients who depended on her, needed her services.

'So where are we going to meet?' she asked.

'Lockleigh House tennis court.'

'Oh?'

'I am continuing your education, Jude. Yesterday

you saw real tennis for the first time. On Wednesday you're going to play real tennis for the first time.'

'But I can't do that.'

'Why ever not?'

'Because I'm fat and in my fifties.'

'Absolutely no bar to playing the game. There were people you saw in the Sec's Cup yesterday who were carrying a lot more weight than you are.'

That was certainly true, but Jude still felt she had to protest, 'I haven't lifted even a proper tennis racket for over twenty years.'

'Jude,' said Piers Targett sharply, 'that is the most offensive thing I have ever heard you say.'

'Sorry?'

'A real tennis racket is a *proper* racket. Real tennis is the *proper* game. "Lawners" is nothing more than a vulgarian upstart.'

Jude hadn't heard her lover speak like this before and wasn't sure whether he was serious or not, so was quite relieved when she heard him giggle from the other end of the phone as he announced, 'Sorry, Jude, but you must get these things right. If you're going to be spending a lot of time round Lockleigh House tennis court then there are certain basic points of protocol you must understand.'

'And who says I'm going to be spending a lot of time round Lockleigh House tennis court?'

'I do. Anyway, the court's at seven forty-five, first booking of the day. Under normal circumstances I'd say I'd pick you up, but I'm not quite sure what my movements will be that morning, so could you meet me at the court?'

'Well, yes, I'm sure I could, but I'm not sure that I want to make a fool of myself in front of lots of—'

'The only person you will be in front of will be me. The professionals don't come on duty till nine. And, anyway, you're far too poised and beautiful a woman ever to make a fool of yourself.' He was silent. 'Cheesy again?'

'Pretty cheesy, yes.'

'Ah well, I'm afraid you'll just have to learn to live with my cheesiness, Jude. Just as you will with many other less appealing aspects of my character.'

'And what are they?'

Piers let out a low whistle of admonition. 'I'm not going to screw up my chances by enumerating them now. Wait till we know each other a bit better.'

'As you wish,' she said. 'Anyway, what about after the game?'

'Sorry?'

'Will you be returning straight to London? Or do we get the chance to spend some time together?'

'We spend all Wednesday together. Including, if I could impose on your hospitality, Wednesday night.'

'Sounds good to me. I will introduce you to the delights of Woodside Cottage.' She was about to suggest an introduction to Carole Seddon as well, but no. Too soon, too soon.

'I look forward to it, Jude.'

'And then?'

'Then?'

'Sorry, it's just me being practical. There are some healing sessions I've got to book for Thursday, but I don't want to cut across any mutual plans we might have.'

'I see what you mean. Well, no, sadly on Thursday morning we face another separation.'

'Oh?'

'I have to go to Paris on business for a few days. Back on Sunday, I hope.'

'And what kind of business is it?'

'Boring stuff,' said Piers Targett airily. 'Money, you know.'

And before Jude could ask for a bit more detail, he went on, 'So the booking at the court's seven forty-five a.m. on Wednesday. Arrive a little earlier to give yourself time to change. And the dress code is strictly white.'

'THAT WAS THE new man, was it?' asked Carole as a somewhat shamefaced Jude returned to the bar.

'Yes. Yes, it was.'

'The one who introduced you to real tennis?'

'Mm.'

Carole Seddon was desperate to ask more about the mystery man, but equally desperate not to be seen to be desperate about it. She looked around the crowded pub. 'Ted certainly seems to be doing good business. Excellent for a weekday, isn't it?'

JUDE WAS QUITE organized that afternoon. She cleared the messages on her answering machine and set up a couple of healing sessions for the following day. There was a third she said she might do, depending on how drained she was after the first two.

But though she felt better for having made the arrangements—and made a desultory gesture towards cleaning Woodside Cottage—she was still uncharacteristically twitchy. She didn't enjoy every aspect of being in love. Though no one realized it, the serenity she showed to the outer world had been hard won. She had thought her emotional equilibrium was secure. The arrival of Piers Targett in her life had made her conscious of its central fragility.

She was also annoyed with herself for not telling Carole about him. She should just have cut through her neighbour's assumed lack of interest and given her the facts. Not having done so left Jude feeling guilty; it was not a sensation that she was familiar with. And not one she enjoyed.

These thoughts were circling unhelpfully around her head when the phone rang. She answered it.

'Oh, hello, it's Wally.'

'Sorry?' She couldn't immediately place the claret-soaked voice.

'Wally Edgington-Bewley. We met up at Lockleigh on Sunday.'

'Oh yes, of course I remember.'

'You probably also remember that I mentioned a little book I'd written.'

'Erm…' She had no recollection of it, but didn't want to sound rude.

'Little, self-published thing. About some of the world's real tennis courts I've visited with some chums. Called *Courts in the Act*.'

'Oh yes,' said Jude vaguely.

'Anyway, I said on Sunday I'd like to give you a copy.'

'Of course.' This time she gave a better impression of knowing what he was talking about.

'Well, I was wondering how to get the copy to you...'

'It shouldn't be a problem...'

'...and then Piers said he was taking you up to Lockleigh for a knock-around on Wednesday.' How quickly news spread in the world of real tennis. 'Which is going to work rather well, because I've got to be up at the court tomorrow, so I could leave a copy for you on the table in the club room.'

'Well, that's very kind, Wally.'

'No problem at all. Be in a brown envelope with "Jude" written on the front in my almost-legible scrawl.'

'Thank you.'

'Incidentally, I'm very glad to hear you're going to take up the game.'

'I'm not absolutely sure that I—'

'You'll love it. Takes about ten years to get used to the dimensions of the court and the scoring and what-have-you.' Exactly what Oenone Playfair had said. 'After that it's plain sailing.'

'Well, I'll certainly do my best to work it all out,' said Jude.

'And, incidentally—' Wally Edgington-Bewley paused and his voice became deeper, more personal— 'I'm so glad that Piers has got you...'

'Oh?'

'...you know, after all he's been through.'

Which didn't do a lot to make Jude feel more set-tled. She was becoming preoccupied with how much she didn't know about Piers Targett.

SIX

ON THE WEDNESDAY morning Jude got a cab from Woodside Cottage to Lockleigh House. She could have asked her neighbour for a lift in her Renault and the request would undoubtedly have been granted. Despite her denials, Carole was infinitely curious about Jude's life and wouldn't have turned down the chance of a visit to Lockleigh House…not to mention the possibility of catching a glimpse of Piers Targett.

But for the time being Jude was inclined to play things close to her chest. If her relationship with Piers continued, there would undoubtedly come a moment when his introduction to Carole would have to be made. But Jude was in no hurry to rush that encounter. Carole had met a few of her lovers over the years, but never one about whom she was so serious.

Following Piers' instructions, Jude had managed to get together a white ensemble suitable for Lockleigh House. It was a while since she'd worn the shorts and she had to breathe in quite severely to get them on. Picking one of many white cheesecloth shirts was less of a problem and the top she chose was voluminous enough to hide her struggling waistline. She also succeeded in tracking down some white socks and a battered pair of whitish trainers. Piers had advised that they'd change at the court, so she packed her kit into a woven straw basket of African origin.

It was a perfect autumn day when the cab dropped her at the gates of Lockleigh House. Though there had been rain during the night, that had gone now. The air felt crisp so early in the morning but with a promise of warmth later. The Victorian mansion looked huge and impressive. The Wardock family must have had many children to fill its fourteen bedrooms, or more likely the space was designed to accommodate all the guests who attended long country weekends. The house looked to Jude like the perfect setting for a game of Cluedo.

The high, wrought-iron main gates of Lockleigh House were locked (though members of the tennis club arriving by car had electronic cards to open them), but Jude had been instructed to enter the premises through a small door to one side of the gates.

Once inside, she looked up at the high rectangular bulk of the real tennis court, standing at some distance from the house. Before the Sunday she wouldn't have had a clue what the building might be used for; now she couldn't imagine it being anything else.

Piers was already there, leaning against the side of his E-Type, basking in the thin October sun. There was one other car parked outside the court, a substantial silver BMW.

His smile of welcome was warm, but somehow strange. After the intimacy of their weeks together, the two days of separation had made Jude feel almost awkward at re-meeting him.

But his kiss was reassuringly familiar. He did have exceptionally full, soft lips for a man.

As they drew apart, he said, 'It's been too long,' in a voice of mock heroics. 'I will never again let you escape my web of enchantment. And soon you will be bound to me closer than ever.'

'Oh yes? How's that?'

'Soon you will have fallen under the spell of real tennis, and then our shared obsession will allow you no escape route.'

'Really?' said Jude drily. 'Suppose I don't like the game?'

'Impossible,' he said as he moved towards the court building. 'I couldn't possibly be in love with someone who didn't like real tennis. Come on, don't let's waste a minute of our booking.'

The door had a keypad entrance system. 'We only have to use this when the pros aren't here,' said Piers Targett. Then he tapped in a code, the door gave and he ushered Jude inside.

After the raucous jollity of the Sec's Cup, the lobby in which they found themselves seemed almost unnaturally silent. The door to the court itself was closed. 'Better get you a racket,' said Piers, and led Jude into a small room just inside the entrance. 'This is where the pros hang out,' he said.

A closed door with a glass panel showed into an office with the usual assemblage of laptops, printers and telephones. In a glass-fronted case in the outer area was displayed a selection of white kit, each item bearing the Lockleigh House logo of crossed rackets with a fish above them. Purple and green stripes also featured. Supported on pegs on one wall was a row of rackets. Piers took one down and felt its heft in his hand. 'A bit heavy for you, I think.' He replaced it and tried another. 'This is a better weight, but it'll probably be easier for you if you have a bigger grip.' He found a racket that met all his criteria and solemnly handed it across to her. 'Take it in your hand and feel the first tricklings of your lifelong obsession.'

Jude grinned. 'We'll see.'

'Just do the lights.' He reached into a cupboard to flick a switch.

'Are they on all day?'

'Pretty much. Switched on by the first person to get to the court in the morning, switched off by the last one to leave in the evening. But they've got sensors to turn them off if there's no activity on court. Keeps the electricity bills down. Lockleigh House tennis court doing its bit for the environment, eh?'

Piers opened the door and led the way along the passageway at the side of the court, down towards the club room and changing rooms. As he did so, he glanced to his left on to the court and stopped stock still.

'Oh, my God!' he breathed.

Lying on the court, more or less in the position where he'd fallen on Sunday, lay Reggie Playfair. He was not wearing tennis whites, but a smart business suit with some kind of club tie.

And the glazed expression on his congested face left no room for doubt about the fact that he was dead.

SEVEN

In her online *Lady in the Lake* researches Carole Seddon had by now weeded out the eccentric, ghoulish and frankly demented references and had found only two leads which, while they might not provide a solution to the problem, did at least offer sanity. The first was a posting from a man called Dmitri Gascoigne, who was convinced that the bones found in Fedborough Lake belonged to his wife Karen. He had set up a rather primitive website called *What Really Happened to Karen Gascoigne?* which had the air of the unvisited. The most recent update was nearly four years previously, so Carole got the feeling that Dmitri Gascoigne's campaign had maybe run out of steam.

The other—and to Carole's mind more promising—lead was to a woman called Susan Holland. Her blog made clear her conviction that the Lady in the Lake was her daughter, Marina, last seen in Brighton over eight years previously. From the way she wrote, Susan Holland came across to Carole as a very level-headed woman, not a hysterical over-reactor. If she suspected the dead body to be that of her daughter, then she had good reasons for those suspicions. Carole was also attracted to the woman by the reference to Brighton and the surname Holland, which was quite common in the Fethering area. Both of these clues suggested that Susan Holland might be a local.

Anyway, having decided that she would contact Susan Holland, once again Carol felt grateful to her laptop. Email was such a satisfactorily anonymous form of communication—and geographically unspecific. In the event that the woman being contacted proved to be dangerous or troublesome, the only address she'd have would be a virtual one.

That knowledge gave Carole Seddon a sense of security as she set out carefully to draft an email about the Lady in the Lake.

JUDE HAD INSTANTLY tried resuscitation, but it soon became clear that nothing could bring Reggie Playfair back to life.

Then Piers had taken charge. He felt in his pocket for his iPhone. 'Damn, I've left it in the E-Type.' He handed across the keys. 'Would you mind getting it, Jude love? In the glove compartment.' Responding to the puzzlement in her eyes, he said, 'Sorry, it's just I've known Reggie so long, I wouldn't mind having a moment alone with the old bugger.'

'Of course.'

Jude gave him a full five minutes of silent communion with the deceased, then went back into the court and handed across his phone. 'Are you going to ring for an ambulance?'

Piers Targett shook his head. 'Arriving at hospital five minutes later or earlier is not going to make much difference to poor old Reggie, I'm afraid. I'm going to ring George first.'

'George?'

'George Hazlitt. He's in charge of the court. He should be informed about what's happened.'

The pro lived at some distance from Lockleigh House, so it was a quarter to nine before he arrived. Fortunately he was just in time to stop at the door the two young men who had the nine o'clock court booking. Not wishing the news of Reggie Playfair's death to spread too quickly, George Hazlitt fobbed the two players off with some excuse about there being a water leak which made the court unplayable (fortunately it had rained during the night, so his story was just about feasible). The young men, who had been relishing their singles encounter, left considerably disgruntled.

As soon as they'd gone, the pro took a closer look at Reggie Playfair's body and started keying a number into his mobile.

'Are you ringing for an ambulance?' asked Jude.

'No, I've got to check things out with Don Budgen first.'

Jude looked interrogatively at Piers who said, 'Club chairman. Remember, it was his wife, Felicity, who presented the trophy on Sunday.'

'Of course.'

'Morning, Felicity. Sorry about the hour. Could I speak to Don?' asked George Hazlitt, getting through on the phone. He then moved into the pros' office to continue his call in private.

Piers looked back at the corpse, then ruefully at Jude. 'Poor old bugger. Mind you, after the number of heart scares he's had, he's been on borrowed time for the last two or three years. And Reggie really loved his real tennis, so dying on the court is probably the way he'd want to go.' He let out a wry chuckle. 'When the news of this gets out, I know the first question a lot of the members here will ask...'

'"What was he doing here at this time of the morning?"'

'What? Oh, I see what you mean. Yes, Jude, one or two people might ask that, but I can guarantee that if I were to say to the average member here, "Reggie Playfair dropped dead on the court", the next thing they'd say would be, "Oh? What chase?"'

'Meaning?'

'Well, I explained to you that the chases are the painted lines on the floor of the court, representing the distances from the back to—'

'Yes, but what's that got to do with Reggie's death?'

'It's a kind of joke. You know, somebody drops dead on court and obviously the first question you ask is: "What chase?", and in Reggie's case it'd be "Hazard better than second" and—'

'I really don't think it's something you should joke about.'

This was a very uncharacteristic thing for Jude to say and the tone of voice she used was out of character too. Certainly in their brief acquaintance Piers Targett had never heard her speak like that before and he was instantly all contrition.

'Listen, Jude. I'm not saying this because I don't care about Reggie. We go back thirty years at least. I'm deeply shocked by the fact that he's pegged it, but I can't pretend it was unexpected. And the members of this club who'll ask which chase he died on, they care about him too. It's just the old thing of a joke making the totally unpalatable just a little bit more palatable. Surely you've come across that syndrome before, Jude?'

'Of course I have.' She was apologetic now, aware

of how unusual it was for her to snap at anyone. 'More interesting to me, though,' she went on, 'is the other question I asked. Aside from the fact that he died there, why on earth was Reggie Playfair on the court in the first place?'

'Well, I'm sure there are many reasons why...' Hearing the door of the pros' office open, Piers Targett left the sentence there and looked questioningly towards George Hazlitt.

'Don'll be here in about half an hour. In fact he was at some dinner in London and stayed up there last night. He's on the train back now, but Felicity's managed to get a message to him, so he'll drive straight here when he gets to Fedborough Station.' The pro looked at his watch. 'I should be in time to put off the ladies' doubles at ten fifteen.'

'Aren't you going to close the court for the whole day?' asked Piers, perhaps trying to demonstrate to Jude that he really did have some respect for his dead friend.

'I'll see what Don says.' And George Hazlitt went back to the office to make the next phone call.

There was more hanging around, waiting for the club chairman. Jude got the impression that George Hazlitt would have preferred her not to be there, but he didn't raise the issue. She was Piers Targett's guest and the pro seemed to show deference to the older man.

As Jude had been told on the Sunday, Sir Donald Budgen was a retired British ambassador, and as such presumably used to dealing with more serious incidents than the discovery of a corpse on a real tennis court.

He took one look at Reggie Playfair's body and

said, 'Poor old bugger.' (This was clearly the default response to death amongst the members of the Lockleigh House Tennis Club.)

Sir Donald Budgen was reintroduced to Jude. He greeted her with the automatic professional charm of a diplomat. 'Of course. We met briefly on Sunday. I'm sorry that you've come into a situation like this. If you'd prefer to go home, I'm sure we—'

'I'm fine.'

This was not the response that Sir Donald Budgen had been hoping for, but he was far too well trained to show that. Instead he went straight into organizational mode. 'The main thing we need to do, George, is to ensure that the news of Reggie's death gets out to the members in the proper way. We don't want any rumours spreading around. We need everyone to get the information at the same time in the correct form.' Jude got the impression that the words 'proper' and 'correct' made frequent appearances in Sir Donald Budgen's conversation. 'I'll draft an email for you to send out to all the members, George.'

'Thanks, Don.'

'But obviously it's important that the message doesn't go out before Oenone's been informed of what's happened.' The ex-ambassador glanced at his watch. 'You say you've put off the ten fifteen booking?'

'Yes. I used the same excuse about a leak on the court. I'll explain it to the ladies later. I'm sure in the circumstances they won't mind my little white lie.'

'No, I'm sure they'll be fine. Who's on at eleven thirty?'

'The Old Boys' doubles. Every Wednesday morning, regular as clockwork. Shall I call Wally to head them off at the pass?'

Sir Donald Budgen gave another look at his watch. 'Hold fire for the moment, George. Wally's only just down the road—he won't need much notice if you have to cancel. Next thing we should do is call an ambulance to take the body away. If that's sorted by eleven, then I can see no reason why the Old Boys shouldn't have their doubles. So, George, you call for an ambulance.'

For a moment the pro looked perplexed. 'What number should I—?'

'It's just a straightforward nine-nine-nine call. Do you want me to do it?' There was a note of sharpness in the ex-ambassador's tone, perhaps an echo of some previous disagreement between the two of them about their respective duties. Jude had noticed that the chairman's manner to the pro was very much that of master and servant...though she reckoned that was quite possibly how he treated everyone.

The power struggle was very short. With a 'No, that's fine,' George Hazlitt went through to the office to make the call.

Jude couldn't prevent herself from asking, 'Don't you think the police should be called?'

'The police?' Sir Donald Budgen echoed. 'What on earth has any of this to do with the police?'

'Well, I'd have thought that any suspicious death—'

'There is nothing suspicious about this death,' he pronounced in the voice which he had used to face down argumentative foreigners during his long government service. 'Poor old Reggie had a long history of heart trouble. It finally caught up with him. That's all.'

'But surely the question of why he was here in the court must be—'

'I said: "That's all."' Sir Donald Budgen was not used to being argued with. He cast a slightly reproachful look towards Piers Targett, as if to say, you really ought to choose your girlfriends more carefully.

And Jude did feel a moment of, not guilt, but regret for having been so premature. The investigation of crimes in the past had made her rather prone to make instant categorization of any suspicious death as murder.

'Then, of course,' Sir Donald Budgen went on, 'there's the small matter of breaking the news to Oenone. As chairman, it's my duty to do that. I'll give her a call and then go to the house.'

'Of course you're welcome to do it, Don,' said Piers diffidently, 'but I think possibly it might come better from me. I've been a friend of the family for over thirty years.'

The ex-ambassador accepted the offer with alacrity. Though in his professional life he had had to take on any number of unpalatable encounters, it wasn't an experience he'd ever enjoyed and he was very happy to be let off the hook for once.

Piers Targett read something in Jude's face that she hadn't realized was there. 'I think this is a job I should do on my own,' he announced firmly.

And Jude, intrigued though she was at finding out more about the Playfairs, couldn't deny that he was right.

As IT TURNED OUT, the Old Boys didn't have their doubles cancelled. The ambulance arrived soon after half past ten and all traces of Reggie Playfair had been removed before eleven. George Hazlitt had checked to see if he'd left anything in the club room or changing room, but he hadn't. Using the keys from the dead man's pocket, Piers and the pro had also checked out his BMW, but found nothing unexpected. Then Piers set off on his difficult visit to Oenone Playfair.

He told Jude that she could either call a cab and go home or stay and he'd join her for lunch in the Lockleigh Arms. Just down the lane from the court. And to kill time, she could watch the Old Boys' doubles. That way she might get more idea of the rules of real tennis.

EIGHT

THE LOCKLEIGH ARMS was the only pub in the village… though to call Lockleigh a village was perhaps straining the definition. Apart from the big house with its real tennis court, there were fewer than a dozen other dwellings. The only sizeable one of these was a farmhouse that had given up its original function in the 1970s when its extensive acres had been turned into a golf course, the club house for which was on the main road, some mile or so away from Lockleigh. The village's other habitations had been built for farm workers, though now they had been modernized and interior-designed to within an inch of their lives to provide weekend retreats for wealthy city-dwellers.

Isolated as it was, the Lockleigh Arms might easily have joined the gloomy and increasing statistics of pub closures, were it not for shrewd management. Building on its natural advantages of a beautiful rural location, the (relatively new) owners had invested shrewdly in refurbishing the place. But they had employed the skills of the restorer rather than the modernizer, so the result was a pub that looked as it might have done fifty years earlier. No muzak was ever heard, there were no television screens or gaming machines. The only places where the modern had been allowed to intrude were out of sight, in the superior-spec toilet facilities and the state-of-the-art kitchen, from which their award-winning chef conjured up wonderful meals.

Just as Ted Crisp had found at the Crown and Anchor, it was the food that brought the punters in. Even in recessionary times, there was still a lot of money in West Sussex, and plenty of well-pensioned couples who enjoyed nothing more than going out for a pub lunch or dinner. The Lockleigh Arms' menu was cleverly traditional. It featured none of the challenging taste combinations and presentational fussiness beloved of television chefs. The menu offered pub favourites—steaks, liver and bacon, sausage and mash, steak and ale pie, fish and chips—but all superbly cooked from the finest locally sourced ingredients. The Lockleigh Arms was not the cheapest pub in the area, but most visitors reckoned that the quality of the food justified the higher prices.

Geographical proximity alone dictated that it was used a lot by members of the Lockleigh House tennis court. And it was there that Jude was joined by Piers at the end of what felt like a very long morning since they had discovered the corpse on the court.

'"Resigned" is the word I'd use,' said Piers Targett wearily. 'Oenone is resigned to Reggie's death.'

'Did she cry when you told her?'

'No, she's made of sterner stuff than that. Oenone may be weeping her little heart out now she's on her own, but she'd never let anyone else see how much she was suffering.'

They were sitting in the bar of the Lockleigh Arms. Jude had been going to order a glass of Chilean Chardonnay, but Piers, being a red wine man, had persuaded her to share a bottle of Argentinian Malbec with him. As ever, he had chosen well. Drinking the fine wine in front of the Lockleigh Arms' blazing fire was warming both physically and spiritually. They were both feeling rather battered by the events of the morning.

And hungry. Jude's fruit and yogurt before the taxi collected her was a long time ago and Piers said he hadn't had any breakfast. From the Lockleigh Arms' limited but carefully chosen menu they had both ordered the day's special, venison casserole. That promised to continue the physical and spiritual thawing process.

'How did you first meet the Playfairs?' asked Jude.

'Can't remember exactly. It was through tennis. You know, Reggie and I had a few friendly games, played in the odd tournament...went out for the odd drink... We were friends. Then started meeting up with Oenone as well and...you know how it is.'

Jude picked up the nuance. 'You mean that you used to meet up as two couples...while you were still married?'

'You're very sharp, Jude. Yes, that's what I meant.'

'You've never told me much about...'

He raised his hands to stop her in mid-flow. 'No, I haven't. I will in time, I promise. But after the morning I've just been through, the last thing I want to do is to talk about my ex-wife.'

'Fair enough,' said Jude. And she meant it. If their relationship was going to survive, then unpacking the baggage of their pasts was going to take a long, long time. 'I'm still intrigued to know why Reggie Playfair was on the court anyway.'

'I'm sure we'll find out in time.'

'And indeed when he got there. Does Lockleigh House have security cameras, because if it does, then there'd be a record of—'

'It doesn't have security cameras.'

'Isn't that rather unusual? For a big place like that?'

'It doesn't have security cameras because, being an old people's home, there's someone on duty all the time. Also a lot of the residents suffer from insomnia. Only an extremely stupid burglar is going to break into a place like that.'

'But if there's someone on duty all the time, then they might have seen when Reggie's car arrived and—'

Again the hands were raised. 'Jude, Jude. I really don't want to talk about this either. I've just lost a very close friend. I need a bit of time to get used to that idea.'

For a moment, to her surprise, Jude wished Carole was with her. Her neighbour would have had no inhibitions about picking through the details of an unexplained death.

But then she looked across at Piers and was overcome by a wave of sympathy. She could see from his face that he really was suffering. Though he erected defences of humour, referring to the 'poor old bugger', asking which chase Reggie had died on, the death had affected him profoundly. Jude reached across and placed her plump hand on his thin one. 'Sorry,' she murmured.

'Don't worry about it,' he said. 'How was the Old Boys' doubles?'

'Fascinating. I really did get more of a feeling of the game from watching them. They don't move about much, but they hit the ball beautifully.'

'They were all pretty good players in their time.'

'And how old are they?'

'Oh, I'm not sure that it's polite to ask that. Still, you reckon you've now got an idea of the rules now?'

'I get some of it. The bit that still doesn't make any sense is why they change ends.'

'But I told you about that. It's to do with the chases. When two chases are laid, or only one if the score has reached—'

It was Jude's turn to raise her hands. 'Please, Piers, please. We've established there are subjects you don't want to talk about at the moment. Well, I've got one too—and it's the rules of real tennis.'

He grinned. 'Very well.' He looked up towards the pub door to see the entrance of four elderly gentlemen. 'Ah, here come the Old Boys themselves. Maybe you'll take being taught the rules better from them…?'

'I doubt it,' said Jude.

She knew the other three elderly gentlemen who entered because Wally Edgington-Bewley had introduced them with punctilious politeness in the dedans before they had started playing. Their names were Rod Farrar, Jonty Westmacott and Tom Ruthven. They all wore a kind of uniform of variegated cardigans and brightly-coloured corduroys.

'My turn to buy the drinks,' said Tom Ruthven.

'I'll have—' Jonty Westmacott began.

'I know what you'll have…unless you've changed the habits of eleven years. I know what you'll all have.'

'Do you mind if we join you?' asked Wally Edgington-Bewley, edging towards the table near the fire.

Piers flicked a quick look at Jude, but she nodded assent. She was rather fascinated by the geriatric foursome and was pleased to see them draw comfortable chairs up to the table.

'Oh, incidentally, you left this,' said Wally Edgington-Bewley, holding out a fat envelope towards her.

'Sorry?'

'Copy of my book. I said I'd leave it for you in the club room.'

'Oh, I'm so sorry. I forgot, what with…' Seeing a negative head-shake from Piers, she didn't mention Reggie Playfair, just concluded: 'One thing and another.'

'Well, I do hope you'll enjoy it. Labour of love on my part. It's about all the real tennis courts I've played on.'

'Which is virtually all the real tennis courts in the world,' said Piers.

'Virtually,' Wally agreed with a modest smile.

'As I know well,' said Piers.

'Oh yes, we've had some jolly jaunts in foreign climes, haven't we?' The old man recollected with a nostalgic smile.

'Well, thanks. I'm sure I'll really like it,' asserted Jude, with possibly more tact than truth, as she took the book. Then she went on, 'I enjoyed watching you play this morning.'

'You didn't see me at my best, I'm afraid,' said Jonty Westmacott. 'Just wasn't seeing the ball today. Tweaked a tendon in my knee a couple of months back and it hasn't really settled down yet.'

'Well, you saw me at my best,' said Rod Farrar. 'Sadly, that's as good as I get these days. Not that I ever was that great. And the new hips and knees, wonderful though they are, never quite match the originals.'

'Have you had them done recently?' asked Jude.

'Most recent knee a couple of years ago. But I have got to second time round on both hips and knees. So what you see before you is a bionic man. All parts in more or less perfect order...though not all the original parts I started out with.' He looked at Jude piercingly. 'Are all your joints your own?'

It was not a question that she had ever been asked before, but she was able to reassure Rod Farrar that her body had not yet been enhanced in any way by the surgeon's knife.

'Lucky you.' Then realizing that actually asking the question might be seen as some lapse from gallantry, he said, 'But of course you are far too young to worry about that sort of stuff. Anyway—' he grinned at her— 'are you hooked yet? Are you going to become obsessed with real tennis like the rest of us?'

'Early days,' she replied cautiously.

'I do hope you'll take to it,' said Rod. 'And it would be really good if you could join us one day for a Wednesday morning doubles.'

'Oh? Why?'

'Because,' he replied, 'you would lower our total age to under three hundred!'

Quickly she did the calculation and realized that, even if Rod Farrar was being rather gallant about her age, all of the men must be in their eighties.

By now Tom Ruthven had returned to the table with the drinks. A red wine for Jonty and for the others halves of bitter (Jude got the feeling that a few years earlier, when their prostates had been in better condition, they would have been ordering pints.)

'Incidentally,' Wally Edgington-Bewley announced, 'George did tell us about Reggie, so if you were delicately skirting round the subject…'

'Thanks for telling us,' said Piers.

'You two found him, I gather?'

'Yes.'

'We should raise a glass to him.' Wally raised his half and said, 'Reggie Playfair.'

All the others around the table did the same and together, as somehow Jude knew they would, they all solemnly intoned, 'Poor old bugger.'

NINE

'HELLO, IT'S OENONE PLAYFAIR.'

Jude was taken aback by the unexpected phone call and hastened to assemble some appropriate words of condolence but Oenone briskly cut through them. 'Yes, well, it was bound to happen one day.' As Piers had said, she wasn't the type to let anyone see her suffering.

'Listen, Jude, the reason I'm calling you is that a great friend of mine is Suzy Longthorne…you know, who runs the Hopwicke Country House Hotel.'

'Oh yes?' Jude knew exactly who was being referred to. Suzy, a former model, had been a friend for a long time.

'Well, Suzy told me that you were very helpful to her when she had an awkward situation of a young man being found hanged in her hotel.' Jude remembered the circumstances vividly. What had looked like a suicide had been proved to be murder.

'She said you and your friend—Carole, is it?— found out the truth of what had really happened.'

'Well, yes, I suppose we did.'

'And I wondered if I could enlist your help…ideally yours and Carole's?'

'Of course. But can I ask what for?'

'To find out what actually happened to Reggie.'

JUDE WAS VERY relieved that Carole had been included in Oenone Playfair's request for a meeting. She was aware of her neighbour's continuing unspoken resentment of the new relationship with Piers Targett. The fact that he had stayed over at Woodside Cottage on the Wednesday night would not have lessened that resentment.

Anyway, Piers had set off after breakfast in the E-Type on his way to Ebbsfleet where he would take the Eurostar to Paris.

So Jude had the perfect opportunity to do a little fence-mending. No peace offering to Carole Seddon could have been more seductive than an invitation to join in another murder investigation.

'I think you should be careful about the words you use,' said Carole when the situation had been explained to her.

'What do you mean?'

'Well, Oenone Playfair didn't use the word "murder", did she?'

'No, she just said she wanted to find out what had happened to Reggie, but surely that must mean…?'

'Not necessarily. I don't think we should mention the possibility that he was murdered until she does.'

It was a wise caution, because as soon as Carole and Jude started talking to Oenone Playfair, it was clear that the recent widow had no suspicions of foul play.

They had agreed to go to her house, Winnows. Though reacting with apparent stoicism to her husband's death, Oenone confessed that she didn't really feel up to going out yet. On the way over in Carole's immaculate Renault, Jude brought her neighbour up to date with the events of the previous day at Lockleigh House tennis court.

Winnows was a large detached dwelling about midway between Lockleigh and Fedborough. Flint-faced like many West Sussex buildings, its size suggested that it had probably once been a farmhouse, which over the years had been expensively refurbished. The whole place breathed money. The garden was immaculately maintained. On the gravel in front of a flint-faced outhouse converted into a double garage stood two BMWs, including the one Jude had last seen outside the Lockleigh House tennis court.

The interior of the house was equally perfect, not flashy in any way but with the kind of antique furniture, upholstery and curtains that didn't come cheap. Like the garden, everything was irreproachably tidy, suggesting perhaps that the Playfairs had live-in staff.

While Oenone went through to the kitchen to make coffee, the two visitors were seated on the large cushions of a sofa whose box-like back and sides were tied at the top with silken ropes. They looked round at the effortless elegance of the recessed fireplace and the grand piano. Jude noted that the only photographs on display, except for some black and white ones of presumably deceased relatives, were of Oenone and Reggie. It confirmed the impression she had somehow received on the Sunday, that the Playfairs didn't have children.

Over the fireplace hung a portrait of a young woman in a green ball dress. The fashion of the gown and a residual likeness declared it to be of Oenone in her twenties.

Entering with the coffee, she saw that they were

looking at the painting and grimaced. 'A lot to be said for putting that in the attic,' she commented. 'A bit masochistic to have such a constant reminder of the ravages of age.'

'Did Reggie commission it for you?' asked Jude.

'No, my parents had it done. Before Reggie and I had met. Part of being a debutante.' She shuddered at the memory. 'It was a vital ingredient in my parents' sales pitch to entrap a suitable husband for me.'

'And was Reggie that suitable husband?'

'Good heavens, no. Not in their eyes. My father was an earl, I'm afraid. When I started going round with Reggie, they very definitely thought I was slumming.'

'Was he of very humble origins?' asked Carole.

'By their standards, not by anybody else's. No title, you see. And only from a minor public school. Then he was very successful in the City, which they thought was a bit *infra dig*.'

'What did he do?'

'Stockbroker.'

'Was he still…?' asked Jude. 'I mean, had he retired?'

'Oh yes, in theory he retired about seven years ago. The company was sold off back then. But Reggie still spent a lot of the time studying the markets and dealing. It was his hobby, really. Though he was doing it with our money rather than other people's.' As if anticipating a question they were too tactful to ask, she continued. 'Very successfully. I have no reason to complain.' She looked around at her beautiful surroundings with some satisfaction.

Carole and Jude were both struck by how composed she seemed for a woman whose husband had died the previous day. But then British aristocrats were not renowned for wearing their hearts on their sleeves.

'Anyway…' Oenone's tone changed to a more businesslike one, 'I told Jude on the phone about the recommendation Suzy Longthorne gave for your investigative skills. I gather up at the Hopwicke you solved a murder for her. Obviously this case is nothing like that—' Carole and Jude exchanged almost imperceptible looks— 'but Reggie's death has left me with some unanswered questions.'

'Including, no doubt,' said Jude, 'the one that's been puzzling me. What was he doing at the tennis court at that time of day?'

'Precisely.'

'I mean, that seems to me to be the most obvious thing anyone would have asked. And yet all the time I was there yesterday morning nobody asked it. And I had lunch with some of the members yesterday…'

'Really? Who?'

'Wally, who you introduced me to on Sunday, and three others.'

'Oh, the Old Boys. Of course, yes, they do their doubles on a Wednesday morning. So you were at the Lockleigh Arms?'

'Mm. And I kept trying to get on to the subject of what Reggie was doing there, but they kind of avoided answering it, almost as if I was asking something distasteful. Even Piers wasn't very helpful when I asked him last night.'

Carole pounced on the little detail. 'Did Piers stay with you last night?'

'Yes,' Jude replied wearily.

'Oh,' said Carole, as only Carole could say 'Oh'.

'That in a way,' said Oenone Playfair, 'is what worries me about the situation.'

'Sorry? What do you mean?' asked Jude.

'The way the men are all clamming up. It suggests to me that they probably do know what Reggie was up to, and it's something he shouldn't have been up to.'

'Isn't it also possible,' suggested Carole, 'that they don't know what he was up to, but they're clamming up because they think he *might* have been up to something he shouldn't have been up to?'

Oenone conceded the possibility. 'Yes, men do that, don't they?'

'Let's work back from when you last saw him,' said Jude. 'Did you see him before he left the house yesterday morning?'

'No.'

'Oh?' Carole was instantly alert.

'No, but I wasn't expecting to. We'd said our goodbyes, such as they were, the previous day.' Catching sight of the expression on Carole's face, she explained, 'There's nothing sinister about it. We have a flat in town. On Tuesday evening Reggie was going to a dinner at his livery company. When he does that he leaves the car at Pulborough and takes the train up to London. So he went off after lunch on Tuesday.' For a brief moment there was a slight tremor in her voice as she said, 'That was the last time I saw him.'

'And do you know whether he actually made it to the dinner?' asked Carole.

'Yes, I called a friend who's a member of the same livery company. Reggie had definitely been there at the dinner—and apparently in raucous good form, as only he can be—could be.' She made the correction automatically, not wishing to give way again to emotion.

'Would there have been anyone at your flat, who might have seen when he left there—or indeed if he arrived there?'

Oenone Playfair shook her head. 'No, there's no concierge or anyone there. And we hardly know the owners of the other flats. I suppose it's possible that someone might have seen Reggie arrive or leave, but it's unlikely.'

'What about the clothes he was wearing? Had he changed after the dinner?'

'No, he hadn't. I…' Again the slightest of tremors. 'I saw him at the hospital yesterday. And they… gave me his clothes. The shirt he was wearing was the one he'd worn to the dinner. Reggie always insists on wearing a clean shirt every day. And clean boxer shorts.'

'So the implication,' said Carole, 'is that he perhaps didn't go to your London flat.'

'He may have gone there. But he certainly didn't sleep there.'

'So he could have gone down to the court any time after the dinner ended,' suggested Jude.

'Well, just a minute, no,' Carole objected. 'Remember he'd left his car at Pulborough Station. Assuming the livery dinner ended too late for him to have got the last train back from Victoria…'

'Which it certainly would have done,' Oenone confirmed. 'I've been to those dinners when they have ladies' nights and, God, do they go on? Also, the friend I spoke to said that when he left, round eleven thirty, Reggie was very much still there, in his customary role as the life and soul of the party.' Some slight nuance in her voice suggested that that was one aspect of her late husband's character she wouldn't miss too much.

'So…' Carole pieced things together slowly, 'unless for some reason your husband got a taxi or a lift from someone down to Pulborough, he couldn't have picked up his car until the first train of the morning had got there. If I had my laptop here, I could check what time that is.'

Except of course, thought Jude, *you never move the laptop out of the spare room at High Tor, do you?*

Oenone Playfair, however, had the relevant information locked into her memory. 'There's a five fifteen train from Victoria—I've had to catch it on a few occasions. Gets into Pulborough at six thirty-four.'

'And how long would it have taken your husband to get from the station to the tennis court?' asked Carole.

'A quarter of an hour, if that.'

'So he could have been there round ten to seven,' said Jude, 'which would be about three-quarters of an hour before Piers and I got there.'

'Did Piers and you arrive together?' asked Carole with some sharpness.

'No, he was there when the taxi dropped me.'

'And how long had he been there?'

'I assumed he'd just arrived.'

'But you don't *know* that?'

'No, I don't.' Jude looked at her neighbour with slight puzzlement. She knew that Carole resented the appearance of Piers Targett in her life, but surely she wouldn't be crass enough deliberately to build up suspicion of him?

Carole seemed to read her thoughts and said, 'I'm

sorry, but these are the kind of questions we'd be asking if there was nobody we knew involved.'

Jude nodded, accepting the point. 'Yes, all right, I don't know how long Piers had been there.'

'But you can ask him,' said Oenone.

'Of course.' But Jude wondered if that was another subject on which she might find her lover evasive.

'Presumably,' said Carole, 'if your husband had caught the train from Victoria, there'd be CCTV footage of him at the station. That could be checked.'

'I don't think that's very likely,' said Oenone.

'Why not?'

'Well, who would check it?'

'The police, presumably.'

The older woman sat back in astonishment. 'The police? Why on earth should it have anything to do with the police?'

'Well, they—'

'There's no crime involved here. Reggie died of a heart attack, there's not much doubt about that, after a dinner where he, typically, over-indulged himself. God knows he'd had enough warnings. Saw the quack only last week and had another lecture about changing his lifestyle.'

'So if he's seen the doctor that recently,' said Carole, 'there won't have to be an inquest.' She was good at details like that.

'Won't there? Thank God for small mercies. Anyway, for heaven's sake, don't get me wrong. I'm not trying to involve you two in a criminal investigation. I'm just—as any widow would be—curious about how my husband spent his last hours. And I thought maybe you could help me out on that.'

'Yes, of course,' said Jude, as she and Carole exchanged covert looks, realizing how much they had let their instincts to see any suspicious death as a potential murder run away with them.

Carole moved into practical mode. 'I suppose an obvious starting question might be whether your husband had any tennis-related reason to be on the court at that time in the morning.'

'How do you mean—tennis-related?'

'I know nothing about real tennis—even less than Jude does, but I imagine, because it's a competitive sport, people do train for it. So is it possible that your husband was there so early to do some kind of training session?'

'Reggie? Training?' Oenone Playfair's grief was not so deep that she couldn't still see the incongruity of the idea. 'For a start there's very little training you can do on a real tennis court on your own. You could practise a few serves, I suppose, that's about it. But the idea of Reggie doing any kind of training is just too incongruous for words. There was a time when he was younger, maybe, when he used to do a bit of running and what-have-you, but back then most of his training just came from playing the game. He'd be up at the court three, four times a week.'

'With Piers?' asked Jude, remembering what her lover had said about a similar period of intense real tennis.

'With Piers, yes. There was a whole bunch of them, all incredibly keen, all incredibly fit. Wally Edgington-Bewley, though a decade or so older than the others, was part of the group. They lived for real tennis, used to go off on jaunts to foreign courts…Bordeaux, New York, a couple in Australia. But that's a long time ago. So no, Carole, there is absolutely no chance that Reggie was on the court for training purposes. Apart from anything else, his kit had been in the wash since Sunday and our help doesn't do the ironing till Friday.'

'Right. I see,' said Carole, who couldn't help feeling that she had received something of a put-down.

Jude picked up the investigation. 'Well, if we can also rule out the possibility that Reggie had simply gone back to the court because there was something he had left there on Sunday…'

'Which we can,' asserted Oenone. 'You may remember I helped him get his stuff together on Sunday. I made sure he'd got everything.'

'That being the case, the only other reason I can think of for Reggie to be there was because he had arranged to meet someone.'

'Yes, Jude,' said Oenone Playfair wretchedly, 'that's what I'm afraid of.'

TEN

CAROLE INSTANTLY PICKED up on the implication. 'You mean there's someone you know who Reggie might have been meeting?'

For the first time in their encounter Oenone Playfair looked embarrassed. Up to that point she had been keeping good control of her emotions, the strongest of which seemed, not surprisingly, to be grief. Embarrassment was new.

'Would you like more coffee?' she asked, playing for time.

They both said that they would like their cups refilled. After Oenone had poured for them and placed the silver pot back down on the silver tray, she began, 'Look, this probably sounds silly and perhaps I am just an old woman maundering on, but although generally speaking Reggie and I had a very happy marriage, there was one time, many years ago, when he hurt me very much.'

'Are you talking about an affair?' asked Jude, always sensitive to that kind of hidden implication.

'Yes. Well, I don't know how far the relationship ever went, but Reggie certainly did fall in love with another woman and it did have a profound effect on us…on me, certainly.'

'The trust issue?'

'Exactly that, Jude. The relationship, affair, infatuation, whatever it was, didn't last very long. I think it may have started when they were both on some trip to Paris, but I really don't know. And I don't believe Reggie was ever actually thinking of leaving. He said he'd never stopped loving me, he'd just been surprised by his capacity to love two women at the same time.'

'Men often say that in such circumstances,' Carole observed drily.

'Maybe. I'm sorry, this sounds ridiculous—a woman in her seventies being as jealous of a man as a schoolgirl protecting her first boyfriend from her predatory friends.'

'It's not ridiculous at all,' said Jude. 'The capacity to fall in love—and to be hurt by the people one loves—that's nothing to do with age. It's just something we're stuck with all the way through our lives. Betrayal doesn't hurt any less in your nineties than it did in your teens.'

'Mm. Anyway, Reggie and I settled down, got back on an even keel. And he was very good to me—he was always very good to me, even when the…relationship was going on. And I suppose the whole thing lasted… well, I don't believe it was more than three months, which in retrospect seems a tiny portion of time.'

'But felt longer while you were living through it.'

'Exactly, Jude. Anyway, at the time, when my head was buzzing with ever more destructive thoughts and imaginings, I became obsessed with the question of where Reggie was managing to meet this woman. I'm sure he'd never have brought her here—I was around most of the time, apart from anything else—and this was before we'd bought the flat in London, so that wouldn't have been available for them. Reggie had let slip that the other woman was married, so I'd have thought it unlikely they'd meet at her place…though I suppose it is possible.'

'Hotels are traditional places for illicit assignations,' Carole pointed out.

'Yes, but…well, I suppose he could have afforded it. Reggie was already doing very well by then. But—oh God, I feel dreadful saying this, particularly in the current circumstances. I went through Reggie's credit card receipts. It's something I'd never have dreamed of doing before. It's amazing how corrosive suspicion can be, turning you into the kind of person you never wanted to become—or thought you ever would become. Anyway, there was nothing. No receipts from stays in hotels that I didn't know about. I felt guilty for being so untrusting, but… Anyway, as I say, I just became obsessed with the question.

'All kinds of silly ideas were going through my head. I knew the local young people who lacked tolerant parents tended to conduct their sex lives in cars… or there was a favoured wooded area on the local golf course, but I thought Reggie would have a bit more sophistication than that. And then the thought came to me…that maybe they met at Lockleigh House tennis court.'

'Really?' said Carole, immediately intrigued.

'Back then the booking hours were much the same as they are now. No one there between, say, ten o'clock at night and seven thirty the next morning. They didn't have the electronic keypad entry system—each member had their own key, so there was no problem about gaining access. And of course,' she concluded sardonically, 'the club room, then as now, does boast those large, extremely accommodating sofas.'

'Are you suggesting,' asked Carole, 'that the woman with whom your husband had an affair was also a member of the real tennis club?'

Once again Oenone Playfair was drowned in embarrassment. 'I think, I mean…I couldn't be sure, but…yes, I think it could have been.'

'There aren't that many woman members, are there?' asked Jude.

'There are quite a few, but not as many as the men, no.'

'So you must have had a pretty shrewd idea of who Reggie's lover was.'

Oenone winced at the word 'lover'. 'As I say, I'm not sure how far the relationship went. He was certainly infatuated with her, but whether they actually…' Her words petered out.

'From what you say,' said Carole firmly, 'you know exactly who the woman was.'

But the widow didn't want to go that far. 'There were one or two lady members who possibly…I couldn't be sure. It was a very difficult time for me. My mind was so confused with lots of different anxieties and suspicions. Sometimes I'd been playing a ladies' doubles and think it could be any one of the other three. I wasn't very rational.'

'But basically,' said Jude, 'you are worried that Reggie might have gone to the court the night before last to meet up with his former—' she avoided the word lover this time— 'infatuation?'

'That's what I'm afraid of, yes. That's what I'd like you to try and find out.'

'If you don't tell us the name of the woman who you think your husband may have been meeting,' Carole contributed tartly, 'you are rather hobbling any investigation we may try to make.'

'I can see that. But I'm sorry, I can't voice my suspicions, in case I'm wrong. It would be awful, particularly with Reggie just dead, for me to go accusing someone completely innocent. They'd think grief had really unhinged me.'

'Mm.' Carole Seddon sniffed. 'Well, if you don't give all the information you have, it is going to make our job very difficult.'

'I'll give you all the information *of which I'm certain.*'

And that was it. Carole tried pushing for more, but got nothing. Jude essayed a gentler approach, but also drew a blank. Some inbuilt sense of honour would not allow Oenone Playfair to give the name of the woman whom she suspected had caused her so much unhappiness.

'If we do pursue the investigation you want us to,' said Carole, 'it's inevitable that we're going to be asking questions of quite a lot of the Lockleigh House club members.'

'I can see that.'

'And do you want us to tell them that we're doing it on your behalf?'

Oenone Playfair winced at the idea. 'I'd rather you didn't…if you can avoid it,' she pleaded.

'We'll do our best,' said Jude.

Though Oenone wouldn't reveal the names of the women she suspected of being loved by her husband, to all the other questions Carole and Jude asked she was extremely forthcoming.

An interesting moment occurred when Carole asked whether Oenone had noticed any differences in her husband's behaviour recently. 'Well, yes,' she replied. 'There was one thing…'

'Oh?'

'He'd got very interested in…' Once again she was embarrassed. 'I suppose I'd have to call it "the occult".'

'Seances and that kind of thing?' asked Jude.

'That kind of thing, certainly, though I don't know whether he actually ever attended a seance. It was more kind of…ghosts and things that intrigued him.'

'Ghosts?' Carole echoed with knee-jerk scepticism. 'Did he actually believe in ghosts?'

'I don't know, but he found the possibility of there being ghosts sufficiently fascinating to do some research on the subject. Which I can see from your expression that you find unlikely, and I agree with you it was. Reggie of all people! I say this as someone who loves him deeply, but the one thing he never had much of was imagination. Wonderful practical skills, very talented with money, but Reggie hadn't much time for anything off the straight and narrow. The books he read—and he only tended to do that when we were on holiday—were all blokeish thrillers. Loved James Bond and other writers of a previous generation— Hammond Innes, Alastair MacLean. I think his favourite book was probably Nicholas Monsarrat's *The Cruel Sea*. God knows how many times he read that.

'So Reggie was a very straightforward "man's man", I suppose you'd call him. No time for self-questioning, no interest in religion beyond putting in a well-oiled appearance at Midnight Mass every Christmas. The idea that someone with his head screwed on that firmly would believe in ghosts is incongruous. And it was an interest that seemed to grow as he got older. Anyone new he'd met he'd ask if they'd ever had any experience of ghosts. Surprising how many had…usually nothing very convincing. Strange noise at night, closed doors being found open, objects moved from where they had last been seen. Nothing to convince the sceptic and yet Reggie always listened with deep attention. It was strange, something happened to him when he was listening to a ghost story. His eyes started to water, almost like tears but without spilling out. I've no idea what caused that.'

'Can you think of any reason,' asked Jude, 'why he was interested in ghosts?'

'I don't know.' But the way Oenone said it made Jude realize that she did. 'Why does anyone believe in ghosts?'

'Because they're deluded,' said Carole characteristically. 'There is no such thing as a ghost and there never has been.'

'Oh, I'm not so sure,' Jude countered.

'What, have you ever seen a ghost?'

'No, I don't think so.'

'What do you mean—you don't *think* so? Either you have or you haven't.'

'I don't think I've seen one, but I've met people who say they have and I've believed them.'

'Jude, there are no ghosts. When people die, they die and that's all there is to it.'

Her neighbour might have been about to take

issue with Carole's blanket scepticism but, realizing where they were, thought better of it and asked Oenone, 'When I asked you what made Reggie believe in ghosts, you said you didn't know, but I got the impression perhaps you do have some idea.'

The older woman grinned wryly. 'You're very perceptive, Jude. All right, I'll tell you. It's not something I often talk about because, well, it's not something I often talk about. The fact is that Reggie and I haven't got any children, which was something we rarely talked about but which hurt us both very deeply. Oh, we went on through life, we kept busy, we became serial godparents. We went to some wonderful places, we did some wonderful things. But I always carried the sadness with me, and it was only in recent years that I realized how much it had affected Reggie too.

'I said—quite carefully—that Reggie and I "haven't got" children. But briefly, very briefly we did have a child. About six months into our marriage, in a very predictable middle-class way, I became pregnant. All seemed fine, normal pregnancy. Went into labour, taken to a nursing home…where things didn't work out as they should have done. Difficult birth, cord round the baby's neck, she was stillborn. And the process had made such a mess of my insides that the doctor decided on an emergency hysterectomy.' The very matter-of-factness with which she spoke the words made them all the more moving.

'Well, I suppose we could have adopted, but…and nowadays I read in the papers that there's surrogacy and… But there wasn't back then. The simple facts were that I had lost a child and there would never be another one. I was soon fit and healthy again and Reggie just…didn't want to talk about it, really. He did say how much simpler our life would be, how much more we'd be able to travel and…I was very hurt by his attitude at the time, but…' Oenone Playfair sighed. Although she wasn't showing much emotion, the narrative was taking its toll on her.

'Anyway, as I say, in a very British way Reggie shut things in, continued to make lots of money, continued to play lots of real tennis, but all the time the sadness was niggling away inside him. And then, about eight years ago I suppose, he told me that he'd seen Flora's ghost.'

'Flora?' prompted Jude.

'Our daughter's name. She didn't live long enough to be christened or anything, but to us she was Flora.'

'And where did he see the ghost?' asked Carole.

'Everywhere. He said he kept seeing her. Not as the baby that we saw for such a short time, but as a grown woman. I told him that it was just imagination, that I'd experienced something similar. It's inevitable. You see a girl whose hair's the same colour as yours and you think, maybe that's what my daughter would look like if she were still alive. She'd be over fifty now if she'd lived, but I still see women who make me think of Flora.

'Anyway, I put that to Reggie, but he said no. He pointed out that I kept telling him he had no imagination, so his mind wasn't going to invent things like that. What he was seeing must be Flora. Or rather Flora's ghost. To cut a long story short, that got him into reading books about ghosts and…he sort of became obsessed by the idea.'

'Well, the obvious question to ask,' said Carole, 'is: are there any ghosts connected with the Lockleigh House tennis court? Might ghost-hunting explain your husband's appearance there the night before last?'

'That's a thought.' Oenone was clearly taken with the idea. Perhaps simply because it was more palatable than her other imaginings. 'Somewhere in the back of my mind that does ring a bell. A story going back a long way...to when the Wardock family owned Lockleigh House. Now when did I hear that?' She tapped at her chin in frustration. 'Oh, when was it? It'll come to me. I must have heard it from one of the members of the tennis club. Who was it?' She waved her hands hopelessly. 'I'll wake up at three a.m. and remember it.'

Oenone Playfair smiled, obscurely comforted. 'It would make sense, though. Much more likely that Reggie had gone to the court on a ghost-hunting search than that he had fixed to meet someone there.'

Neither Carole nor Jude was about to point out the inaccuracy of this assessment. If he was interested in its connections with ghosts Reggie Playfair could have inspected the Lockleigh House tennis court on many occasions. His presence there two nights before was much more likely due to an arrangement to meet someone.

And both Carole and Jude knew that the words she had just articulated would only give Oenone a brief respite. Her worries about her husband betraying her would soon return.

Which gave an extra urgency to their mission to

find out precisely what had drawn Reggie Playfair
to the tennis court that night.

IT WAS CAROLE who had asked permission to check out
the BMW. Oenone admitted that she hadn't had the
strength to look inside it. 'So much Reggie's car—
it'll still smell of him, like he's popped out and is just
about to come back in. But you two do look in it by
all means.'

She had also explained to them how the car had
got back to Winnows. 'George Hazlitt—you know,
the pro—he drove it over. With his junior, Ned, following in another car to take them back.'

She gave them the keys, saying, 'Obviously if you
find anything of interest, let me know. Otherwise,
just drop the keys back through the letterbox. I think
I might go and put my feet up for a while.'

And they both realized how desperately exhausted
Oenone Playfair was. In spite of her overt stoicism,
the events of the past days had taken a heavy toll on
her. And the long conversation with Carole and Jude
couldn't have made her any less tired.

She saw them to the door and added, 'Oh, and by
the way, do let me know if you find Reggie's mobile
phone in the car. I couldn't find it in the clothes that
came back from the hospital...not that I really looked
that hard. I was...' The strain was beginning to show
more forcibly now. 'As I say, I'm just going to put my
feet up for a while. Then I'll have to address myself
to the subject of funeral arrangements.'

They could both tell that she was now just desperate
to be on her own, so they said their hasty goodbyes.

And as soon as Oenone had closed the front door, they started their inspection of the BMW.

'Be very handy,' said Carole, 'if we did find his mobile phone, with a text on it from someone arranging to meet him at the tennis court.'

'Well, don't hold your breath,' said Jude. 'The business of investigation, as we have found out, is seldom quite as simple as that.'

And so it proved. The BMW did not contain a revelatory mobile phone. Nor a note setting up an assignation with an old flame. Nor indeed anything else that one wouldn't have expected to find in the car of a wealthy married man in his seventies.

As SHE SEDATELY drove her sedate Renault back to Fethering, Carole Seddon observed, 'There's one thing that's struck me as particularly odd in everything I've heard today.'

'Something Oenone said?'

'No. Something you said.'

'Oh?'

'When we were driving over to Winnows. You said when you arrived at the tennis court yesterday morning Piers Targett was standing beside his Jaguar...'

'The E-Type, yes.'

'And where was Reggie Playfair's BMW?'

'Parked by the wall of the tennis court, a little bit further along.'

'But Piers didn't refer to it before he went into the court?'

'No.'

'You said they were great friends, though, didn't

you?' Jude nodded. 'So Piers would have recognized Reggie's car?'

'Yes,' Jude agreed unwillingly.

'Which must mean that Piers knew Reggie was at the court before you found his body.' There was a silence. 'Mustn't it?'

Jude felt very wretched.

ELEVEN

WHEN CAROLE SEDDON got back to High Tor, her Labrador, Gulliver, looked extremely reproachful. She hadn't been out long, but his expression was that of a child whose mother had abandoned him at birth. Though he'd had his normal early-morning walk, Carole couldn't resist the baleful pressure to take him out for another blow on Fethering Beach.

So it was only after she'd done that that she checked her emails on the laptop incarcerated in her spare bedroom. And found one from the Susan Holland she had contacted about the Lady in the Lake case.

Yes, the woman would be happy to meet. She lived in Brighton, had a part-time job and no car, so it would be easier if they could meet there. She worked afternoon and evening shifts at a nursing home, but was free most mornings. There was a coffee shop in Brighton called Bean in Love that would be a good place to meet.

The email gave no impression of the kind of woman Susan Holland was. It was properly spelled and punctuated, but offered no indication of age, social standing or any other details of her life.

Seizing the moment before her mind started to dither and equivocate, Carole sent back an email wondering whether Susan Holland might be free to meet at Bean in Love the following morning at, say, eleven o'clock…?

She was gratified to receive a reply within minutes, assenting to the rendezvous. It had been sent from a Blackberry. For a moment Carole considered the possibility that this meant Susan Holland was rich. But only for a moment. Everybody has Blackberries these days.

Having set up the meeting gave her a warm glow. This was an investigation she was doing without Jude. And though she had been included in the request for help from Oenone Playfair, Carole was still feeling a little resentful towards her neighbour. Not only was Jude getting into far too serious a relationship with Piers Targett, she was also bound to be the major player in any investigation into Reggie Playfair's last hours. It was Jude, after all, who had found the body, Jude who had the contacts at Lockleigh House tennis court.

All in all, Carole Seddon was quite glad she had a case of her own to investigate.

It was the following morning, the Friday, that a call came through to Woodside Cottage.

'Hello, is that Jude?'

'Yes.'

'It's Oenone Playfair.'

'Oh, how good to hear you. How are you bearing up?'

'I'm fine. The only possible thing to be said in favour of organizing a funeral is that at least it keeps you so busy that you can't think about other things. No time to brood.' She was in a more forceful, less twittery mood that morning, though Jude rather doubted whether she was feeling any better deep down.

'Also I've had so many letters and cards and what-have-you. I had no idea what a lot of people were fond of the old bugger.'

'Well, on very brief acquaintance, I can see why everyone would have liked Reggie. He seemed very straight, very honest.'

'Yes.' Was there a slight hesitation in the monosyllable? Had 'honest' not been the right word to use in the circumstances? Whether it was or not, Oenone did not allow anything to stop her flow for long. 'Anyway, in the middle of the night I suddenly remembered.'

'Remembered what?'

'What we talked about yesterday morning. You know, your friend Carole asked if there were any ghost stories attached to Lockleigh House and I said it did ring a vague bell, but I couldn't remember who I'd heard it from. Well, in the middle of last night I did remember.'

'Oh, well done.'

'I knew it was one of the tennis club members and I suddenly recalled a conversation from…ooh, way back, and it was Tom who mentioned something about some old rumour.'

'Tom?'

'Tom Ruthven.'

'The one who plays in the Old Boys' Wednesday doubles?'

'That's the lad. I can't remember any details, but I know it was he who mentioned it. He's got some family connection with the Wardocks…you know, the ones who used to own Lockleigh House. Anyway, if you want to follow up, Tom's your man.'

'Do you have a number for him?'

'Oh, just a minute, Reggie's membership list is around here somewhere. God, he was so untidy.' Not, thought Jude, from what she had seen of the interior of Winnows. Or indeed his car. But then maybe his wife had always followed round tidying up after him.

'Ah, here it is,' announced Oenone triumphantly from the other end of the phone. And she gave the number. 'Tom's retired, so he's around a lot of the time. You shouldn't have any problem making contact. Unless, of course, he's out playing golf.'

'Well, thank you very much for the information. I'll certainly talk to him.'

'Oh, and incidentally, Jude…'

'Yes?'

'Don't feel you have to come to the funeral.'

'Oh.'

'I mean, you hardly knew Reggie. Piers obviously will be there, but don't feel you have to tag along.'

'I won't, unless Piers specifically asks me to do so.'

'Good wheeze. Where is Piers at the moment?'

'He's in Paris, got some business there.'

'Oh yes, of course. Fingers in many pies, as usual, our Piers.'

In different circumstances Jude would have asked for elucidation of that enigmatic remark, but it didn't seem to be the moment, as Oenone went on, 'It's on Thursday, by the way, the funeral. A week today. I could have arranged it for Wednesday—the vicar would have preferred that—but I didn't want the Old Boys to miss their doubles.'

TWELVE

CAROLE SEDDON ARRIVED at Bean in Love before Susan Holland. It was one of those laid-back coffee shops with lots of sofas and an air of aggressive informality that always made Carole feel tense. Service seemed to happen from the counter rather than from waitresses. As she approached, she looked up at the infinite variety of coffee types and cup sizes on the chalkboards.

'Good morning. What can I get you?' asked a girl with a butterfly tattooed on the side of her neck and a badge reading 'Barista Celine'.

'Just a black coffee, please?'

'Would that be an Americano, espresso or filter?'

'Just ordinary black coffee, thank you.'

'Filter.'

'If that's what ordinary black coffee is, yes.'

Carole took the white mug to a table and opened her *Times* to the crossword page. But her eyes kept glancing off the clues, refusing to let her brain engage in unpicking their logic. She was nervous. What was she doing, a middle-aged woman setting herself up as some kind of superannuated private eye, poking her nose into things that didn't concern her?

'Hello. Are you Carole?' She looked up at the sound of the voice. It hadn't occurred to her that Susan Holland might go and get her own coffee before greeting her, but that's what the woman had done. Her ease in the Bean in Love environment suggested that she was a very regular customer.

Susan Holland was one side or the other of fifty. She was shortish, dressed in black leggings and a grey fleece. Her features were strong and dark, suggesting perhaps some Hispanic blood in her genetic make-up. Shortish hair, coloured to a chestnutty sheen, perhaps to hide the incipient grey.

'First thing I have to ask,' she said very directly as she took a seat opposite Carole, 'is what your interest is in the Lady in the Lake?'

'A perfectly legitimate question. And one to which I feel it is difficult to give a simple answer.'

'You will understand my caution. A lot of rather dubious people involve themselves in missing-person cases. There are plenty of weirdos out there, people with their own bizarre agendas, some whose interest is distinctly unhelpful.'

'You don't have to tell me that. I've read a lot of the stuff that's been posted on the Internet.'

'So you understand, Carole, why my instinct is to be extremely careful.'

'I understand completely.'

'Then why've you contacted me?' The woman could not keep the neediness out of her voice any longer. 'Have you got any new information? Have you got any proof that the Lady in the Lake was Marina?'

Carole felt guilty now. She should have thought, should have realized how desperate the woman would be for news of her daughter. Her email contact had been unwittingly cruel, raising hopes where there were none.

'I'm sorry. I have nothing like that to offer you.'

The younger woman looked predictably crestfallen. 'It's just that I live in Fethering, so obviously I heard about the discovery of the Lady in the Lake up at Fedborough and I just…thought maybe it might be worth doing some investigation into it.'

Stated like that, her intention did sound painfully woolly.

'I'm presuming you're nothing to do with the police?' said Susan Holland.

For a brief moment Carole considered mentioning her former career in the Home Office, but she knew it was irrelevant, so she replied, somewhat shamefacedly, 'No.'

The reaction that prompted was better than she feared. 'Thank goodness. They're a useless bunch of tossers. When I asked them to make enquiries into Marina's disappearance, they treated me like I was an idiot, just another menopausal mother who'd had a spat with her teenage daughter.'

'On thing does strike me,' said Carole. 'Surely it would be very simple for the police to find out whether the Lady in the Lake was Marina or not. They'd find a DNA match with you.'

'That wouldn't have worked.'

'Oh?'

'Marina was adopted. I don't know anything about her birth parents.'

'But that information must be available somewhere? Through the adoption agency?'

'You'd have thought so, but Marina had a rather unusual early life.'

'In what way?'

'She was found drifting in a rubber dinghy in the

sea off Brighton. Only about two at the time, so very little language to give a clue to where she came from. The view was that the dinghy had belonged to a larger boat that had been smuggling in illegal immigrants. Whether that's true or not is impossible to know. As is whether the larger boat sank, taking down her parents with it. Some people reckoned from her looks— pale blue eyes, high cheekbones—that she came from somewhere that used to be part of the Soviet bloc. No idea if that was true. All conjecture.

'The facts, on the other hand, are that Marina was taken into care. Her name, incidentally, was given to her because the dinghy was found floating near Brighton Marina. The press at the time came up with the nickname, and it stuck.

'Anyway, I was married back then, and it was becoming clear that we weren't going to be able to have children, and I was keen to get on with adopting before the authorities thought we were too old. So Marina became our daughter.'

'And your husband? Is he still on the scene?'

Susan Holland let out a derisive 'Huh', then added, 'He went the way of all men. Or at least all the ones I get involved with.'

'So how old was Marina when you adopted her?'

'Five. And those years in care hadn't done her much good, which, added to God knows what traumas she'd suffered before that, meant... Well, Marina was never the easiest child. Her father walking out didn't help either.'

'But going back to the DNA, surely there must have been things of hers in the house that the police could have got a match from? A toothbrush or...?'

'I'm sure there were. Still are. But persuading the police that they should be channelling valuable resources into doing those kinds of tests was never going to happen. As I said, they'd written me off as the hysterical mother of a grumpy teenager.'

'Susan, what makes you think that the remains found in Fedborough Lake might be those of Marina?'

'Timing as much as anything. That dry summer was the year after Marina disappeared.'

The two women looked at each other. Both knew how flimsy Susan Holland's reasoning was. And both knew the level of neediness that made her clutch at so fragile a straw.

But Carole Seddon didn't comment. Instead she asked, 'Could you tell me the circumstances of Marina's disappearance?'

Apparently relieved at the direction of the questioning, Susan Holland was more than ready to reply. 'All right. We're talking seven years ago, more than that now, nearly eight. Marina was sixteen going on twenty-six. A seething vat of hormones and confusion. Every teenager reaches a point where they question their own identity. They don't know where they're going, they want someone to define them. They're full of questions about who they are, what their place in life is. Well, given her complex background, Marina had more of those questions than most kids of the same age.

'Iain—that's my ex-husband—had walked out about a year before and, though she'd never admit it, Marina had been very hurt by that.'

'Were they close?'

Susan Holland screwed her face up as she tried to find the right words. 'They were, in a way. Iain had been very fond of her when she was small. She was a pretty little thing and I think he saw her as a kind of accessory. He'd show her off, at the same time demonstrating to everyone what a great dad he was. But as she grew older, the relationship changed.'

'You don't mean…?'

'Oh God, nothing like that. He never touched her or anything. There are a lot of harsh, uncharitable things I could say—and have said—about my ex-husband, but I'd never accuse him of that. No, I think he turned against Marina just when she became less biddable. You know, suddenly she wasn't the adorable little moppet who thought everything her daddy did was wonderful. She started to develop a mind of her own and gave us both a hard time. Pretty soon she only had two default settings—asleep and stroppy. Well, I took most of the flak. Iain just—am I allowed these days to say "in a very masculine way"?—avoided confrontation with Marina and lost interest in her. By coincidence perhaps it was also around the same time that he lost interest in me.' She spoke these words with grim resignation. 'Are you married?'

In some circumstances Carole might have resisted giving personal information to a stranger, but she was keen to bond with Susan Holland so readily replied, 'Divorced.'

'So you know where I'm coming from.'

'Perhaps.'

'Anyway, Iain was off, developing his career, finding a new wife, getting a new set of kids—kids of whom he was the birth father—which didn't do much for my confidence, as you might imagine. He was generally starting over—and beginning to make a lot of money.'

'Oh? Doing what?'

'He's in the stationery business. Started very small, just bought this one ailing store and we worked very hard to turn that around.'

'You were in the business with him?'

'Yes. But don't worry, I'm not about to get into that routine of "I worked my fingers to the bone for that man, but when the business started to take off, I got dumped and…" True though it happens to be. But I'm not bitter about it—well, not more bitter than I am about other aspects of his behaviour. And the fact that Iain's now got a chain of stationery stores across the south coast and his kids are in private school and he's even got time to dabble in local politics and… Don't get me started.'

To Carole it seemed that she already had got Susan Holland started, so she quickly asked, 'Did your ex-husband keep in touch with Marina?'

'Not as far as I know. I don't think he wanted any links with the past. He wanted to start with a new squeaky clean sheet.'

'So you don't think he might know what had happened to her?'

'No. He might have been sufficient of a bastard to keep that kind of information from me, out of sheer bloody-mindedness, but he wouldn't have lied to the police—and they interviewed him quite a lot around that time. No, I'm sure he didn't know anything.'

'But he didn't take much positive action to find out what had happened to his daughter?'

'I think her disappearance probably suited him

quite well. Reducing the number of skeletons in his closet to one—namely me.'

'Hm.' Carole nodded thoughtfully. 'Let's go back to the time when your husband walked out, and the effect it had on Marina.'

'Well, she'd never have admitted it, but she was very upset. Which, of course, affected her behaviour. She was getting well out of hand. I was doing the job at the nursing home back then, like I am now, and that involves quite a few evening shifts, so I wasn't able to keep as close an eye on her as I should have done. So I think Marina was getting in with the wrong crowd... and there are quite a lot of wrong crowds in Brighton.'

'Are you talking about drugs?' asked Carole.

Susan Holland grimaced. 'Probably. They're certainly easily available round here. I don't know. Marina was very defiant towards me. She wanted to hurt me. She seemed to blame me for her confusion. If Iain and I hadn't adopted her, she said, her life would have been more straightforward. She could have, as she kept putting it, "gone back to her roots". Though, poor kid, neither she nor anyone else had any idea what her roots were. But I've heard adopted children can often entertain the fantasy that they were born to better things. And there were a lot of things better than being brought by a harassed, hard-up single mother in one of the less salubrious areas of Brighton.

'Marina was quite attracted by the idea that she was Russian by birth. An exotic Russian...I suppose in the nineteenth century she might have thought she was a princess. Now what? The daughter of a Russian oligarch? Who was going to appear one day in a Rolls-Royce, claim her as his rightful child and whisk her away from the squalor of Brighton and of me. Poor kid.

'Oh, I understood a lot of what she was feeling. But there's only so much understanding a busy working mother can give. And I didn't want to let my own life and needs become completely subservient to hers. Of course there were lots of arguments.'

'I did ask you about drugs.'

'Yes, I was getting there, sorry. Marina told me she was taking drugs. She told me she was having sex too. Both things may have been true, but the way she said them to me, it was more a kind of defiance. As if she was challenging me, seeing how far she could push me before I snapped and said something unforgivable to her.'

'Something unforgivable?'

'Yes. Like that I didn't love her. That's what she wanted to hear from me. She kept telling me she hated me and she wanted me to hit back in the same way. She said I couldn't love her—not properly—because I wasn't her real mother. According to Marina, the only reason I'd taken her on was because I wanted a baby, any baby. It wasn't her specifically. And the love I gave her was the love I would have lavished on whatever baby I happened to end up with.'

'It sounds exhausting even just to hear it described.'

'Believe me, Carole, it was. The same arguments time after time, sawing away like a serrated knife through broken flesh. I was dead on my feet by the time she finally disappeared.'

'And what caused that? Why did she finally go? Did you have some even more enormous row?'

Susan Holland was silent. She'd been swept along

by the momentum of her narrative, but now her grief and bewilderment caught up with her. 'No. I wish there had been something. I wish there had been one enormous flare-up, a bigger one than all the others, something I could have looked back to and said, "That was it. That's where I went wrong. That's what did it."

'But I don't have that satisfaction. Oh God, I've asked myself that so many times. What did I do? What was the trigger? In what Marina would have regarded as the long catalogue of my offences what was the one thing that pushed her too far, the one thing that made her go?'

'And you're sure she did go of her own accord?'

'As opposed to what?'

'As opposed to being abducted. If you are thinking of Marina being the Lady in the Lake, then you're thinking of a murder victim.'

'I see what you mean. No, she left home of her own accord.'

'How do you know that?'

'There was a note.'

'Had she ever done anything like that before?'

'Left a note? Oh yes, she was always doing it. I'd come back from an evening shift, find a note on the kitchen table saying she hated me and she'd left and she never wanted to see me again. The first few times I panicked. After that I got used to it. She was always back within twenty-four hours. Back when she was hungry. Or needed clean knickers. Very fastidious Marina always was about personal hygiene.'

'And where do you think she went those nights when she was away?'

'Slept over at a friend's house.'

'Boyfriend?'

'I don't think so. That's what she wanted me to think. She wanted me to be shocked. But I think it was probably just one of the girls from school.'

'And then there was this one time when she didn't come back.'

'Yes, Carole. At first I thought it was the same routine as usual, but as the days went by, I realized this was different.'

'Was the note she left that time any different?'

'God, I've asked myself that so many times. I've looked at it and looked it, trying to find some secret message. You try, by all means. A fresh eye may make all the difference. You see if you can find what I've been missing for the past eight years.'

Susan Holland reached into her handbag and produced a transparent plastic folder containing a much-creased sheet of paper. She handed it across.

'May I take it out?'

'Be my guest.'

A piece of A4 copy paper, worn and frail along its folds. The writing in blue ballpoint was pitifully faded but in a tidy, firm hand. And it read: *Goodbye. I hate you and I know that you really hate me. I'm going to find someone who really appreciates me. And this time I really won't be coming back.*

Carole observed, 'The last sentence sounds pretty final.'

'She wrote that every time. If I hadn't thrown them away, I could show you another dozen notes with virtually identical wording.'

'And you sure it's Marina's handwriting?'

'Yes. That's one of the things that I thought too—

that someone had abducted her and forged the note. So I went to a graphologist who checked it against other stuff Marina had written and yes, it's hers. She wrote it.'

'Hm.' There was a long silence, then Carole Seddon said, 'You've been very open with me, Susan.'

'Why shouldn't I be?'

'Well, as you said right at the beginning of our conversation, there are a lot of strange people out there and you don't know me from Adam—or should that be Eve?'

'No, but you do seem to be genuinely interested in what might have happened to my daughter—and it's a long time since I've met someone with that qualification.'

'It's the only qualification I do bring to the table, I'm afraid.'

'Don't worry about that. If you think you really can find out something about Marina…'

'I don't know whether I can. But I'm prepared to try.'

'Well, it's probably hopeless. It all happened so long ago, and the few trails there ever were have gone very cold. But if you would like to pursue it further, Carole…'

'I would, Susan.'

'Why?'

'I don't know. I suppose I'm just nosy.'

Susan Holland grinned. 'Nosy is good,' she said.

THIRTEEN

'Ah, hello. Is that Tom Ruthven?'

It was the Friday evening. Jude had tried the number Oenone Playfair had given her a few times before, but this was the first time she'd got more than an answering machine.

'Yes, it is,' the precise elderly voice at the other end of the line confirmed. 'Who is it speaking?'

'My name's Jude. We met on Wednesday with Piers Targett at the Lockleigh Arms after your game of doubles.'

'Oh yes, of course. And after that morning's terrible shock.'

'Mm.'

'Well, it's delightful to hear from you. You're not ringing to say you'd like to join us next Wednesday, are you?'

'No.'

'Pity. We're one short. Jonty Westmacott has injured his toe. At least he says he's injured his toe, but I rather think it's a recurrence of his gout.'

'I'm sorry to hear it. But why did you think I might be offering my services?'

'Well, I've tried ringing round a few of the usual suspects, but without any luck, so I asked George Hazlitt if he might try to fix us up with a fourth. I thought he might have asked you.'

'But I don't even know how to play the game. And I'm not a member of the club.'

'Not yet,' said Tom Ruthven.

'I may never be.'

'You will if you stay with Piers. No way he'd tolerate having a girlfriend who didn't play real tennis.'

'Well, we'll see.'

'Anyway, if it's not about tennis, to what do I owe the pleasure of your call?'

'It's to do with something Oenone Playfair said to me.'

'Oh? How is the poor darling? She must be in a terrible state. In spite of the rather cavalier way Reggie treated her at times, the pair of them were absolutely devoted to each other. I've been meaning to write to Oenone, but I keep procrastinating. Difficult to put into words what you feel for a bloke like Reggie. Poor old bugger.' Jude was beginning to wonder whether those three words would be what ended up carved on Reggie Playfair's tombstone.

'Oenone and I were talking about Reggie's interest in ghosts.'

'I didn't know the old reprobate had an interest in ghosts.'

'Well, apparently he did, and Oenone was wondering whether that might have had something to do with why he had gone to the court that Wednesday morning.'

'Really?' For the first time there seemed to be a note of caution in Tom Ruthven's voice.

'Well, do you have any idea why he might have been there?' It was worth asking.

But she didn't get much by way of return. Tom

Ruthven replied rather woodenly that perhaps Reggie had left something behind after his unexpected exit from the Sec's Cup.

'Oenone said he definitely hadn't.'

'Then I've no idea why he might have been there.' The old man's tone made it clear they'd come to the end of that particular line of questioning. Once again Jude got a sense of closing ranks. The men who played at Lockleigh House tennis court looked after their own. They might entertain their own suspicions about what Reggie Playfair had been doing, but they were not about to share them with anyone else.

'Going back to the ghosts, though…'

'Yes, Jude.' Tom Ruthven sounded relieved that the conversation had moved on.

'Oenone said you'd once mentioned some ghostly sighting at Lockleigh House, or the tennis court or somewhere around. Does that ring any bells?'

'Distantly. Oh, goodness, that was years ago. I'm surprised she remembers that far back. It was something I was told by some relative of mine called Cecil. I can never remember whether he's my great-uncle or second cousin. Cecil's a Wardock.'

'Oh, from the family who built Lockleigh House?'

'Yes. So I might have some connection to them as well, though I'm not sure what. Some ancestor of mine married into the Wardocks, I think, but I've never bothered to check the details. Yes, Cecil did tell me some vague story about a ghost, a woman who topped herself, I can't remember the details.'

'Might Cecil himself remember them? That is, if he's still around.'

'Oh yes, he is still around. Just. Mind you, he's seriously old.'

Coming from a man in his eighties, Jude wondered just how old that might be.

'Is there any way of contacting him?'

Tom Ruthven chuckled. 'Well, that couldn't be easier.'

'Oh?'

'Cecil is an inmate—no, that's not what they call them—he's a resident, that's right, of Lockleigh House. You know it's now an old people's home?'

'Of course. And is he still…?' Jude hesitated.

'*Compos mentis*, is that what you're asking? Well, the old marbles roll about a bit, but on a good day he's still got most of them. I go to see him from time to time, what with him being a relative. Not as often as I should.'

'Would it be possible to introduce me to him?'

'What, to talk about his Lockleigh House ghost story?'

'Yes.'

'The old boy'd love it. Nothing he likes better than maundering on about the past. Particularly maundering to ladies.'

'When could it be arranged?'

'Well, when I visit him, it tends to be on a Saturday. Would tomorrow be too soon for you?'

'No,' replied Jude. 'It wouldn't be too soon at all.'

THAT AFTERNOON, as she was folding up her treatment table, Jude felt pleasantly exhausted. Exhausted because healing always took more out of her than she could ever possibly explain to someone who hadn't had the experience. And pleasantly so, because the session she had just finished had been successful. The client had been a high-flying female solicitor who had suddenly been struck down by ME. This was the third session she had had and she was now finally beginning to recognize the fact that she was genuinely ill. She was coming to accept that her sudden inability to function was not her fault. The woman was by no means cured—that would take a long time—but Jude felt they had made a start on the road to a cure.

She was about to go upstairs to wash away her weariness in a bath with aromatic oils when the phone rang.

'Hello?'

'Ah, is that Jude?' Another elderly man's voice, pernickety like a stage lawyer. She could not immediately place the speaker, but he was quickly identified for her. 'I'm Jonty Westmacott. We met at the tennis court on Wednesday.'

'Yes, of course. And at the Lockleigh Arms.'

'Mm.' He hesitated, ordering his thoughts. 'I hear from Tom Ruthven that you've been enquiring about Reggie Playfair's death.' Once again Jude was struck by how quickly news spread in the world of real tennis.

'Yes.'

'Is that because you think he may have been murdered?'

Jude was quick to deny that she had ever considered such a thing, although of course it had been her first thought.

'Hm. Well, I wouldn't be too sure about that.'

'Jonty, are you saying you think he was murdered?'

'It wouldn't surprise me.'

'Why not? Is there some information you have that makes you say that?'

'More suspicion than information. I mean, everyone in the Lockleigh House club knew that Reggie had a weak heart.'

'Yes.'

'So anyone could have lured him down to the court and given him some terrible shock there, which would have been enough to give him another heart attack, a big final one.'

Jude was intrigued. 'Yes, that could have happened. But the major questions that raises are: who lured him down to the court? And: why did they want to kill him?'

'Yes, those are the major questions, I agree.'

These words were spoken with an air of finality, and there was a silence before Jude asked, 'And do you have an answer to them, Jonty?'

'Oh, no. But I got the impression from Tom that you were some kind of investigator.'

'Well, not in any professional way.'

'Professional or amateur, if you're an investigator, then you've got to investigate.'

'Ye-es.'

'So let me know when you come up with something.'

'Yes, of course I will. But, Jonty, just to check again… You do genuinely believe that Reggie Playfair was murdered?'

'Yes.'

'Can I ask why?'

'I have an instinct for these things.'

It wasn't the most helpful answer that had ever been

given to an investigator, professional or amateur. But Jude did find it interesting that she and Carole were not the only people whose first thought had been that Reggie Playfair's death was murder.

FOURTEEN

JUDE HAD HAD no problem in persuading Tom Ruthven that Carole should join them on their Saturday visit to Lockleigh House Nursing Home for the Elderly. 'The more the merrier,' he'd said. 'Cecil likes an audience—particularly if it's a female audience.'

So they went together in the Renault to meet Tom, as arranged, at two thirty. The plan was to visit Cecil Wardock in his room, but when Tom announced them the smartly-suited woman on reception said, 'If you don't mind waiting for a moment. The nurses are just tidying things up for you upstairs.' Whether it was the room or Cecil himself who was being tidied up for them they had no means of knowing.

So they waited in the rather splendid hall of Lockleigh House. This area had not been updated, but rather restored to its former glory, recreating what a Victorian country house should feel like. And though the reception desk gave it the air of a public rather than a private dwelling, it felt more like an upmarket hotel than an old people's home. There wasn't even a whiff of urine or disinfectant.

'So did Cecil ever actually live here?' Jude asked Tom. 'I mean, while the Wardocks still owned the place?'

'No. He was a different branch of the family. Visited quite a bit as a child, I believe. Then worked and lived in London most of his life. Was in publishing, quite successful, I think. Not that it's a world that I know much about.'

'What was your world?' asked Carole. 'You know, before you retired?'

'Oh, I worked in a bank. Back in the days, I hasten to add, before bankers became the pariahs of society they are now. I enjoyed it, spent my entire working life in the City. Very healthy pension, retired down here, I can't complain.'

'And did Cecil have connections to this area before he moved in here?'

'Yes. While he was London-based, they bought a weekend place in Smalting and moved in there full-time when he retired. Then his wife died a few years back and he was getting to the point where he couldn't manage on his own. So he moved into what he refers to as "the family house".'

'Did he ever play real tennis?' asked Jude.

Tom Ruthven chuckled. 'I don't think so. I'm sure he would have mentioned it to me if he had.'

They might have heard more about Cecil Wardock's background, had not the woman on reception told them that he was now ready to receive his visitors.

There was a lift for the more infirm residents and guests, but they took the broad oak staircase instead. Tom Ruthven led them along the landing to a door with the number seven on it. He tapped and a thin voice shouted, 'Come in.'

The room was luxuriously appointed, maintaining the Victorian country house feel of the hallway below. Large windows looked out over the gravel driveway and main gates of Lockleigh House. The panelled

walls on one side were completely obscured by high
bookshelves. On the other hung half a dozen water-
colours of shorelines. They looked to be by the same
artist and they looked expensive. There was no bed,
so presumably the bedroom and bathroom lay beyond
the interior door. The only details that suggested the
room was part of a nursing home were the wheelchair
neatly folded up by the wall and the pair of crutches
propped against the owner's high armchair.

Whether it was thanks to the nurses' tidy-up or his
own efforts, Cecil Wardock looked extremely dapper.
He wore a gingerish tweed jacket and smartly-creased
grey corduroy trousers, a blue shirt and a bow tie with
stripes the colour of salmon and cucumber. The ensemble was only slightly let down by the fleece-lined
and Velcro-strapped slippers on his feet.

His thin hair was neatly parted and combed back
over his head. Thick-lensed glasses with heavy frames
balanced on the narrow bridge of his nose. In spite of
his bulky clothes, Cecil Wardock still looked painfully thin. He seemed to have been stacked into the
chair rather than sitting in it.

'Afternoon, Tom,' he said in a cultured, slightly
reedy voice, 'Forgive me, ladies, for not rising to greet
you. I'm afraid getting out of this chair is one of the
many things I seem unable to do these days.' The
words were not spoken self-pityingly, but with wry
resignation.

Tom Ruthven effected the introductions and Carole said she hoped Cecil didn't mind his afternoon
being invaded by two women he'd never seen before.

'Mind? Why'd I mind? I'm starved of female
company in this place. I don't mean that there aren't

women here, but they do tend to be…how shall I put it graciously? Rather on the mature side? So it's unalloyed pleasure for me to have my afternoon invaded by two considerably less mature and beautiful women.'

Jude grinned and Carole blushed. They both recognized that Cecil Wardock must have been quite a charmer in his day. 'A wonderful collection of books you have,' said Jude, gesturing to the shelves.

It was the right thing to say. The old man beamed as he responded, 'Yes, and do you know, every one of them I published myself.' Carole looked more closely at the books. There were quite a few literary names she recognized amongst them. 'When I retired, I had those bookshelves made specially to accommodate every title into whose publication I had some input, you know, starting from when I was just a humble editor, then when I was publishing director and finally as MD. And I've spent a large proportion of my retirement rereading the books.'

'And never reading anything new,' said Tom Ruthven.

'Exactly. Those bookshelves are my personal Forth Bridge. As soon as I get to the end bottom right, I start again at the beginning top left. And in fact, you know, I'm actually speeding up on my reading now.'

'How's that?' asked Jude.

'One of the effects of getting older—which some people regard as a curse—is the fact that you don't need so much sleep. At least I don't. And rather than as a curse I regard that as a blessing. Enables me to read my books quicker, you see.'

'Don't you ever get bored reading the same stuff time and again?' asked Carole.

'Good Lord, no. You see—' he let out a mischie-vously complacent chuckle— 'I was a very good pub-lisher.' He looked around the room. 'Now, ladies, Tom, can I order up something for you? Tea? Coffee? Rich tea biscuits? The staff are very good at organizing that kind of thing.'

His visitors said that they'd all had coffee recently and didn't require anything.

'Well then,' said Cecil Wardock, 'what can I do for you, ladies? Tom was exceedingly mysterious on the phone.'

'We really wanted to ask you,' said Jude, 'about any ghost sightings there may have been in Lock-leigh House.'

'Good gracious me.' The old man chuckled again. 'So am I in the presence of the West Sussex Spiritu-alists' Association?'

'No,' replied Jude. 'You are just in the presence of two nosy middle-aged women.'

Carole winced a little. Though she undoubtedly was middle-aged, she thought it a little indelicate to draw attention to the fact. But she was relieved that Cecil Wardock didn't ask more about the reasons for their investigation. They'd agreed that they wouldn't talk about Reggie Playfair's death unless Cecil initi-ated the subject. Tom wasn't sure how open the lines of communication were between Lockleigh House's nursing home and its tennis court. It was quite pos-sible that Cecil Wardock had heard nothing of the re-cent tragedy.

'And Tom,' Jude went on, 'seemed to recall hear-ing you mention something about a ghost attached to Lockleigh House.'

'Hm.' Cecil Wardock was silent for a long time and the two women worried that he might be unwilling to share his story with them. But in fact he was only marshalling his thoughts and eventually he began. 'Yes, there is a rumour, which I heard through family connections. As Tom may have told you, I was a distant cousin of the Wardocks who used to own this place. Whether there's any truth in the story I have no means of knowing and the cousin who told it to me was a bit of a fantasist, so I'm sure he embellished his tale in the telling…that is, assuming he didn't just make the whole thing up.

'Anyway, it went back to before the First World War. One of the daughters of the house was called Agnes—Agnes Wardock, of course. From all accounts she was a very beautiful young woman—I've seen a photograph, actually, pure English rose, long blonde hair, quite a stunner—and she was courted by a good few of the local gentry. A good prospect in many ways—the Wardocks were still pretty well heeled at that time. But Agnes was her own woman and didn't want to take advice from her parents as to whom she should marry. She was, I gather, a romantic, waiting for Mr Right to come along, and confident that she'd recognize him when he did.

'And I think she enjoyed a happy life in that Edwardian dream world which so many writers have evoked in novels of varying quality. In fact, there was one I published back then…beautiful, sensitive novel about a young man growing up in a world of shooting parties and regattas and…it's on the shelf over there. I'll be reading it again in a couple of months—can't wait. Just so exquisitely done.' He sighed fondly for a moment. 'Charming author who sadly was taken too young, by breast cancer, before she fulfilled her undoubted promise.' He shook himself out of his reverie.

'But sorry, I digress. Agnes Wardock, yes. Not finding Mr Right and, in her parents' view, getting rather close to being left on the shelf. I mean, she was probably only twenty-four or twenty-five, but back in those days…the ideal was for a young woman to be engaged by the end of her first season.

'Anyway, finally, Agnes does meet a young man who…what's that expression people use so much these days? "Ticks all the boxes", that's right. And…this'll amuse you, Tom, Agnes actually met her Mr Right through real tennis.'

'Excellent.' The (marginally) younger man smiled. 'Can't go wrong with the kind of chap who plays real tennis.'

'So you keep telling me. I really must get round to learning how to play it one day…though maybe I have left things a little late.' Cecil giggled for a moment. 'Now I don't know much about Agnes Wardock's young man, not even his name, but apparently he was a university chum of one of her brothers. They'd both played the game at Oxford, I believe, I don't know where.'

'Merton College,' Tom Ruthven supplied.

'Ah, knew I could rely on you to have all the facts at your fingertips. Anyway, Agnes' brother invited his chum down here to have a game, the two young people met and that was it. For Agnes it was undoubtedly love with a capital L. Young man was equally keen. Her parents had hoped for someone with a title perhaps, but they recognized a good thing when they saw it and didn't make any objections.

'So the engagement was official, wedding date set for the following May, notice in *The Times*, all that stuff. But then for that particular young couple, as for so many people round that time who felt confident that the Edwardian summer idyll would last forever, things changed.

'Small matter of some Austrian archduke being assassinated in Sarajevo…I don't need to spell it all out, do I? Well, caught up in jingoistic fervour, Agnes' fiancé joined up at the first opportunity. Never any doubt he would, being an honourable young man—' Cecil Wardock winked at Tom Ruthven— 'not to mention a real tennis player. And since everyone knew that the war would be over by Christmas, no need to change the wedding plans. The fiancé would go off and sort out the Boche, return to England probably decorated for conspicuous gallantry and everything'd be tickety-boo for him to walk Agnes up the aisle in May.

'Except of course that wasn't what happened. On the fifth of September, 1914 began the Battle of the Marne… Actually an author of mine wrote a splendid novel on the subject…rather better than more recent, over-praised works of fiction covering the same period…' His eyes strayed towards the bookshelves, before he returned with slight reluctance to his narrative. 'Battle went on for a week and was actually an Allied victory. Not that that was much comfort for the seventeen hundred-odd British casualties…amongst whose number was included…yes, you guessed it, Agnes Wardock's fiancé.'

The old man was silent for a moment. Though he was enjoying having an audience for his story, the effort of telling it was taking it out of him.

'There were a lot of young women who were bereaved in that way,' prompted Carole, with surprising gentleness.

'Oh yes. And a lot of them stiffened their upper lips and got on with life, channelling the love they had lost into good works or whatever. But that didn't happen with Agnes Wardock. She fell to pieces in a very un-British way. Her parents, her friends tried to comfort her, but nothing could break through her carapace of grief.

'Within a week of hearing the news of her fiancé's death Agnes Wardock hanged herself. And because it was on the Lockleigh House real tennis court that she had first met the young man, that was where she did the deed. Wearing the wedding dress which she had already had made for the following May.'

After a long silence Tom Ruthven asked, 'Where did she do it?' For a moment Jude feared that he was going to ask which chase the girl had died on, but fortunately he was not so crass, and continued, 'Was it from one of the high walkways up by the windows?'

Cecil Wardock nodded.

'So,' asked Jude, 'it is Agnes Wardock's ghost who is said to haunt Lockleigh House?'

'Yes. Or more specifically, she is said to haunt the tennis court adjacent to Lockleigh House.'

'Presumably there have been sightings of her over the years?'

'Presumably. Though, as ever with ghost stories it's hard to get proper evidence. The imaginations of people who regard themselves as psychic are extremely fertile. A rumour very quickly takes on the mantle of fact. One of my authors—' he gestured again to the bookshelves— 'did an excellent study of the ghosts of West Sussex, but although I pointed him in the direction of Agnes Wardock, he didn't include her.'

'Why not?'

'Lack of evidence. He made a rule that for inclusion in the book a ghost had to have had at least two sightings, authenticated either by the individual who had seen the apparition or by some written record. He couldn't find even one for Agnes Wardock.'

'But within the family...' said Carole. 'You said it was a cousin of yours who mentioned the idea of the ghost. Had he seen it?'

'He claimed to have talked to one of the housemaids who'd seen a female figure in a long white dress on the tennis court.'

'What would a housemaid have been doing on the court?' asked Tom Ruthven.

'According to my cousin, she was there after dark to meet one of the boot boys. For an assignation of a carnal nature, I fear.'

Carole and Jude exchanged looks. It seemed the court might have a long history of the kind of rendezvous that Oenone Playfair had worried about her husband arranging.

'I think it's quite possible, though,' Cecil Wardock went on, 'that the housemaid invented the story of the ghost to divert suspicion from what she was really up to.'

'And that's the only sighting you know of?' asked Carole.

'Yes. Maybe members of the Wardock family who actually lived here might be able to provide more detail… if there were any of them around to ask.'

'And are there?'

'Sadly, no. I'm afraid the line dies with me. My marriage was blessed in every way possible, except in the matter of children. So no, when I go…which cannot by the law of averages be too far into the future… that will be the final pruning of the Wardock family tree.' Though the thought might be a melancholy one, it was spoken with great cheerfulness. 'Getting old isn't as bad as some people say, you know. It has its consolations. In fact, I published a slim volume written by a philosopher friend of mine on that very subject.' Another gesture towards the bookshelves. 'Very thoughtful piece of work. It brings me renewed comfort each time I get round to reading it again.'

'Cecil, we can't thank you enough for telling us all this,' said Jude.

'No hardship for me at all, my dear young lady. I love telling stories. That's why I went into publishing. And it's nice for me to have such an attentive audience. I'm afraid back in the days when I used to lord it in the coffee room at the Garrick Club…' He gestured to his salmon and cucumber bow. 'Recognize the tie, do you? Anyway, back then most of the members had heard all my stories before, so it's a pleasure for me this afternoon to know that I haven't repeated myself.'

'There is one thing I'd like to ask,' said Carole.

'Ask away. I'm not about to go anywhere.'

'Tom said you mentioned the story of Agnes Wardock's ghost to him some years ago…'

'Yes. I hope you're not going to ask me how many.

When it comes to time these days I always have to double the number I first thought of.'

'No, that wasn't going to be my question. I just wondered whether you'd told the ghost story to anyone else more recently?'

'Funny you should ask that, because there was a chap came to see me within the last month who seemed extremely interested in Agnes Wardock's ghost. You probably know him, Tom. He's a member of the real tennis club.'

'Oh? What's his name?'

'Reggie Playfair,' said Cecil Wardock.

It HAD STARTED to rain while they had been talking, so the other two waited under the porch of Lockleigh House while Carole went to fetch the Renault from the car park.

'Cecil didn't seem to know about Reggie Playfair's death, did he?' Jude observed.

'No. Otherwise he'd have been bound to mention it when the poor old bugger's name came up.'

'There didn't seem to be any point in saying anything.'

'Absolutely not. He'd only met Reggie the once.'

There was a silence. The rain looked set in for the afternoon.

'Pity you haven't started playing tennis yet,' said Tom Ruthven.

'You still looking for a fourth for your Wednesday doubles?'

'That's it. I suppose Jonty's gout might be better—he's such a hypochondriac with his ailments, and not above using them for a bit of gamesmanship too—but I'd like to have a back-up.'

Jude had a good idea. Her lover was due back from Paris the following day. She didn't know his plans for the next week, but he always seemed ready to drop everything for a game of real tennis. 'Why not ask Piers?'

'Oh, I asked him. He couldn't do it. Some business meeting, he said.'

'In Paris?'

'He didn't mention Paris.'

Jude felt a disturbing trickle of anxiety. 'Did you speak to him on his mobile?'

'No, his home number.'

'In Bayswater?'

'No, no. Down here. In his house at Goffham.'

'When was this?'

'Yesterday evening.'

But Piers Targett was supposed to be in Paris till Sunday. Jude's manner gave no sign of the turmoil in her mind as she said lightly, 'Thank goodness you mentioned that, Tom.'

'Oh? Why?'

'Well,' she lied glibly, 'I'd made an arrangement to meet Piers at the house this afternoon. Make sense if I went straight there now. Trouble is, I'd made a note of the address, but I left it at home. You don't know it, by any chance, do you, Tom?'

Tom did.

FIFTEEN

JUDE DIDN'T GIVE any hint of her feelings as Carole drove them back through the rain to Fethering. They talked about what they had just heard from Cecil, and the possibility that Reggie Playfair's fascination with the ghost of Agnes Wardock might have been the reason for his final visit to Lockleigh House tennis court. It didn't seem likely, but then none of their other lines of enquiry were leading anywhere so the notion was worth exploring. Carole was unaware of her neighbour's preoccupation and didn't notice that she was doing most of the talking.

When the Renault dropped her outside Woodside Cottage, Jude said she just had to dash out to get some shopping at Allinstore, Fethering's uniquely inefficient supermarket. Carole went into High Tor to face the baleful looks of a disgruntled Gulliver, a process of blackmail that would almost inevitably lead to his being taken for another walk on Fethering Beach.

Jude didn't go to Allinstore. Instead she cut across the village to the railway station, beside which was a Portakabin displaying the legend 'Fethering Cars'. A minicab was procured and she gave the Goffham address that Tom Ruthven had passed on her. Fortunately the driver had no desire to engage in conversation because, atypically, Jude didn't feel like talking that afternoon.

IN THE SPARE bedroom at High Tor, Carole found on her laptop an email from Susan Holland. She wrote that she had enjoyed their meeting at Bean in Love and, if Carole was genuinely interested in helping find out what had happened to her daughter, she gave a phone number for one of Marina's best friends from school, Donna Grodsky. Susan had talked to the girl endlessly in the immediate aftermath of the disappearance. Donna hadn't been able to provide much information then, but maybe her lack of cooperation had been due to simple teenage bolshiness. Perhaps, now a few years had passed, and if the girl was approached by someone different, she might be more forthcoming.

Carole Seddon checked her watch. It was five forty-five. Not a respectable time on a Saturday to ring someone you hadn't met before. Particularly someone young. Young people—young women, certainly—would be busy preparing for the evening ahead. Choosing the most revealing minidress, the most vertiginous heels, and loading up with cheap supermarket vodka to set them up for a night of excess. Though Carole took *The Times*, many of her preconceptions were more likely to have come from a *Daily Mail* reader.

She would definitely ring Donna Grodsky, she decided. Just not then.

THE COTTAGE OUTSIDE which Jude's minicab drew up was on the edge of the village of Goffham. There was an air of neglect about it. The paint on the window frames was peeling and the rough grass in the front garden had not been mown all summer.

But it had been an attractive house and, with a little care and attention, could be again.

On the weed-ridden gravel in front of the house stood Piers Targett's E-Type. In the manner of the Royal Standard flying over Buckingham Palace, it was a bright red announcement that the owner was in residence.

Jude paid off the driver, still with mercifully minimal dialogue and, as the car eased away, walked towards the house.

One of the hinges had sheared off the garden gate and she had to lift the upright out of a rut to open it. The unwillingness with which the gate gave suggested that not many people had been through recently.

Jude walked boldly along the weed-fringed brick path to the front door. She was hardly thinking, certainly not planning how she was going to conduct the conversation that lay ahead. She seemed to be on automatic pilot, but she knew that she couldn't take any other course than the one she was taking.

She lifted the discoloured brass knocker on a front door whose green paint had blistered and flaked, and let it fall. There was a silence, then she heard the sound of someone approaching from inside.

The door opened. And when Jude said, 'Good afternoon,' the expression on Piers Targett's face was one which she had not previously seen during what she now realized had been a very brief relationship.

PIERS WAS EXTREMELY fluent in his explanations. No surprise there, he'd always been good with words.

No, he hadn't lied to her about going to Paris. He had caught the Eurostar from Ebbsfleet as planned on the Thursday morning. But the business he was due to do in France hadn't taken as long as anticipated, so he'd returned to England on the Friday afternoon.

They were sitting in the kitchen. Jude had refused his offer of 'tea, coffee or maybe something stronger...?' She was struck again by how shabby the place looked. The interior matched the exterior— not squalid but with an air of neglect. Though it was starting to get dark outside, she could still see the dust and cobwebs on the windows. The mess of the house was in such sharp contrast to the antiseptic neatness of his Bayswater flat that Jude couldn't help feeling that the difference must express something in Piers Targett's personality. Another secret perhaps, something else that would require explanation.

In spite of the circumstances, she hadn't stopped finding Piers attractive. There was something impossibly engaging, almost vulnerable, about the way his white hair flopped down over his ears. The temptation had been strong when she first arrived to throw herself into his arms, listen to whatever he said, believe whatever he said. But she had confined their contact to a chaste kiss on the lips. She forced herself not to succumb to his charms until she had heard what he had to say for himself.

'So this business you were conducting in Paris?' she asked. 'Am I allowed to know what it was?'

'Oh, just...stuff.' He shrugged airily. 'To do with money. Boring but necessary.'

'Oenone Playfair said you had "fingers in many pies".'

'Did she? Well, as ever, Oenone was spot on. And, given the current economic situation, it looks like I'm going to have to find a lot more pies to dig my grubby little fingers into.'

'Hm,' was all that Jude said. There were so many questions that she wanted to ask, she didn't know where to start. And the tone of too many of them would sound like the peevish huffiness of a woman scorned. Which was not an image that Jude had ever wanted to present.

Fortunately Piers took the initiative, divining the thought that was uppermost in her mind. 'What you want to know, I dare say, Jude, is why I didn't tell you I was going to come back earlier.'

'The thought had crossed my mind.' Keep it light, keep it at the level of banter.

'The fact is—' he looked awkward— 'there were one or two things I needed to sort out down here, so I wanted to get those sorted and then pick up where I left off with you...sort of, with a clear mind.'

'Are you sure you don't mean a clear conscience?'

'Absolutely bloody sure! Look, Jude, if you think I'm trying to keep something from you, if you're even suggesting that I might have something going on with another woman, well, you're totally barking up the wrong tree.'

'I'm glad to hear it. But you must see why, if I were the kind of woman who's prone to paranoia, a few anxieties might be kicking in.'

'Why?'

'Oh, come on, Piers. Don't pretend to be more naive than you really are. Everything you do is shrouded in such secrecy.'

'I thought we'd talked about this, Jude, about not wanting to live in each other's pockets. If I could quote your own words back to you, I seem to remember your saying, "I don't want to be part of one of those couples where each of them knows exactly what the other's doing every minute of the day."'

She couldn't deny it. She had said that. 'All right, all right, take your point. And I don't want to be like that. But I still can't help finding it odd that you didn't tell me that you were going to come back from Paris two days earlier than you'd intended.'

'I told you. I had stuff to do here.'

'What kind of stuff?' Jude hated herself for asking the question.

'Just stuff. Nothing that would interest you.'

'If it wouldn't interest me, then there's no reason why you shouldn't tell me about it.'

'One thing I've never wanted to do in our relationship, Jude, is to bore you.'

'Oh, very slick.' Jude grinned. 'The old silver tongue working overtime again.' Her expression changed. 'What was this "stuff" that was so important you couldn't ring me or text me to say that you'd come back from Paris early?'

Piers Targett looked at her ruefully, then sighed. 'All right.' He gestured round the kitchen. 'It's this place. I want to put it on the market. Which means contacting estate agents, sorting out a cleaner to do a basic tidy-up, a gardener to make the outside look vaguely presentable. That's what I've been doing this morning…well, most of the day, actually. All that stuff…which, as I say, is not very interesting.'

'And none of this was to do with Reggie Playfair's death?'

He looked totally shocked by the question. 'No.

Why should my putting this place on the market have anything to do with poor old Reggie?'

'I didn't mean that. I meant has any of the other "stuff" you've been doing had anything to do with his death?'

Piers Targett shook his head in a manner that contained puzzlement and also some other emotion that Jude could not quite identify.

'Sorry about that,' she said. 'Going up a blind alley. But there is one thing I do want to ask.'

'Ask away.'

'Why have you suddenly decided you want to put this house on the market? From all accounts, you've owned it for quite a while, not used it much, spent an increasing amount of time in London. So why now? Why do you suddenly want to sell now?'

He grinned wryly. 'Partly it's financial. Some of my investments—some of my "pies" as Oenone calls them—have proved to have less filling in them than I'd hoped. So realizing a bit of capital and then going off to find more lucrative pies to dip my fingers into, well, that's part of the reason.

'The other bit—' he turned the full beam of his deep blue eyes on her— 'is to do with you.'

'In what way to do with me?'

'Look, Jude, this place represents a different part of my life. This is where I lived when…' The supremely articulate Piers Targett seemed to run out of words.

'When you were married?' Jude suggested.

'Yes. And well, as I told you, I still am technically married. Not divorced, anyway. But I couldn't move on. I couldn't get rid of this place, even though I was hardly ever here, even though I've let it become such a tip. Every time I considered doing something about the place, inertia overcame me. It was all too much effort. Then I met you, and suddenly I had a reason for wanting to close that chapter of my life. Suddenly I had a reason to want to move on. And I felt I had to set that whole process in motion before I could get back in touch with you. Does that make any kind of sense, Jude?'

'Yes,' she said, her voice thick with emotion. 'Yes, it does, Piers.'

Their eyes interlocked and they were drawn ineluctably towards each other. But before they touched, they both froze at the sound of the front door clattering open and shut.

A woman with long blonded hair appeared in the kitchen doorway.

'Ah,' she said. 'So this is the new one, Piers?' She looked Jude appraisingly up and down. 'First time you've gone for bulk.' And almost before the insult had had time to sink in, she announced, 'I'm Jonquil Targett. Piers' wife.'

SIXTEEN

'So what's he told you about me?' demanded Jonquil Targett. 'Nothing, if I know Piers. Presenting himself as the poor, suffering divorcé, finally having got over the trauma of the relationship in which he'd invested so much emotional capital and at last ready to take the first stumbling steps towards a new one? Only needing the love of a good woman? Is that the image he's projected to you?'

'No,' replied Jude with more coolness than she felt. 'Piers has not told me he's divorced. He's made no secret of the fact that he's still technically married.'

'Technically? Huh, I like that. Reducing me to a small technicality in his life. I hope he hasn't pretended to you that you're the first of his girlfriends.'

'No, he's never suggested that.'

'Though I think you're the first he's brought back to this house, the house that we jointly own.'

Jude tried to think back to what Piers had actually said about his emotional history and realized that it had been very little. They'd been so caught up in the happiness they'd found in each other that most other things had seemed irrelevant. They'd both known that there were big subjects that they would have to deal with eventually if their relationship progressed. But shelving such discussions for the time being had suited both of them.

'Jonquil, just leave her alone,' said Piers in a voice Jude hadn't heard from him before. There was a note of despair in it. Gone was the urbane articulacy. In his wife's presence Piers Targett seemed immobilized, struck down by the same inertia that he had said prevented him from selling the house.

Jonquil knew the power she had over him, and gloried in it. She was an attractive woman, probably about the same age as Jude, but thin as a rake. The long blonded hair, though perhaps a bit too young for her, had been expertly done. She was dressed in the kind of tight sweater and jeans that people with her figure could get away with.

'Piers,' said Jude, 'I think I'll go now.'

'No, don't.'

'I think I should.'

He didn't argue any further. Jonquil had drained the will out of him. 'Look, I'll give you a call,' he said. 'I can explain.'

As she went out through the front door, Jude wondered how many men had used that pathetic, hopeless expression over the years. 'I can explain.' And how many women had accepted those explanations, knowing all the time that they were as false as the lies that had got the man into the position of needing to explain in the first place?

It was nearly dark, but at least the rain from earlier in the afternoon had stopped. Jude didn't know exactly where she was, but she remembered the car going through the small village of Goffham just before they reached their destination. And in that small village there had been a pub. She'd walk back there, have a glass of wine—no, a large Scotch—and phone for a cab to take her back to Fethering.

Untidily parked on the gravel outside the house there was now a Nissan Figaro, presumably the car in which Jonquil Targett had arrived. Its baby-blue paint looked somehow ineffectual beside the classic scarlet of the E-Type. As she walked past, Jude noticed something white draped haphazardly across the Figaro's back seat.

It was a wedding dress.

MID MORNING ON the Sunday, Carole rang the number Susan Holland had given her for Donna Grodsky. When the phone was answered there was a baby crying in the background. She explained that she was trying to find out what had happened to Marina.

'Are you police or something?' asked the suspicious voice from the other end of the line.

Carole was only fleetingly tempted to lie. 'No,' she said.

'Good. Because they were bloody useless when Marina originally disappeared.'

'I was wondering if you would be prepared to talk to me about what might have happened to her?'

Donna Grodsky didn't sound keen. 'What do I get out of it?' she asked.

The only answer Carole could come up with sounded a bit feeble to her. 'I could buy you lunch.'

As it turned out, that was spot on. 'Yeah, all right. I never get out of the bloody house these days, what with the baby and everything.'

She gave the name of a pub, the George's Head in the Moulsecoomb area of Brighton, and they agreed that Carole would appear there the following morning at twelve. 'It's a good time, because sometimes the little bugger has a kip round then.'

As she put the phone down, Carole felt a warm glow. She did get a charge out of conducting an investigation independently of Jude. Yes, they worked very well together, but Carole didn't really need Jude. With her Home Office background, it was Carole Seddon who supplied the intellectual rigour in their investigations. Her neighbour's method had always been based more on intuition and outrageous good luck. Not that she was jealous, of course, but Jude did just swan through life so easily.

Little did Carole suspect that next door at Woodside Cottage her neighbour was still crying.

JUDE'S MOBILE RANG on the Sunday evening. The number calling was Piers Targett's. She answered it instantly, but it wasn't Piers at the other end.

'Hello. I'm calling on Piers' mobile. It's Jonquil. We met earlier.'

'I remember.' What on earth did the woman want? To pour out more poison about her husband? To hurt Jude even more?

'I gather you were with Piers when he found Reggie Playfair's body at the tennis court...'

'Yes.'

'Did you see him take the poor old bugger's mobile phone?'

'What? No, I didn't.'

But the scene came back very vividly. Finding Reggie lying on the court... Then Piers sending her off to fetch his iPhone from the car...because he wanted

a moment alone with the corpse of his old friend…
If he planned to purloin the dead man's mobile, he'd
created the perfect opportunity.

'Well, Piers has got it. I saw it in his jacket pocket,
recognized it straight away—Reggie had this case specially made for it in purple and green stripes—the
Lockleigh House club colours.'

And Jonquil Targett echoed Jude's thoughts exactly
as she went on, 'Now, why on earth would Piers want
to take Reggie's mobile?'

SEVENTEEN

BRIGHTON IS A big city and Carole Seddon only really knew the centre of it. The sea front, the Pier, the Royal Pavilion, the intricate trendy thoroughfares of The Lanes, the Marina, all of those were familiar to her. But she'd never been to Moulsecoomb before.

She was characteristically early for her meeting with Donna Grodsky, drawing the Renault neatly into the pub car park just before eleven forty-five. The George's Head did not look at all Carole Seddon's sort of pub. It was painted white, but every outside feature—window frames and surrounds, doorways, mock-Tudor beams and guttering were picked out in a garish red. An array of colourfully chalked blackboard signs stood outside, offering happy hours, meal deals, senior specials, karaoke nights and the inevitable Sky Sports.

Carole, whose attitudes had changed since she became a regular at Fethering's Crown and Anchor, went instantly back to her default position of not being 'a pub person'. Still, she was at the George's Head in Moulsecoomb in the cause of investigation, so she swallowed her prejudices and entered.

She was surprised by how noisy it was at that time of day. Part of the sound came from the massive screens at each end of the bar, one of them apparently tuned to sport and the other to a pop-music channel.

But there were also a lot of customers in there, all talking loudly and none paying any attention to either of the televisions.

Elderly couples sat at tables, consulting menus with great concentration as they tried to decide which senior special to opt for when orders started to be taken at twelve. Standing at the bar were quite a few of what Carole thought of as 'workmen' (in other words men with faded tattoos in sleeveless T-shirts), but also around the tables a good few of what she thought of as 'single mothers' (with buggies and rather newer tattoos). It was this demographic that Carole expected shortly to be joined by Donna Grodsky.

She advanced awkwardly to the bar, feeling every eye in the place was on her (though actually nobody showed any interest). Agonizing over whether a pub like the George's Head in Moulsecoomb would stock Chilean Chardonnay, and indeed whether she should have an alcoholic drink when she was not only driving but also investigating, her thoughts were interrupted by a shout of 'Hi! Are you Carole?'

She turned to face what had to be Donna Grodsky. The girl, as she had said she would be on the phone, was dressed in a gold hoodie and jeans with a lot of diamanté on them. Her hair with blonde highlights was scraped back into a scrunchy so tight that it was flat against her head. The face was heavily made up with eyelashes too long to be real, and a silver stud pierced her lower lip.

In the buggy beside her, in immaculately clean blankets and Babygro, with a tiny blue baseball cap on his head, lay her baby, angelically sleeping. Carole wouldn't in the past have been much good at estimating infant's ages, but up to speed thanks to Lily's appearance in her life, she would have estimated he was about four months old.

'Hello, you must be Donna.'

'Dead right.'

'How did you know it was me?'

Donna Grodsky looked around the pub and grinned. No one else was wearing a Burberry raincoat. Or such sensible shoes. 'I just knew.'

'Now, can I get you a drink?'

'I've got one.' The girl indicated what looked like a Coke in front of her.

'Oh, you shouldn't have—'

'Don't worry. I've started a tab for you with Vin at the bar.'

'Oh?'

The girl took a long swig from her drink. 'And actually I'm ready for another.'

'Coke, is it?'

'With a large voddy in, yes.'

Vin, the girl at the bar, knew about 'Donna's tab' and knew she'd want a 'large voddy and Coke'. Carole wondered idly what 'Vin' might stand for. The girl didn't look like her idea of a 'Lavinia', but she couldn't think of anything else.

Carole had by now decided that she was definitely going to need a drink. To her surprise the George's Head turned out to have an extensive wine list and she got her Chilean Chardonnay.

Back at the table she found Donna Grodsky studying the huge A3-size menu. 'Better order quick. Hell trying to eat once the little bugger wakes up.'

'What's his name?' asked Carole.

'Kyle.' The girl looked at her defiantly. 'And I love him to bits.' She put down the menu. 'I'll get the sirloin steak, medium rare, with everything and extra onion rings.'

It was the most expensive item on the menu. Carole wondered briefly if she was being taken for a ride. On the other hand, all of the prices at the George's Head were extraordinarily cheap. And if Donna Grodsky did have any useful information... She gave in the order at the bar, adding a tuna and cucumber baguette for herself.

Carole was disarmed when she returned to the table by Donna saying, 'Thanks for picking up the tab and that. I used to be quite a girl for the clubs and the pubs, but since I've had Kyle...' She raised her unfinished first glass, said 'Cheers' and gulped down what was left. 'Real treat for me these days, this is,' she went on. 'Getting out of the flat, seeing people who aren't Kyle or my mum.'

'His father...?' asked Carole tentatively.

The girl let out a bitter chuckle. 'What do you think? He scarpered soon as he knew I was up the duff. Not that I mind. I wasn't in love or anything like that. He was quite fit but, anyway, he served his purpose.'

'You mean you wanted to get pregnant?'

'Too right I did. Always wanted to have something I could really call my own. Now I've got Kyle. Anyway, council wouldn't have given me the flat if I hadn't got the baby.'

Carole bit back various *Daily Mail* responses that were rising up towards her lips. 'If we could talk about Marina...'

'Sure. I liked her. That's why I hope nothing bad's happened to her.'

'Her mother thinks she was murdered.'

'I know. But there's lots of things that can happen to girls of her age that aren't murder.'

'That would cause her to disappear?'

'Yeah. I know plenty of girls down here in Brighton who just moved out of their homes. Mostly from a long way away, Scotland, the North. They just couldn't stand the way their parents kept going on at them. Nobody knows where they are, but they haven't been murdered. They've just started leading different lives.'

'And you think that's what happened with Marina?'

'I think it's more likely than her being murdered.'

'You're probably right. Susan—Marina's mother— talked about her having a lot of sleepovers with her school friends…'

'Nothing odd in that. We all did.'

'Did she stay at your place?'

'Coupla times. Look, I know what you're going to ask next.'

'Oh?'

'Did she stay with me the night before she went missing?'

The girl was brighter than her appearance might suggest. 'How did you know I was going to ask that?'

'Because the police did too. It's the obvious question to ask.'

'You said on the phone you weren't very impressed with the police's enquiries into Marina's disappearance.'

'No, well, they just went through the motions. Don't blame them really. Marina was sixteen, over the age of consent. If she wanted to move in with a boyfriend, well, that was her business, wasn't it?'

Carole was very quick to pick up on that. 'And is that what she did? Move in with a boyfriend?'

Donna Grodsky blushed. She'd said more than she intended. 'I don't know,' she stuttered. 'I mean, that's what she said she wanted to do, but I don't know if it was kind of just an idea or if she'd actually got someone in mind.'

'Did you tell the police what she'd said?'

'No, of course I bloody didn't!'

'Why not?'

'Because she was my mate. Look, if she's moved in with some bloke to get away from her mum, I'm not being much of a mate if I set the police off investigating that possibility, am I?'

'And for the same reason you didn't tell her mother?'

'Of course I didn't.'

They were interrupted at that moment by the arrival of Vin with their food. The portions were massive. Donna's steak and accompaniments hardly fitted on her plate. And Carole's baguette was served with chips, which she hadn't expected. But they did look rather good chips.

Carole noticed that both their glasses were empty. 'I don't know if you…?'

'Yeah. Vin, get me another large voddy and Coke. And same again for Carole.'

'Oh, I'm not sure that I—'

'Go on, get 'em, Vin.' As the barmaid went off, Donna Grodsky demanded, 'Why're you looking at me like that, Carole?'

'I'm not looking at you like anything.'

'Yes, you are, and I know exactly what you're thinking. Third double vodka and she's meant to be in charge of a baby.'

'No, I wasn't—'

'You don't think I'm breastfeeding the little bugger, do you?'

'No, I—'

'Look, I'll have you know this is the first drink I've had for three weeks. I can't afford booze on the pittance of a handout the government gives me. So when someone offers me a drink, I'm not going to say no, am I? And it's not like you're not getting what you asked for. I'm answering your questions, aren't I?'

'Yes. I'm very grateful for—'

'Then why're you looking so bloody disapproving?'

'I'm not deliberately doing it. I just think,' Carole confessed, 'that I've got the kind of face that does rather...tend to look disapproving.'

Donna Grodsky looked at her and then suddenly burst out laughing. 'I think you're right, you know. You've hit the nail bang on the head there. You were born looking disapproving, weren't you?' She looked down sharply to the buggy where Kyle was starting to move his little arms. 'Better get a move on with the eating. He'll be waking up in a few minutes. Then he'll want to be picked up and have his bottle.'

'Do you mind if we get on with the questions too?' asked Carole.

'Not if you don't mind.'

'Why should I mind?'

'Well, my mum always told me—and I'm sure your

mummy told you, and all—that it was bad manners for me to talk with my mouth full.'

Carole realized that she was being sent up. She grinned. Donna grinned back. Maybe there had started to be something of a bond between them.

'The obvious next question,' said Carole, 'is whether you have any idea whether Marina really did have a boyfriend and if so, who he was.'

'I agree,' Donna replied through a mouthful of steak and onion rings. 'That is the obvious question. And the answer is, I don't know. Marina never gave me any name or anything like that. But I think I know the kind of boyfriend she would have liked to have.'

'What do you mean?'

'Listen, Carole, I don't know if you know about where Marina come from…'

'Her mother told me about her being found in a rubber dinghy.'

'Yeah, so you know the basics. Anyway, Marina was convinced that her real parents were Russian. That's why she was drawn to me. As you might have deduced from my surname, I am not one hundred per cent through-and-through British. My dad was a Russian sailor, came home to see my mum between trips off round the world. Well, he did for a while. Then he buggered off, rather in the manner of Kyle's Dad. Do you detect a pattern here, Carole?'

'I'm not quite sure what you—'

'It's a pattern called men, that's what it is.'

The baby in the buggy was beginning to twitch and make little grunting noises. Carole didn't have the young mother's undivided attention for a lot longer.

'So are you saying that Marina had a Russian boy-friend?'

'No, but I'm saying if she was looking for a boy-friend, she'd have tried to link up with Brighton's Russian community.'

'Is there much of a Russian community in Brighton?'

'A bit, yeah. There is in most big cities. You know, they've got their social clubs, that kind of thing. Restaurants, pubs they go to.'

'Did Marina know about these places?'

'I'd told her a bit, yes. My mum knew about them, from when she and my dad…well, we're talking some time back obviously. Probably the places she knew had closed, but other ones had come along. Anyway, Marina was fascinated by all this stuff. She was convinced that she really was Russian and, well, if any Russian boy had come on to her, she'd have let him do anything to her.'

'And did any Russian boy come on to her?'

Donna Grodsky shrugged. 'I've no idea.'

'Did she mention any Russian boy's name?'

'She mentioned a few, but, look, I'm not going to remember them, am I? We're talking over eight years ago.'

'Are you sure you can't remember a name?'

The girl screwed up her eyes with the effort of recollection. The lashes looked as if two large black moths had settled on her face. 'Oh, there was one boy Marina talked about. Vladimir, I think…Vladimir… oh, God, what was the surname? Mind you, I don't know if he even existed. Marina was a great one for her fantasies. Lived in a kind of dream world, you know, where somehow her Russian heritage was going to claim her back at some point. I took everything she said with a large sack-load of salt.'

'Vladimir…? Vladimir…?' prompted Carole patiently, hoping to stir Donna's memory for a second name.

But she was only rewarded by a shake of the head and the eyes reopening. 'No, it's gone.'

'Are you sure you don't know the name of—'

'I've told you, I don't *know* anything. It's just, as I said, if I was trying to find out what'd happened to Marina, I'd check out the Russian connection.'

'Right, thank you.'

'And the other thing I'd check out,' said Donna Grodsky as she swept up the juices of her steak with the last few chips, 'is Marina's Dad.'

'Iain Holland?'

'Yeah.'

'Why?'

'Because I always thought he was a shifty bastard. And though he treated her like shit, Marina still kind of worshipped him.'

'Susan said she was as rude and bolshie to him as she was to her.'

'Doesn't mean she didn't worship him. There's something about fathers and daughters. My dad treated my mum like shit, treated me like shit, and all…' The grotesquely long eyelashes tried to flick away tears. 'Doesn't mean I wouldn't like to see him again. Doesn't mean I don't miss him.'

Kyle was now wide awake and crying. Donna Grodsky shoved the last chip into her mouth and swigged down the remains of her third voddy and Coke. 'Good timing, eh? God knows I've had enough practice. Oh, what's the matter with Mum's lovely boy then?'

Carole, aware that the last sentence wasn't addressed to her and that her time was very short, asked, 'Do you have any way of contacting Iain Holland?'

'Haven't got an address or anything, but shouldn't be too difficult to track him down.'

'Really?'

'He's all over the local paper every week.'

'Why?'

'Because he's a very important local councillor. New squeaky-clean wife, new squeaky-clean kids, new squeaky-clean social conscience. Oh yes, round Brighton, Iain Holland is very definitely a pillar of the community.'

CAROLE SEDDON DROVE back to Fethering, sedately careful in her Renault, with three strong impressions. One, that Donna Grodsky was an extremely intelligent young woman. Two, that she was also a very good mother. And three, that the prices in the George's Head in Moulsecoomb were really very reasonable.

And she didn't at all regret the twenty-pound note she had pressed into the girl's hand as they parted.

EIGHTEEN

JUDE WAS STILL in a bad way. She'd had two clients booked in for sessions on the Monday morning, but postponed both of them. She knew from experience that healing required all her focus and energy. When she was preoccupied with something else it just didn't work.

And she felt bad about what was preoccupying her. The laid-back manner and serenity she displayed to the world were genuine, but they had not come to her without effort. Though the carapace she had built around herself was less instantly visible than Carole's, she too had created a protective layer to keep her from the worst excesses of her emotions. And one of the ways in which she had shielded herself was by not falling in love.

There had been a good few lovers in Jude's past— though not as many as her next-door neighbour fantasised that there were. And of course there had been the two marriages. But since she'd moved to Fethering her life had been quieter. She'd indulged in the odd one-night stand, the occasional nostalgic coupling with an ex-boyfriend, and then she had nursed a former lover, Laurence Hawker, till his death from cancer. But that period of her life with Laurence, though painful, had had an elegiac quality to it. Not the heady mania of a new love affair.

But that was what she had tumbled straight into with Piers Targett, and now Jude felt stupid for having been so precipitate. Both of them knew that there were stories from their pasts that must at some point be told. But they were both so enjoying the moment that they didn't want to spoil it. For Jude and Piers love had come first; getting to know each other could wait.

Not any more. Jude had gone over again and again the scene with Piers and Jonquil Targett. His wife had spoken of 'the house we jointly own'. Did that mean they still cohabited there? Was that why Piers had hardly mentioned the place to Jude? And why he had made no attempt to invite her there?

On the other hand, the Goffham cottage's state of neglect did not suggest that it was regularly occupied. So maybe Jonquil Targett's arrival there on the Saturday had just been a coincidence? Or maybe Piers had summoned her there to have a final confrontation, to get her agreement to his putting their shared property on the market?

Jude tried not to dwell on it, but she couldn't help remembering what Piers had been talking about just before Jonquil's arrival. He'd said that what made him want finally to sell the house was having met her. Jude. He wanted to 'close that chapter' of his life. Did that mean he was looking forward to a new life that included her?

These thoughts circled infuriatingly round and round in her head and she despised herself for letting them. It was so unlike her. This wasn't the Jude she felt comfortable with, the strong Jude she had so carefully constructed over the years. She hated behaving like a snivelling schoolgirl.

Shilly-shallying wasn't in her nature. Her instinct was to get everything out in the open, have a confrontation if necessary, but at least not bottle things up. A hundred times on the Sunday she had contemplated just picking up her phone and ringing Piers. But each time she restrained herself, thinking, no, the ball's in his court. When he's sorted out whatever he needs to sort out with his wife, then he'll get back to me.

By the Monday morning the temptation to ring Piers hadn't weakened. In fact, through Jude's largely sleepless night it had got stronger. But still she resisted it.

She was hugely relieved, though, when mid-morning the phone rang. She pounced on it, feeling sure it must finally be Piers.

It wasn't. The voice was the extremely cultured one of a mature woman who had been to all the right schools and moved in all the right circles.

'Good morning. Is that Jude?'

'Yes.'

'This is Felicity Budgen. We met at Lockleigh House tennis court during the Secretary's Cup.'

'Yes, of course, I remember.'

'I'm sorry to trouble you, but it's in connection with dear Reggie Playfair's death.' Felicity Budgen was far too genteel to use the expression 'poor old bugger'.

'Oh yes?'

'Now, Oenone Playfair's a very dear friend of mine, and I understand from her that you were actually with Piers Targett when he discovered poor Reggie's body...'

'Yes, I was.'

'I'm so sorry you had to experience that. It must

have been a terrible shock.' She spoke with the practised empathy of an ambassador's wife comforting
the bereaved.

'Yes, it was a shock, but don't worry, I'm fine.'

'I'm very glad to hear that. Now, I don't know
whether you know, Jude, but Reggie's funeral is on
Thursday.'

'Yes, I had heard.'

'I don't know whether you'll be coming with
Piers…?'

No need for Jude to say that the two of them were
currently not communicating. 'He hasn't mentioned
it. And it's not as if I knew Reggie Playfair well. Just
met him very briefly on that Sunday.'

'Yes, of course. Well, needless to say, Oenone's up
to her ears with arrangements for the funeral, and I'm
trying to take any burdens I can off her back.' There
was a silence, as if the woman was making prepara-
tions for her next sentence. 'Now there is one thing
that's worrying Oenone and, as I say, she's got more
than enough on her plate at the moment, so I'm making enquiries on her behalf.'

Jude had had enough of this diplomatic circumlo-
cution. 'What's it about?' she asked.

'It's about Reggie Playfair's mobile phone.'

That wretched mobile phone. There seemed to be
no way of escaping the subject.

'What about it?'

'Well, Oenone hasn't been able to find the thing.
She's checked through Reggie's belongings that came
back from the hospital, and she's looked through his
car. She'd got George Hazlitt to check out around the
tennis court. No sign of it. So I was just wondering

whether you actually saw a mobile phone near Reggie's body…you know, when you…' Graciously Felicity Budgen didn't spell out the details.

'No, I'm afraid I didn't see any sign of it.'

'I thought that would probably be the case, but it was worth asking. As I say, anything that can be done to save Oenone further distress…'

'Of course.' Jude had a moment of hesitation before she went on, 'It might be worth asking Piers. I wasn't with him all the time when we were at the court. He might have seen something I didn't.'

'Yes, what a very good idea. I'll give him a call.' But Felicity Budgen didn't sound as if that would be the first thing on her agenda. 'Anyway, it's been a pleasure to talk to you, Jude. And I probably won't see you Thursday…?'

'Probably not.'

'No. Well, hope to see you round the tennis court with Piers on another occasion.'

I wouldn't count on it, thought Jude bitterly.

THE CALL SHE was waiting for came through late that afternoon, by which time she had to some extent got her head together. She had done some special yoga exercises, which calmed her, and by the end of them she'd reconciled herself to the idea that she was never going to see Piers Targett again. The thought didn't make her happy, but at least it was the first broad stroke of the thick black line she was determined to draw under the whole episode.

Then Piers phoned her and her embryonic defences crumbled instantly.

'"I can explain",' he quoted ironically. 'I'm sorry,

Jude, but I can't let the last words you ever hear from me be the cliché response of every guilty husband in every dreadful farce ever written—"I can explain".'

His description so exactly matched what she had thought of the words when he'd said them on the Saturday afternoon that Jude couldn't prevent the eruption of a small giggle. It was also relief, relief at finally hearing his voice after the torture of the previous days.

'But can you?' she asked.

'Explain? Well, I can give you some relevant information.'

'Something which has been rather lacking from you since we first met.'

'*Mea culpa*. On the other hand, I don't think you can be completely exonerated from the same charge.'

'Fair enough. I agree, there's a lot you don't know about me.'

'Well, maybe we should get together and barter chunks of our pasts…?'

Two minutes before Jude had been determined that she would never see Piers Targett again. But it didn't take long for her to say, 'I think that'd be a very good idea.'

'Where? Some kind of neutral ground? A pub? A bar?'

'No.' Jude felt too emotionally fragile to conduct their next meeting in public. 'You come round here.'

NINETEEN

'THE FACT IS that Jonquil is bipolar,' said Piers. 'The condition's kind of contained so long as she takes her medication, but I'm afraid she's sometimes very perverse about taking her medication.'

'But are you still married to her?' asked Jude.

'Yes. I've never denied I am.'

'I meant, are you still cohabiting?'

'What, at the house in Goffham? God, no. Neither of us lives there. Surely you could see that from the state of the place?'

'Then why were you there?'

'For the reasons I told you. Look, I'm not a liar, Jude. I told you I was down there to get on to an estate agent, to get the place on the market as soon as possible—and that's true.'

'All right, let's change the question a little. Why was Jonquil there?'

'Ah.'

There was a silence. They hadn't touched since Piers arrived at Woodside Cottage, not a peck on the cheek or even a handshake, but Jude could still feel the magnetism of his presence. Slowly he answered her.

'Jonquil, as I say, is very volatile. She can agree to something one day and then totally disagree the next. For a long time I've been trying to get her to agree to the sale of the Goffham house. But she's kept being resistant to the idea.'

'Is that because she thinks it represents your marriage? That once that's sold, it will be a kind of acknowledgement that the marriage is really over?'

'God, no. Jonquil was the one who wanted the marriage over, at least initially. She was the one who kept on having affairs and saying how claustrophobic she felt in the relationship. For a long time I thought I could somehow still make it work.'

'And do you still think that, Piers?'

'No. For years now I've really known that it was over. But I dithered. Because of her mental state, Jonquil can be very vulnerable at times. I didn't want to do anything that might push her over the edge.'

'What do you mean by "push her over the edge"?'

'I mean: make her do something stupid.'

'And you're using "do something stupid" in the traditional sense of attempting suicide?'

'Yes, I suppose I am. It wouldn't be the first time.'

'Jonquil has attempted suicide before?' He nodded. 'Genuine attempts, actually trying to kill herself, or just as a means of gaining attention?'

'In retrospect I'd have said the latter. But that didn't make them any less scary at the time. And didn't make me feel any less guilty.'

Of course it was going to be true, thought Jude again, that nobody gets to our age without accumulating baggage. And it seemed like Piers Targett had got a serious amount of baggage. 'You still haven't told me why Jonquil came to the house on Saturday,' she reminded him.

'No. Well, as I say, she's very inconsistent, but I'd

spoken to her when I got back from Paris on Friday evening.'

Jude couldn't stop herself from remembering jealously that he hadn't found time to ring her the same evening. God, she was pathetic.

'Anyway, I was feeling really positive and I said it was daft for us to go on doing nothing about the house and we really ought to sell it. And Jonquil actually agreed with me. She was very calm and rational and she said she couldn't imagine why we hadn't put the house on the market years ago.'

'Any particular reason why she had changed her mind?'

'She's got a new chap.'

'Do you know who he is?'

'No idea. When we were living down here, in quite a lot of cases I did know who her men were, because they were people in our circle. Since she's moved to Brighton, I've no idea who she consorts with.'

'But if she's now in a good relationship, then maybe that'll take the pressure off you, and she'll finally get out of your life…?'

'Jude, I've been here before. Many times. With Jonquil every new relationship is going to be The Big Thing. And so it is for a few weeks, months sometimes, years in my case…and then she starts getting unsettled and jealous…and pretty soon she's off with someone else. It's a recurring pattern with her, one that I'm afraid never gets broken.'

'So why did she appear at the house on Saturday?'

'Because she'd changed her mind. Whatever she'd said on the Friday evening, on the Saturday she no longer wanted to sell the house. She could have told me on the phone but, being Jonquil, no, of course she had to do it in person. She knew I'd be there, so she decided to give me the latest in a long, long line of shocks.' He sounded infinitely weary. 'The fact that she found you there when she arrived was…I don't know, whatever the opposite of "serendipity" is. Shit, probably.'

'And what did she say after I'd left?'

'Basically that she'd never agree to our selling the house. And a whole lot of other stuff.'

'Like?'

'Old stuff, infinitely recycled recriminations. Believe me, Jude, you really don't want to know.'

She really did want to know, but there'd be time enough in the future to ask those questions. Jude rose from her draped armchair, went across the room and kissed Piers gently on the forehead.

'Now,' she said, 'how about a drink?'

'Do you know what I'm going to do?' said Piers Targett drowsily, after their emotional rapprochement had been followed by a physical rapprochement. He turned over in the bed and looked down at Jude. Her blonde hair was spread in beautiful disarray over the pillow.

'Tell me,' she murmured.

'I'm going to fix for you to have a real tennis lesson with George Hazlitt.'

'Really? Do you think you should?'

'Why not?'

'Well, I wonder if I put a jinx on that tennis court. Remember what happened last time I went there.'

'Hm.' He was silent for a moment, reminded of his old friend's death. 'Incidentally, Reggie's funeral is on Thursday.'

'Yes, I heard from Oenone.'

'Jude…'

'Hm?'

'I'd very much like it if you would come with me to the funeral. I think it's going to be an emotional strain for me. I'd feel better if you were there.'

'Well, if that's what you want I'd be very glad to come.' But even in the peacefulness of love the small idea formed in her mind that she would see a lot of the Lockleigh House tennis court members at the funeral and might be able to advance her investigation a little.

'Anyway, this lesson of yours with George. I'll set it up and let you know when.'

'All right,' said Jude softly. 'Though I don't think I'll ever understand that business of chases…'

'It's very simple,' Piers protested. 'The chase lines are marked in yards parallel with the back wall both ends of the court. If the ball lands *nearer* the back wall than the chase, you say it's *better* than whatever number the chase is. If it lands *further away* from the back wall you say it's *worse* than the…'

Jude was already asleep.

TWENTY

As DONNA GRODSKY had suggested, Carole didn't have any difficulty in finding information about Iain Holland online. He had his own website and there were lots of reports about him from local newspapers. He could also be contacted or followed through LinkedIn, Facebook and Twitter, though these were not avenues she was likely to go down. The day that someone as secretive and paranoid as Carole Seddon might expose secrets of her life to all and sundry over the Internet was the day when hell had not only frozen over but was also hosting the Winter Olympics.

It was clear from all the references that Iain Holland was a Conservative local councillor for one of the Brighton wards. It was also clear that he was an expert at self-promotion. From the amount of events he managed to attend and be photographed at, he must have handed over the day-to-day running of his stationery empire to managers. Fêtes, prize-givings, openings of new buildings, protests, demonstrations, hundredth-birthday cake-cuttings in old people's homes, Iain Holland's smiling face was seen at all of them.

And his CV was everywhere. The story of how he had been educated through the state system, with the help of long after-school hours spent in his local library: how he'd rejected the possibility of university because he 'wanted to get straight into the business of making a living'; how he'd borrowed from his parents to buy a stationery shop that was about to go belly-up; how by dint of sheer hard work and entrepreneurial flair he'd built up that business and gradually added others until he was in charge of one of the country's most recognizable stationery brands.

His devotion as a family man was also stressed. Any photo opportunity that could include his wife and two children was seized upon. It was because of Iain Holland's respect for 'old-fashioned family values' that he had naturally gravitated towards the Conservative Party. He had 'been lucky' in his own business career, and it was now his ambition to 'iron out the inequalities in our society and improve the lot of those to whom life had been less generous.'

There was no doubt that the personality of Iain Holland combined the best qualities of Jesus Christ, Mother Theresa and Margaret Thatcher.

Of his first marriage there was no mention. Susan and Marina had been completely airbrushed out of Iain Holland's history.

Carole Seddon was thoughtful. There was certainly not going to be a problem contacting her quarry. His website seemed to be crying out for everyone in the world to get in touch with his saintly figure. They had only to do that for their problems to be at an end… assuming, that is, that their problems concerned his particular ward in Brighton. But the implication in all his self-aggrandizing self-advertisement was that local politics for Iain Holland would only be a stepping stone to greater things. He was on the right committees within the Conservative national organization. He was a coming man. It appeared to be only a matter of time before he would be standing for some constituency as a prospective MP.

This information—or rather implied information—prompted two thoughts in Carole. One, that Iain Holland had a lot to lose if anything were to come out that might tarnish his squeaky-clean image. And two, that he would be aware of that and would guard himself against indiscretions, being careful about whom he had contact with. If she was going to take the obvious next step in her investigation, she was going to have to be very circumspect.

Her approach to Iain Holland needed a lot of thought. Gulliver was delighted to get the bonus of another walk on Fethering while his mistress worked through her problem.

JUDE FELT A little nervous when Piers dropped her from the E-Type at Lockleigh House tennis court on the Wednesday morning. Not about their relationship. They'd done a lot of talking on the Tuesday when they'd had a Fethering day, walking on the beach, having lunch at the Crown and Anchor, dinner at the local Chinese. It felt more like being a couple and, if anything, their rift over the weekend and subsequent making up had strengthened the feelings they shared.

Piers had even talked about how he made his money, which was chiefly by investing in small companies in Britain and the rest of Europe (hence his trip to Paris). His early career had been in PR. He'd built up his own agency and sold it, clearly for a great deal of money, some five years previously.

He talked about Jonquil's financial affairs too. She had inherited a substantial amount when her parents died, which was why the half-share she'd get from the sale of the Goffham house wasn't of great importance to her.

So when Piers had airily told Jude that on the Wednesday he had to go up to London for 'various meetings, boring money stuff, wouldn't interest you', she was unsuspicious and didn't feel the need to ask for any more detail. They were beginning to recognize the areas of their lives that would overlap and the ones that wouldn't.

But Piers was keen that real tennis should be one of the things that they shared. Which was why he'd set up the lesson with George Hazlitt for Jude that Wednesday morning.

And it was the prospect of that that was making her feel nervous.

Piers had booked the ten fifteen court for her lesson and because of the timing of his London meetings had left her at the court with about half an hour to spare. He had lent her one of his rackets, which lay across her kit and towel in the African straw basket. As she let herself in through the small door to Lockleigh House, Jude looked up at the main building. Above the portico was a window that she reckoned must belong to Cecil Wardock's room. She imagined the old man sitting in there, rereading all the books to which he had devoted his working life.

As Jude entered the court and walked past the pros' office, George Hazlitt looked up from sewing yet another tennis ball to greet her. He glanced at his watch. 'Morning. In good time.'

'Want to get myself in the right frame of mind,' said Jude.

'Good idea.' He grinned. 'You know where the changing rooms are?'

'Sure.'

'And do you know about the etiquette of when you can walk down there?'

'Wait until the players on court change ends.'

'Very good.'

'Piers gave me very specific instructions on that.'

'Excellent.'

'Though he still hasn't managed to explain satisfactorily to me *why* they change ends.'

'Don't worry. All will be clear by the end of your lesson.'

Jude went through the door into the court and waited in the proper manner at the end of the walkway that ran along the length of it. She recognized the player at the other end as Ned Jackson, the junior professional, but the wall prevented her from seeing his opponent. What she didn't recognize was the game they were playing. Her experience of watching the Sec's Cup and the Old Boys' doubles had not prepared her for the speed and power of a high-class singles match. Ned seemed to anticipate every return, taking a few small steps to position himself, plucking the ball out of the air with his racket and redirecting it with incredible accuracy. One of his balls came rocketing straight towards her and she was glad of the netting that stopped its progress. As the shot hit home, a hanging bell rang and Jude congratulated herself on remembering that the ball had found the winning gallery.

'Forty-thirty,' said Ned Jackson. 'Chase better than two.'

Still for no reason that made any sense to Jude, this was apparently the signal for the two players to change ends. While they did so, she made her way towards the club room. She could now see Ned's opponent, whom she didn't recognize but he, like the junior professional, looked supremely fit, without a spare ounce of fat on him anywhere.

When she was changed into her over-tight shorts, white cheesecloth shirt, socks and trainers, she sat in the dedans, clutching the racket Piers had lent her, and watched more of the young men's game. She was again impressed, not only by their athleticism, but by their retrieval skills. From anywhere in the court, even the lowest and tightest corners, they seemed able to pick the ball out and return it with interest. She came to realize that real tennis was a serious sport, not just a leisure activity for old fogies. Also the vowels of Ned Jackson's opponent suggested that it wasn't just a game for toffs either.

During one of her marriages Jude had played quite a lot of lawn tennis. Not at a very competitive level, it had been purely social, but she wondered how much of it would come back to her when she stepped out on to the court. She also wondered, the longer she watched the young men play, how much use anything she remembered from her old skills might be. Real tennis really was a very different game from 'lawners'.

It was ten past ten. Ned and his opponent had got to five-all in what appeared to be the deciding set, so Jude was reckoning either she'd have to wait for her lesson or the young men wouldn't finish their game. From her experience of lawn tennis, she knew that the winner of a set had to be two games clear. But then at forty-thirty ahead, Ned Jackson sent another shot zinging into the winning gallery and his opponent capitulated. He slumped forward and shouted, 'Lovely shot!'

'Thanks!'

'Should help get your handicap down.'

'That's the aim of the exercise.'

The two young men clasped hands across the net. 'You're on fire today, Ned,' said the vanquished one. 'Is that because you're going to see Tonya tonight? Another of your "love-all" assignations?'

'Maybe, maybe not,' the junior professional replied enigmatically.

'You dirty dog,' said his opponent and they both roared with laughter.

JUST AS CAROLE SEDDON would not in a million years have gone near LinkedIn, Facebook or Twitter, she was also very circumspect about her email address. Her name did not appear in it; instead she used her house 'High Tor' with a combination of numbers that had featured in her staff ID when she worked for the Home Office. This precaution might have seemed excessive, given that most of her email communication was with Stephen and Gaby, but, when it came to approaching Iain Holland, Carole was glad of her anonymity.

She had run through a lot of ideas on Fethering Beach the previous day, but it was not until the Wednesday morning that she had decided on the wording that would go into her email to the contact box on the local councillor's website.

The message read simply: 'I am interested in the

whereabouts of your daughter Marina Holland. If you are also interested, get back to me.'

Carole was aware of the ambiguities in her words. They implied greater knowledge than she had. And the word 'whereabouts' might suggest an unsubstantiated belief that Marina Holland was still alive. Carole was taking a risk, but reckoned that risk was worthwhile. The worst that could happen—and indeed the most likely thing to happen—was that Iain Holland would ignore her email and send no reply. But there was the distant possibility that her message might provoke a response.

Carole Seddon took a deep breath and clicked on the 'send' button.

TWENTY-ONE

WHEN JUDE'S LESSON started and they were standing at the net by the entrance to the court, the first thing she asked the track-suited George Hazlitt was about the scoring. 'In real tennis,' he explained, 'it's different from lawn tennis. You only need to be one game ahead to win the set. Get to six-five and you've won it.'

'Any other differences?'

'Well, you still go fifteen—thirty—forty—game, like in lawn tennis. But you call the score of the person who's won the last point first.'

'I beg your pardon?' said Jude, whose hope that there couldn't be any further perversity in the rules of real tennis had just been disappointed.

'Well, you see, Jude, in lawn tennis the players take the service in alternate games. In real tennis the service can change any number of times in a single game.'

'So that's what happens when they change ends?'

'Exactly.' George Hazlitt nodded encouragingly.

Now for the big one. 'But *why* do they change ends?'

'Ah well, this is to do with chases.'

Jude raised her hands in horror. 'Please, not chases. Piers has tried to explain chases to me more times than I care to remember and—'

'Don't worry.' The pro grinned. 'Forget about chases. We'll come to that later. Let's start with just the basics—hitting the ball.' He reached down to a circular recess in the court floor and picked up the basket full of balls that nestled there. 'Look, I'll go down the service end—that's where the dedans is—and you go down the hazard end and I'll just send a few balls down to you and see how you go. You say you have played a bit of lawn tennis?'

'Not for a long time.'

'Well, the first thing you're going to notice is that the bounce of a real tennis ball is very different.' He picked one out of the basket and slammed it down with considerable force on to the stone floor of the court. It bounced up about his shoulder height. 'See? Now if I'd done that to a lawn tennis ball, it would have shot up into the air, way over my head. So you're going to get much less bounce and you're going to have to bend down really low to reach a real tennis ball. Let's try some. As usual, doing it is much more useful than talking about it.'

They took up their positions. 'Stand about a couple of yards in front of the back wall, in the middle,' George Hazlitt shouted down the court, 'and I'll send a few down.'

He had the basket of balls on the floor beside him, picked a couple out and sent the first one fluently down the centre of the court. Jude swung Piers' racket over it and missed by about a foot.

'And another one.' The pro's second ball followed exactly the same trajectory. Jude's stroke was about six inches too high for that one.

The third ball she actually hit. Well, that is to say it made contact with her racket and went spinning off into the wall.

By the time George Hazlitt had sent down the entire basketful—between forty and fifty balls—she had managed to return two over the net. The rest lay scattered on the floor of the hazard end.

'Not bad at all,' said the pro, as he returned the basket to its hole and used his racket to shovel balls back into it.

'Not bad in the sense of really dreadful?' suggested Jude.

'No, I've seen many people do worse on their first hit. And I can see you've played lawn tennis. There it's all about following through with the racket. In real tennis you want to stop once you've hit the ball. Think of it as a chopping movement, like you're bringing an axe down on the side of the ball as it makes impact. And the lower the ball is in its trajectory when you hit it, the better. Don't worry, it takes a while to get used to the basics.'

'Ten years is the figure that's been quoted to me.'

George Hazlitt grinned. 'It needn't be that long.'

So they progressed and Jude began to realize that the pro was really a very good teacher. He showed her the required body positions, standing sideways rather than facing front to take the ball. He taught her a couple of basic serves. And he got her nearer than Piers ever had to understanding what a chase was. He gave her just enough encouragement, not undiluted praise but words that made her feel she was achieving something.

They ended the session by playing a couple of games, something Jude would not have believed possible a mere hour before. She knew full well that George Hazlitt was holding back for her, missing a couple of her returns that he could easily have reached. But he managed to do it without making her feel patronized.

The lesson only lasted an hour of the hour-and-a-quarter booking period, but by the end of it Jude was glowing and she knew her face was red and sweaty. Though, in spite of its bulk, her body was supple from the yoga, this was a different kind of physical activity and had used muscles unexercised for a long time. She had enjoyed the experience, though, and even begun to taste the obsessive attraction of real tennis.

George Hazlitt came to shake her hand over the low part of the net, as if they'd played a genuine game rather than him just popping dolly shots to her. Jude was effusive in her thanks but even at that moment couldn't curb her investigative instincts. 'A rather happier experience than last time I came to the court,' she observed.

The pro looked puzzled for a moment before what she said fell into place. 'Yes, poor old bugger. I'm sorry that was your introduction to the game.'

'Well, I'd also been here on the Sunday, for the Sec's Cup.'

'Of course. I'd forgotten. There are so many people around for an event like that.'

'Oh, I wasn't expecting you to remember. And of course I saw Reggie fall on the court then, too.'

'That's right. You know, I wouldn't be surprised if that had been caused by a minor heart attack too. He was in a pretty bad way.'

'Presumably you have to have some kind of first aid training to do this job?'

'You bet. With regular update sessions to see we're

not getting out of touch. Oh yes, I'm a little devil with the defibrillator.'

'I'm sure you are. Will you be at the funeral to-morrow?'

'Of course. Reggie Playfair had been a member for years.'

'Piers Targett has asked me to come along.'

'Good, I'll see you then. And if you want to book another lesson or fix up a game for yourself…'

'I'm not ready to play a game.'

'Don't you believe it. Some of those returns you were doing towards the end were pretty damned good.'

'Well, thank you.'

'There are plenty of beginners in the club, I'm glad to say. And a lot of young players, which is also good news. I've been working hard to lower the average age of the members here.'

'Yes, one does get the impression that to play here you have to be in your sixties, from the right public school and preferably with a hyphenated surname.'

George Hazlitt shook his head with something close to annoyance. 'That's the image of the game. Hampton Court, toffs… It's really not like that any more. We've got our fair share of Old Etonians and Harrovians here at Lockleigh, but we've also got builders, decorators, farmers. The membership's not all out of the top drawer by any means. Not all rich either. We've got a guitarist, we've even got a writer, so neither of them have got two pennies to rub together.'

'And how do you get the younger ones in?'

'I've got relationships with a couple of the local schools, do regular coaching sessions with them. Then I've been round the local state schools with

Lady Budgen—we've got a good little double act going there, you know, talking about the game. We've had a bit of interest from that area. Have you met Tonya Grace?'

'Not exactly met, but I saw her when Piers was partnering her in the Sec's Cup.'

'Of course he was, yes. Well, she's a very promising young player, and just from a comprehensive in Brighton. Felicity's sort of taken Tonya under her wing and been encouraging her. I think she and Don may even be helping her financially, subscription, court fees, travel expenses, that kind of stuff… But please don't mention to anyone that I told you that. So the game really is moving away from its elitist image.'

Jude grinned. 'It certainly will be if I start playing.'

'Well, we must see to it that you do. Give me a call. There are lots of people round your standard you could have a really good knock with. You have to remember, Jude, real tennis has this extremely cunning handicap system, which means you can have a competitive game, whatever your standard.'

'Yes.' While she still had George Hazlitt on his own, Jude wondered how she could possibly get the conversation round to the identity of the real-tennis-playing woman with whom Oenone Playfair suspected her husband had had an affair. But before she could embark on that rather tricky manoeuvre, a voice from the walkway called out, 'Morning, George. Morning, Jude.'

It was Jonty Westmacott. Of course, thought Jude, the Old Boys' regular Wednesday eleven thirty doubles. A fixture on the calendar so important that

Oenone Playfair had even postponed her husband's funeral to accommodate it.

When Jonty had passed through into the club room, Jude said, 'His gout must've got better.'

'Oh?'

'I saw Tom Ruthven over the weekend. He was trying to get a fourth for today because Jonty was a doubtful starter.'

George Hazlitt grinned knowingly. 'Gout this time, was it?'

Jude was puzzled. 'Oh?'

'I'm afraid Jonty is one of those players who's not above a bit of gamesmanship. If he plays badly, there's always a reason other than his own incompetence.'

'Actually, last week he was complaining of a tweaked tendon in his knee.'

'Yes, there's always something with Jonty. Injury, or of course something wrong with the equipment. I've strung his racket too tight or…the balls.' George Hazlitt raised his eyes to heaven. 'I probably get more complaints about the balls than anything else in this club. They're not completely spherical, the bounce isn't true, they're too soft…I've heard them all. And because Ned and I make the balls by hand—a new set of sixty every fortnight—well, the members know who to complain to, don't they?'

The pro looked at his watch. 'I must go, got some calls to make. But I'll guarantee you one thing…'

'What?' asked Jude.

'That sometime during the next hour and a quarter Jonty Westmacott will summon me out of the pro's office because there's something wrong with the court.'

'And will there be something wrong with the court?'

George Hazlitt shook his head wryly. 'Will there hell? But I will have to take the complaint seriously because I'm afraid that's part of what the job of being a pro is about. And also…I can't help feeling a bit sorry for old Jonty. I mean, he was a really good player. Handicap down in the twenties in his prime. Even then he wasn't above a bit of gamesmanship. But now…it's frustration because he can't play like he used to, that's what makes him do all this stuff. Age, the dreaded age. Heigh-ho, it'll come to us all.' He moved towards the walkway. 'Anyway, I'll see you, Jude.'

'Yes. Just one thing, George…'

But Wally Edgington-Bewley, Tom Ruthven and Rod Farrar had just arrived. The window during which Jude might have pursued her enquiry had closed.

SHE WAS GLOWING with health after she had showered and changed, but she also knew that the following day she would feel all the bending and stretching she had done. Particularly in her knees and the back of her calves. She hoped, though, that this wouldn't be her last time on a real tennis court. The bug had begun to bite.

Remembering the etiquette of the game, she waited in the dedans until such time as the players had to change ends. She watched Rod Farrar serve to Jonty Westmacott, who hit his return into the net. 'Thirty-love,' said Tom Ruthven.

Rod Farrar served again, with exactly the same result. 'Oh, this is ridiculous!' spluttered Jonty West-macott.

'What's the trouble this time?' asked his partner, a very patient Wally Edgington-Bewley.

'Well, it's the height of the net, isn't it? I mean, I don't normally put that many into the top of it.'

'The rest of us seem to be getting the balls over all right,' observed Tom Ruthven.

'Yes, but you've always tended to sky them rather,' said Jonty. 'My game's always depended on my returns going very low over the net.'

'So what do you want to do about it?' Wally looked resigned. This ritual—or something very similar to it—had been carried out every Wednesday morning for eleven years.

'I'll have to have a word with George,' replied Jonty Westmacott and bustled off the court towards the pros' office. The three men left on court sighed and raised their eyes to the heavens.

Because there was a break in play Jude could have left straight away, but she lingered to see how this little scene would play itself out. George Hazlitt, looking suitably serious, came out of his office, carrying a marked stick. Jonty Westmacott followed.

The pro solemnly set the stick upright against the lowest point of the net's sag. Even from the dedans Jude could see that the height was perfectly correct. Three foot. But rather than pointing that out, George Hazlitt went to the side of the court, reached into one of the galleries nearest the net and pulled out a metal bar. It was about a foot long with a square hole in one end. He fitted this over a metal nub sticking out of the pillar supporting the net and cranked it up a couple of notches. 'Oh, I've done it a bit too far,' he announced, and then cranked back the other way exactly the same number of turns.

Ceremoniously, he went back to the centre of the net and checked its height against his measuring stick. 'There, I think you'll find that better, Jonty.'

'Thank you so much, George. Sorry to be a bother, but that kind of thing can make quite a big difference to my kind of game.'

'Of course. No problem.'

George Hazlitt turned on his way back to the office just as Jude was passing along the walkway. Catching her eye, he winked. And she realized that being a real tennis pro was as much about public relations as it was about sport.

TWENTY-TWO

CAROLE SEDDON HAD an email back from Iain Holland around five on the Wednesday afternoon, with text at the bottom reading: 'Sent from my iPad.'

The message read: 'I don't know who you are and since my daughter disappeared I've been contacted by a lot of cranks. But if you genuinely do have information about Marina's whereabouts, then we should meet and talk about it.' There was a mobile phone number.

Carole was shocked by the speed of the response. Not expecting it, she hadn't prepared her next step in the investigation. She felt a little frightened, too. Iain Holland had interpreted her message to mean that she actually had information about his daughter. How would he react when he discovered she knew nothing?

For a moment she was tempted to put the whole thing on hold. It had been a stupid idea to become involved in the Lady in the Lake mystery, and she was getting out of her depth. Better to pull the plug on the whole operation.

On the other hand…Jude was getting ever more deeply entangled with Piers Targett and the affairs of Lockleigh House tennis court, and though she'd done her best to get Carole participating in that enquiry, it was Jude who had the contacts. She was the one who would be going the following day to Reggie Playfair's funeral; there was no justifiable reason why Carole should attend. And funerals are traditionally fruitful hunting grounds for both police and amateur investigators. Overheard conversations, family rows, revelatory body language from suspects…how many times had those been used as stepping stones towards the solution of a case?

So no, Carole Seddon couldn't deny that her nose was a little out of joint. She'd started the Lady in the Lake investigation intentionally as something she was doing on her own. Without Jude. She'd just been offered an open door to the next stage. She couldn't give up now.

Carole decided that she'd make the call from a public phone box. There seemed now to be infinite numbers of ways to track people down through their phone numbers and she didn't want Iain Holland to know where she lived.

A few years before there had been a row of red telephone boxes on the parade at Fethering. Now, with the growth of mobile-phone usage, there was just one. And that wasn't in a proper box. Only in a three-sided screen which, in the event of bad weather, depending on which way the wind was blowing, might protect someone from the waist upwards. Soon, Carole reckoned, that booth too would disappear.

It was with considerable trepidation that she dialled the number from the email. It was answered immediately. 'Hello. Iain Holland.'

There was a brashness in his tone, but also a wariness. It was a confident voice, with no taint of public school, the proper voice for a man of the people.

'Hello. I've just received your email.'

'In what connection is this?'

'About Marina's whereabouts.'

That had its effect. Carole heard him raise his voice and call, 'Sorry, got to take this in the other room.' Presumably that was addressed to his new squeaky-clean wife and his new squeaky-clean children.

There was a silence, the sound of a door closing, and his voice was more urgent when he came back on the line. 'Who are you?' he asked.

She had thought about her answer to this. She had no intention of giving her second name, but nor was she going to go down complicated routes of inventing a pseudonym or answering with something like 'a well-wisher'. 'My name's Carole,' she replied.

'And you know something about Marina?'

'I know that she disappeared eight years ago.'

'Everyone knows that. It was all over the media. You implied that you had some new information.'

'Did I?' Carole was advancing cagily, trying to assess how Iain Holland had read her message.

'Listen, I haven't got time to play games. There's quite a lot at stake here, probably more than you realize. So if you've got some information, tell me about it. If not, let me get back to my evening with my family.'

'I do have some information,' Carole boldly lied, 'but I think I should tell you about it face to face.'

She couldn't quite explain why those words had emerged from her lips, and she fully expected them to be greeted by a blast of scepticism. Instead, Iain Holland said, 'When do you want to meet?'

'Soon as you like.'

'I could do a half hour this evening.'

'All right,' said Carole. Her voice sounded cool, but that was no reflection of her thoughts. Everything was moving so quickly. She was normally a very cautious person, agonizing over even the smallest decision. And here she was being swept along manically into who knew what embarrassment or danger.

Iain Holland said there was a pub in Brighton called The Two Ducks. It had a private room that he quite often used for meetings with residents in his ward. He could be there at eight o'clock. Carole said that she could too. She told him she had grey hair, rimless glasses and would be wearing a Burberry raincoat.

When she put the phone down, Carole Seddon was left with two questions. One, why had she totally lost her marbles? And two, why had Iain Holland agreed so readily to a meeting?

THE TWO DUCKS was in Kemptown, another part of Brighton that Carole didn't know well. Though she had no reason to spend time there, she had been put off the place by reading somewhere that it was the gay centre of the town. Carole wasn't exactly homophobic, she just didn't feel at ease in cultural environments different from her own. Finding herself in a gay pub would prompt the same anxieties as being at a Catholic church service, not sure when to stand up and sit down. Carole Seddon's primary fear was always of drawing attention to herself by doing something wrong.

Whether or not the Two Ducks was a gay pub was hard to tell. Certainly there were men in there, but there were also women. And there was nothing particularly camp about the barman to whom Carole gave her order. Fizzy mineral water. She needed all her wits about her for the forthcoming encounter.

She sat at a small round table and sipped her drink. Nobody seemed to take much notice of her. In characteristic Carole Seddon style she had got to the Two Ducks at a quarter to eight.

On the dot of five to, Iain Holland entered the pub. It was clearly somewhere where he was known. He addressed the barman by name as he ordered: 'A J2O— the orange and passion fruit one.'

Carole recognized him from his website. He was a good-looking man, fiftyish like his ex-wife. His neatly-cut hair carried a dusting of grey and his face still had a residual tan, perhaps from a summer holiday. He was dressed in smart leisurewear—green polo shirt under a brown leather blouson, Levi jeans, moccasins.

Carole thought he had clocked her when he first entered the pub, but Iain Holland waited until he'd got his drink before turning and moving towards her. 'You must be Carole,' he said.

His handshake was firm, his expression bluff and honest, demonstrating the automatic charm of a politician. He called across to the barman, 'Is the upstairs room unlocked?'

'Sure, Iain.'

As he led her up the narrow staircase, Iain Holland told Carole how useful this room had been to him. 'You know, when I'm meeting someone in my ward who's got a problem, a lot of them prefer an informal chat in a pub. Less intimidating than coming to my office or attending one of my official surgeries. Oh, by the way, here's one of my cards, got all my contact details on it.'

He very effectively projected the image of a councillor who could not do enough for the people he represented. Iain Holland was all concern, altruism and transparency.

But the minute he had closed the door and they were alone inside the small function room, his manner changed. Immediately he demanded, 'Do you know where she is?'

There are two ways in which that question could be posed by the father of a missing child. The first is with eager anticipation, hoping against hope that there might be some prospect of being reunited with someone believed to be lost forever. The second is with an edge of fear, frightened that the secret of where the missing child is might have been breached. Iain Holland's intonation was definitely of the second kind.

Carole really was flying by the seat of her pants. She had known that question—or something very like it—was bound to arise, but though she had tried to plan a response, nothing had offered itself.

So, outwardly calm, she said, based on no evidence at all, 'Well, I certainly don't think she's dead.'

'You're in the minority there. The general consensus seems to be that she is.'

'And what is your view?'

Iain Holland shrugged. He was doing quite a good impression of nonchalance, but Carole could sense the tension in him. He was probing at her, trying to find out whether she did genuinely know anything. 'My view,' he said at length, 'is that Marina probably is dead.'

'You don't know how or where?'

'No. It's just in this day and age, with all the means of contact and surveillance we now have, it's diffi-

cult for someone to vanish off the face of the earth.'
More or less the exact opposite of what Donna Grodsky had said.

Iain Holland looked at her sternly. He wasn't both-
ering with the politician's charm any more. His voice
took on the bullying tone of someone used to getting
his own way as he said, 'Look, I'm a busy man. If
you've got anything to tell me, tell me. If not, I think
we should both conclude that this meeting has been
a waste of time.'

'Then why did you so readily agree to meet me?'

'Because I didn't at the time know that you didn't
have any new information.'

'Ah, but perhaps I have,' said Carole. She was
floundering, and it was only a matter of time before
he realized just how much she was floundering.

But she was let off the hook for a moment. Still
worried that she might actually know something, Iain
Holland's manner changed again. He became more
conciliatory. 'Listen, obviously if there is any prospect of finding Marina alive, well, that would be great
news for me. Great news for any father. But I've written off the possibility for so long that it's hard for me
to take the idea on board. My situation's changed since
I split up with Marina's mother. And I'm sorry that
went wrong, but I'm not the first person in the world
who's got married too young. Now I'm in a new relationship, got two lovely kids, business going well. I'm
all right. And I don't want to go back to how things
were before.'

'Are you saying that finding Marina alive would
take you back to those times?'

'No, of course I'm not. It'd be brilliant. Like I say,

every father's dream. But it would take some adjust-
ment. Not everyone knows much about my past, but
there is a kind of acknowledgement that there has been
some great sadness there.'

'The loss of your daughter?'

'Exactly. And if that situation changes, well, yes,
obviously there'd be some adjustments.'

'You mean you might lose some people's sympathy?'

'No. Not exactly that. Look, Carole, the fact is that
I'm increasingly interested in politics, hoping to spend
more of my time, you know, doing some good, helping people out.'

'Do you mean on the national stage?'

'It's not impossible. Some high-ups in the Conservative Party have been quite impressed by the difference I've been making down here in Brighton. It's not
impossible that I might be shortlisted as a candidate at
the next election.' He couldn't keep the note of pride
out of his voice.

'And you're afraid,' said Carole, 'that your perfect
image with the "high-ups in the Conservative Party"
might be a little tarnished if they found out you had a
living daughter from a previous marriage, a daughter
who perhaps has gone to the bad?'

'No!' Iain Holland blustered. 'Of course that's not
what I mean.'

But Carole Seddon knew that it was.

'Anyway, you've still said nothing that convinces
me you have any proof Marina's alive.' He looked at
his watch. 'And unless you do have something new to
tell me, I think we should draw this meeting to a close.'

She had been let off the hook once, but she couldn't

see history about to repeat itself. Iain Holland had risen from his chair and was moving towards the door. Carole thought back desperately to her conversation with Donna Grodsky and blurted out, 'What intrigues me is Marina's Russian connection.'

It had been a complete shot in the dark, but it found its target. Iain Holland froze, then slowly turned back to face her. The slick confidence of his expression had been replaced by something very close to fear. 'What do you know about Marina's Russian connection?'

Absolutely nothing was the answer inside Carole's head, but what she said was, 'I know that she suspected her origins to be Russian. I know that she was very much drawn towards the Russian community here in Brighton.'

Iain Holland processed this information for a moment. He was considerably shaken by what she had said. Then he asked, 'What more do you know?'

The only tenuous piece of information she'd gleaned from all her investigations was one first name. Still, she had nothing to lose by mentioning it. 'I know about Vladimir.'

His immediate reaction showed Carole that she had hit home, but he quickly covered it up and asked sceptically, 'Vladimir who?'

It was the question she had been afraid he might ask. And of course the one to which she had no answer. Realizing that, though she'd got Iain Holland on the back foot, her only hope was to bluff her way out, Carole Seddon smiled smugly. 'I think that's enough for the time being.'

'But you've told me nothing.'

'I know about the Russian connection. And Vladimir.' So confident was she now of the power reversal that had taken place that she rose to her feet. 'Maybe I should be on my way.'

'No, no!' Iain Holland put a hand on her arm to stop her. 'Just sit down again for a moment. Please.'

Carole did as he requested. He sat too and put his hands flat on the table as if to begin a process of negotiation. 'Presumably,' he said, 'you want money to make you keep quiet about this?'

'Actually, I—'

'How much?'

TWENTY-THREE

PIERS TARGETT CAME back to Woodside Cottage after his London meetings and wanted a full debrief on Jude's experience of a real tennis lesson. It seemed really to matter to him that she should like the game and she found his enthusiasm infectious. If anyone had suggested a month before that she might seriously be about to take up a game she'd hardly heard of, she would have laughed in their faces. But it was strange how quickly things could change when love was involved.

Their relationship took another step forward that evening, in that Jude cooked a meal for Piers. Up until then all their eating had been done out—in fact, Piers always ate out. The idea of his pristine kitchen in Bayswater being sullied by anything other than wine bottles and a corkscrew was unthinkable. Jude wondered if he ever had cooked for himself, whether indeed he had any domestic skills. Maybe when he and Jonquil were cohabiting, they had had a normal home life, but it was a subject she did not yet want to discuss. There'd be time enough for that, particularly since this new domestic phase of their relationship somehow seemed to promise a longer future.

She cooked a Thai green chicken curry, one of her specialities. Jude's range of cooking was wide and random. She was just as likely to do a fry-up as something more exotic. And whereas in the next-door kitchen at High Tor every ingredient would be weighed out exactly to the last scruple, Jude's approach was instinctive. She didn't have a recipe book in the house. On the other hand, she had for a while run a restaurant, so she did possess all of the necessary skills.

They drank a lot of wine with the dinner. Indeed, they always seemed to drink a lot of wine when they were together, Piers probably downing a couple of glasses to every one of hers. But she had never seen him drunk. He just seemed cheerfully to go on topping himself up. And he didn't go in for any of that what he called 'nonsense about not drinking and driving'. She'd often seen him take the wheel of the E-Type with a bottle of wine inside him, but she never felt in any danger.

That evening she lit a fire in the Woodside Cottage sitting room. The October night wasn't really cold enough to justify it, but the warmth and the glow were comforting. After they had eaten (and Jude, with a laxness that would have appalled Carole, had not even thought about taking their dirty plates through to the kitchen), Piers had removed his jacket and they'd slipped naturally down from the sofa to the floor. Equally naturally, snuggling and sipping wine had led to lazy love-making.

Which, later, they continued upstairs. Then, in what was now becoming a jokey ritual for them, Jude asked Piers to explain how a chase was laid on a real tennis court. And she was soon blissfully asleep.

JUDE DIDN'T KNOW what time it was when she woke up. Having someone sharing her bed at Woodside Cottage felt strange. Not unpleasantly strange, just unfamiliar.

She lay there, still, drinking in the welcome un-familiarity of Piers' presence, his breathing, steady, deep, just on the edge of a snore. She thought back over the day, particularly the evening, and everything felt good.

But she was wakeful. She knew she wouldn't go back to sleep for at least half an hour. Had she been on her own, she might have switched on the bedside light and read. Or done some of the personalized stretching exercises that she had developed from yoga. Even gone downstairs and made a cup of herbal tea. But she didn't want to wake Piers.

Inevitably, as she lay there, she found herself thinking about Reggie Playfair's funeral in the morning. And from there it didn't take long for her thoughts to home back in on the circumstances of his death.

That, however, prompted an unwelcome memory, which for the past few days she had been, sometimes consciously and sometimes unconsciously, suppressing. The call she'd had from Jonquil Targett about Reggie Playfair's mobile phone. Probably nothing, probably just an attempt by a severely unstable woman to plant suspicions about her estranged husband. Or was there more to it than that…?

Jonquil said she'd seen the phone in Piers' possession. And it had a distinctive cover, specially made in the colours of the Lockleigh House tennis club.

She said she'd seen it in the pocket of Piers' jacket. And Piers' jacket was at that moment lying downstairs in the sitting room of Woodside Cottage.

Jude hated the direction in which her thoughts were turning. It went against her every instinct to be suspicious of someone she loved. And particularly now, when she had just regained a feeling of reassurance after her doubts of the weekend. She tried to shift concentration on to some other subject, but still Jonquil Targett's words sawed away at her mind.

She tried to reason against what the woman had said. Even if Piers had had Reggie's mobile in his jacket pocket, he was likely to have moved it by now. Or he'd be wearing a different jacket. And even if she did find the mobile, its battery would have run down during the past week, so she wouldn't be able to gather any information from it.

Jude now knew that she would have no peace until she had behaved like some archetype of the jealous lover, till she had gone downstairs and checked through Piers Targett's jacket pockets. Hating herself for what she was doing, she edged out from under the duvet. When she was standing by the side of the bed, she froze for a moment, but there was no interruption to the easy regularity of her lover's breathing.

She slipped on a towelling dressing gown and crept from the bedroom, knowing how to move the half-open door without making it squeak, knowing which creaking step to avoid on the staircase.

The last embers of the fire still cast a meagre glow around her sitting room. Jude moved straight to the sofa on the arm of which Piers' jacket had been casually abandoned. Now she had made the decision of what she was about to do, there was no point in delaying the inevitable.

She felt in one pocket and her hand closed on the hard rectangle of a mobile. Extracting it, she was relieved to recognize the counters of Piers' iPhone.

She replaced that and felt in the other jacket pocket.

There too she felt a familiar shape and weight. She took it out. The dying glow of the fire gave enough light for her to see the coloured stripes of the cover.

While Piers Targett had sent her on an errand to his E-Type outside the tennis court, he'd taken Reggie Playfair's mobile.

TWENTY-FOUR

JUDE PUT THE light on and inspected the phone. Switched it on, nothing happened. Of course it would have run out of power. She almost didn't want to find out that the mobile was a Nokia, like her own. And that her charger would fit it. But it did.

Grimly she plugged the charger in. The screen took a moment to come to life. No password was required, she just had to press a function key to unlock the phone.

She went straight to Messaging, and opened the inbox. The last text Reggie Playfair had received was sent at 12.37 am on the day of his death.

It read: 'Something important's come up. Meet me on the court as soon as you can, like we used to.'

The sender had not identified him- or herself. Nor did the number the text had been sent from mean anything to Jude. But she made a note of it.

As she was scribbling the number down on the back of an Allinstore receipt, she looked up to see Piers standing the doorway from the hall. He had thrown on an orange silk dressing gown of hers. Far too small, it made him look faintly ridiculous.

'Ah. So you found the phone,' he said.

'You hadn't made much attempt to hide it.'

'True.' He sounded weary as he came across to sit at one end of the sofa. She sat at the other end. The void between them seemed incongruous after the intimacy they had shared there only a few hours earlier.

'I suppose you want some explanations,' said Piers Targett.

'Wouldn't hurt.'

'No.' He sighed. 'Well, I took it from Reggie's pocket when I sent you out to get my mobile from the E-Type.'

'I assumed that was what had happened.'

'But of course you want to know why.'

'Wouldn't hurt either.'

'I did it to protect Reggie.'

'Bit late for that. He was already dead.'

'True. Perhaps it would be more accurate to say that I did it to protect Oenone.'

'Oh?'

'If the mobile had come back to her and she had found the text message which had summoned him to the court...' He grimaced at the thought of the consequences.

'On the other hand, Piers, you could simply have erased the text message before the phone got back to Oenone, and your problem would have been solved.'

'Yes, I can see that now. At the time I wasn't thinking very straight. The urgent thing seemed to be to prevent Oenone from getting the phone.'

'Hm.' Jude didn't disbelieve him. His behaviour was consistent with the kind of messy, illogical ways people react in a crisis. 'You've presumably read the text message that summoned Reggie down to the court?'

'Yes.'

'And you presumably know who it was from?'

'Yes.' He gave her a shrewd look. 'Why, don't you?'

'There was no name, the number didn't mean anything to me and I hadn't had a chance to check through the phone's address book before you came down.'

'Right.' Slowly, with deliberation, Piers Targett rose from the sofa. He unplugged the stripy-jacketed mobile and put it back into the jacket pocket whence Jude had taken it.

'The text message,' he said slowly, 'was from Jonquil.'

'Really?' Jude hadn't been expecting that.

'So she told me.' Piers spread his hands against his forehead and pressed them sideways as if trying to wipe away some memory. 'Look, as I've said before, Jonquil is never the most rational of beings. In her down periods she's almost catatonic. When she's up, she's capable of all kinds of bizarre behaviour.'

'I thought you said the medication controls that.'

'It does—providing she takes it. But she always thinks the time will come when she doesn't need any medication. So when she's feeling good, like when she's at the beginning of a new relationship—like she has been recently—she won't touch the stuff.'

'And that makes her behaviour even more bizarre?'

'Precisely. Anyway, there's a bit of history between Jonquil and Reggie.'

'Oh?'

'I told you fidelity was never her strong suit. And after the few months of honeymoon period after we got married…well, her promiscuous side took over.'

'So she and Reggie…?' Some people might have thought the idea of the fat man in his seventies having an affair incongruous, but Reggie Playfair had been young once. And Jude knew that passion was not always diminished by age.

'I don't actually know for a fact that they did. But Jonquil certainly slept with other members of the club round that time. And I think she wanted to add Reggie to the list. Whether he was strong enough to resist her, I'm not sure. I've a feeling Reggie was one of those old-fashioned chaps who genuinely believed in the sanctity of the marriage vows. But one thing I know for a fact—if he did resist Jonquil's advances that would have made her absolutely furious. She liked getting her own way—particularly when it came to men.'

'You and Reggie never discussed it?'

'No. Very British of us, wasn't it? He knew—and Oenone knew—that Jonquil was making a fool of me with other men, but the subject was never mentioned. So, needless to say, the subject of whether Reggie himself was actually one of her conquests…well, that wasn't mentioned either.'

Jude felt a surge of pity for Piers, being saddled with Jonquil, the kind of woman who would never be completely out of his life. She felt pity for Jonquil too, as she would for anyone suffering from mental illness, but not as much as she did for Piers.

'If Jonquil sent the text message,' she began slowly, 'and Reggie reacted instantly, in the middle of the night, that must suggest quite regular contact between them, since the time that they…well, if they did have an affair.'

Piers shrugged. He looked almost pathetic, inadequately wrapped in orange silk. His deep blue eyes were tight with pain. 'Jonquil was strange about keeping in touch with people. Suddenly someone'd be her new best friend and she'd be phoning and texting them all the time. Equally suddenly, they'd drop out of favour. Or she might, out of the blue, one day call someone she hadn't spoken to for years. Just another example of her volatility. Trying to second-guess what Jonquil is about to do next is a very exhausting business—as I know to my cost,' he concluded with feeling.

'And do you know whether she had been in touch with Reggie recently?'

He nodded. 'They never really lost touch. There was a professional relationship, apart from anything else.'

'Reggie acting for her as a stockbroker?'

'That's it. As I mentioned, Jonquil's always been pretty well heeled, and she came into a lot when her parents died. Reggie looked after her portfolio, did very well for her in fact. But, according to Jonquil, they'd recently found another interest in common.'

'Oh?'

'She picks up new fads and ideas with the same randomness that she does people. None of them last very long. But her latest obsession is with ghosts.'

'Ah.' Now, Jude felt, they were getting somewhere. 'Which of course is a subject that Reggie was very much into.'

'How did you know that? You only met him once.'

'Oenone told me.'

'Really?' Piers didn't ask why Jude had been in contact with Reggie's widow, but he was clearly puzzled by the idea. Still, he moved on. 'Well, there is a ghost story attached to Lockleigh House tennis court.'

'Agnes Wardock,' said Jude.

That really did shake him. 'How the hell do you know that?'

'I was told about it by Cecil Wardock.'

'And who's he?'

'Relative of Tom Ruthven. Tom introduced me to him.'

'And he told you the Agnes Wardock story? Goodness, Jude, you seem to know everything.' He gave a shudder that was only half in jest. 'Being with you is like spending time with an amateur detective. I feel as if you're constantly investigating me.'

She added no comment to that. Instead she asked, 'So do you think that Jonquil summoned Reggie down to the court on a ghost-hunting mission?'

'I'm rather afraid she did. When she's in one of her manic moods Jonquil's sense of humour is sometimes totally inappropriate.'

'Sense of humour?' Suddenly something slotted into place in Jude's mind. Something she'd seen in Jonquil Targett's car outside the house at Goffham. 'Oh, she didn't…? It wasn't the wedding dress, was it?'

Piers looked at her aghast. 'You know about that too? My God, is there anything you don't know about?' Gloom spread over his face as he admitted, 'Yes, that was Jonquil's idea of a joke. She thought it would be amusing to summon Reggie Playfair down to the court, telling him that she had seen the ghost of Agnes Wardock. And of course he went. Jonquil would have loved the idea that he did that. Nothing gives her more pleasure than having power over men.'

'So the ghost…?'

'Was Jonquil wearing a wedding dress. The dress in fact that she wore at our wedding.' He shook his head in bewilderment. 'I asked her what on earth possessed her to do that, and as I did I realized that "possessed" was absolutely the right word. When Jonquil's in a manic phase, she is possessed.

'As she explained it to me, she said Reggie was so keen on seeing Agnes Wardock's ghost that she thought she'd make his dream come true. She thought she'd "give him a surprise".'

'And it turned out to be a surprise that killed him?'

Piers nodded. 'The way she told it, she arrived at the court before he could possibly have got down from London.'

'How did she get in?'

'She knows the keypad code, which doesn't get changed nearly as often as it should do. Jonquil used to be a member. Well, still is a member actually, though she doesn't play much now. So she went through to the club room, put on the wedding dress and waited. She heard the main door open, she saw Reggie's torch-light coming down the side of the court, then she saw him go on to the court itself. That's where she'd said she'd meet him.

'Jonquil took that as her cue to enter the dedans area. At a distance, in the white dress, with her long blonde hair, her image slightly blurred by the netting in the dedans...I'm sure Reggie Playfair thought he was looking at the ghost of Agnes Wardock.'

'And the shock killed him?'

'Yes.'

There was a long silence. Then Jude asked, 'When did Jonquil tell you all this, Piers? Over the weekend?'

'No, she told me that morning.'

'Oh?'

There was shame in his expression when he said, 'When things go really badly for Jonquil, I'm afraid it's still me she rings. Seeing Reggie's corpse on the court, beginning to realize what she'd done, Jonquil rang me. I went and got her off the premises.'

'So when you went in with me later, you already knew that we would find Reggie there?'

'Yes,' he replied soberly.

'Well, why the hell didn't you say something?' demanded Jude in uncharacteristic anger. 'Why haven't you said anything since? Why haven't you told the police?'

'I couldn't do that, Jude. Jonquil's so unstable. Having enquiries into what she did is just the kind of thing that might push her over the edge.'

There was another long silence. Finally Jude said ruefully. 'You are so far from being over her, aren't you, Piers?'

TWENTY-FIVE

REGGIE PLAYFAIR'S FUNERAL took place at St Peter's, Goffham, in whose parish Winnows lay. Oenone had arranged everything with exemplary efficiency, and all those attending were invited back to the house afterwards.

Sir Donald Budgen did a bible reading, but the encomium, delivered by one of Reggie's former partners in his stockbroking business, made only a glancing reference to real tennis. The emphasis was more on the deceased's professional life and his involvement in charities, particularly the good works he did through his livery company. The strange circumstances of his death were not mentioned and, because they were in church, no one in the congregation said, 'Poor old bugger.' Though there was no doubt that most of the real tennis fraternity felt it.

Oenone Playfair was dressed in an immaculate black linen suit and a black straw hat rather in the shape of a Beefeater's. She stood, bold and brave in the front pew and, whatever emotions she may have been feeling, she betrayed no sign of any of them.

There was no coffin at the funeral. A cremation had taken place earlier in the day, attended, at her request, only by Oenone.

At the end of the service at St Peter's she followed the vicar up the aisle and stood at the door, greeting

her guests with the manners of a well-schooled hostess. Outside the church, one or two of the Lockleigh
House tennis court members did say, 'Poor old bugger.'

The array of parked cars bore testament to the
wealth of the Playfairs' circle. To add to Piers' E-Type,
there were BMWs, Jaguars, Range Rovers and even
a couple of Rolls-Royces. As the church emptied, the
cars filled and everyone drove the half mile to Winnows.

Needless to say, at the house, too, everything was
punctiliously organized. In the sitting room where
Jude and Carole had talked to Oenone, the furniture
had been pushed back against the walls and a large
trestle table set up. The food that was being served
from there was substantial, a proper meal rather than
nibbles. But then the funeral had ended at one o'clock,
so it was lunchtime.

The food and the drink were served by smart young
girls in black uniforms. On arrival in the front hall
the guests were greeted by two of these, holding trays
loaded with flutes of champagne. Jude heard Oenone
saying to someone, 'Reggie wouldn't have wanted
anything less. Always loved a good party. His only
disappointment with this one would be that he can't
attend it. And he'd definitely have wanted it to be a
celebration rather than a wake.'

Piers seemed to know everyone. Again Jude enjoyed his company and she felt that their being together at an event like this, albeit a sad occasion,
marked another advance in their relationship. And
because of the real tennis players she had met through
Lockleigh House tennis court, she didn't have to stay

at his side all the time, dependent on him for introductions.

She saw Wally Edgington-Bewley, who raised a glass of red wine to her. 'Glad to see that Oenone's brought out Reggie's best claret. I'm never that bothered about champagne, you know. Give me a robust red any day. That of course is one of the many advantages of going to the tennis court in Bordeaux—can always fit in a visit to the odd chateau. Oh, but of course you know about that, don't you, Jude?'

'Do I?'

'Sorry, maybe you haven't had a chance to read it yet.'

At last she understood what he was talking about. 'Oh yes, of course, the book you lent me. No, sorry, Wally, haven't got round to it yet, but I will, I will. Why, do you need it back?'

'Good heavens, no. That copy's for you, Jude. Think of it as a rich gift from Wally Edgington-Bewley.' He blushed. 'I have actually written in it for you.'

'That's very kind.'

'Don't worry, I still have plenty more copies.'

'Oh.'

Tom Ruthven came across to join them. After a bit of chat, Jude asked if he'd seen Cecil Wardock again since the weekend.

'The eyes and ears of Lockleigh House? No, I might go again on Saturday. But he does get other visitors you know. Felicity Budgen goes there quite regularly… she's very dutiful on the good works front. Visits a lot of the old crocks at Lockleigh House. But why were you asking about Cecil?' He chuckled. 'You haven't seen the ghost of Agnes Wardock, have you?'

Jude too chuckled at the pleasantry, though after what she had heard from Piers the night before, she wasn't that amused by the idea.

They were joined by Jonty Westmacott.

'Hello,' said Jude. 'How are you?'

Too late she remembered that he was not the person to put that question to. 'Well, I woke up this morning,' Jonty replied, 'with a bit of a twinge in my lower back. I think that's probably why I wasn't at my best in the doubles yesterday.'

'I thought,' said Wally Edgington-Bewley, dead-pan but with the slightest twinkle, 'that you played badly yesterday because the net was the wrong height.'

'Well, that didn't help, obviously. I'm surprised you didn't notice it, Wally. But then I suppose your game's always been less precise than mine…you know, you do all those shots ballooning over the net. But I think it was my back that was affecting me more yesterday. You remember I had that problem with a slipped disc a couple of years back and it never really got properly sorted and then I…'

Jude managed to drift away and found herself beside Sir Donald and Lady Budgen, both gracefully black-suited. 'I enjoyed your reading,' said Jude.

The former ambassador inclined his head. 'Thank you.'

'Oh yes,' said his wife. 'Don can always be relied on to do the right thing on a public occasion.'

Jude wondered whether there was an edge of irony in that remark but, looking at Felicity Budgen's face, she could see none. And when she came to think of it, she couldn't imagine irony—or indeed humour of any kind—playing much of a part in the Budgens' marriage.

'You'd presumably both known Reggie for a long time?' said Jude.

'Oh yes,' replied Sir Donald. 'Though Felicity tended to see more of the Playfairs than I did. When I was on foreign postings, she came back home to settle the various children into schools, that kind of thing. Reggie and Oenone were very generous to you when you were here on your own, weren't they, darling?'

Felicity Budgen agreed that yes, they had been, darling.

Jude couldn't believe the formality of the couple. She had a vision of them being exactly like that all the time, always saying the right thing, never letting their hair down, never letting their masks slip. The idea of the two of them in bed together was almost comically incongruous.

'Oh,' said Jude, making conversation, 'Tom Ruthven was just saying that you sometimes visit Cecil Wardock in Lockleigh House.'

'Yes.' Felicity Budgen smiled sympathetically. 'I go and see quite a few of the residents there. Very few have that many visitors. How do you come to know Cecil Wardock?'

'Tom introduced me to him.' Felicity still looked at her quizzically, requiring a little more explanation. 'I wanted to ask him about…' She paused, realizing that it might be better not to get going on the whole Agnes Wardock ghost story. 'About things that had happened on the tennis court.'

'Oh, I see,' came the apparently satisfied response.

As the wine flowed, the guests—with the exception, obviously, of the Budgens—began to relax, and the noise level rose. Jude, queuing at the table to get her lunch plate loaded up, heard more than one person refer to the late Reggie Playfair as 'poor old bugger'.

Because seats were needed when the guests were eating, the party had spread out of the sitting room into adjacent spaces. Jude found herself drifting towards a conservatory and, just as she was about to enter, she heard what sounded like an argument conducted in low tones.

She hovered for a moment. A voice she recognized as George Hazlitt's was saying, '...and I thought last time we spoke about it, we agreed you wouldn't do it again.'

'Look, I haven't got anywhere else to go,' protested a younger voice. 'You know what Kelly's like about that kind of thing.'

'That's not my problem. If anyone on the committee found out what you'd been doing, they'd—'

'They won't find out. That lot're so dozy they—'

'You going to eat through there?' Piers had suddenly appeared behind Jude, with a piled-up plate, to which a glass of red wine was attached by a plastic holder.

'Yes,' said Jude and they walked through into the conservatory. The conversation inside immediately stopped.

But Jude saw that the person George Hazlitt had been talking to was the junior pro, Ned Jackson. Joining up a few links of logic in her mind, she thought she might know what they had been talking about. And

she wondered how she might engineer an opportunity
to find out if she was right.

Because, if she could, it might offer a whole new
perspective on Reggie Playfair's death.

TWENTY-SIX

OENONE PLAYFAIR WAS AMAZING. Though no one doubted the depth of her pain, during the post-funeral party she was a model of affability and good cheer. There was something to be said, Jude thought, for old-fashioned breeding. Oenone Playfair and Felicity Budgen had come out of the same mould. The qualities required of them on public occasions were charm and interest in the doings of others. Emotions should be contained, restricted to the private arena and, in the case of the club chairman's wife, Jude wondered whether they were even expressed there. As for Oenone, she had no doubts about the darkness that would engulf the new widow when she was on her own, when she no longer had the logistics of organizing the funeral to keep her mind occupied. But equally she knew that no other human being would ever be allowed to see Oenone Playfair cry.

George Hazlitt had gone to get some more mineral water (perhaps he never drank alcohol, a necessary deprivation for a professional sportsman). Then Piers went off to top up their glasses with Reggie's excellent claret. Leaving Jude alone in the conservatory with Ned Jackson, who was finishing up a large plate of coronation chicken.

She'd never have a better opportunity. Moving a

little closer to the junior pro, she said, 'Sounded like George was giving you rather a hard time.'

He looked up with some alarm and for the first time Jude noticed how long his eyelashes were. With his straight black hair and his greyhound-thin body, he really was a very attractive young man.

'What do you mean?' he asked sharply. 'Jude, isn't it?'

'That's right. What I mean is that just as I was coming into the conservatory I heard what George was saying to you.'

'Oh.' Ned Jackson looked positively scared now. 'But you're not going to tell anyone about it, are you? I mean, if anyone on the committee found out, my job could be on the line.'

Her ploy had worked. He evidently thought that she had heard more of the conversation than she actually had. But how was she going to find out about the bit she'd missed? Jude was going to have to advance with some subtlety.

'No,' she said breezily. 'No reason why I should tell anyone on the committee.' She held a silence. 'I might mention it to Piers, though.'

'That'd be as bad. He knows everyone on the committee. It'd be sure to get to them.'

'All right, I won't tell Piers,' she said lightly, as if it couldn't matter less. She played out another silence, then said, 'I'll keep quiet about it on one condition…'

'Oh?'

'That you tell me exactly what did happen.'

'Well, I—'

'Give me your phone number,' said Jude, her man-

ner more assertive than its default setting of amiabil-
ity, 'and I'll call you.'

Silently, Ned Jackson reached into his jacket's breast
pocket and handed a card across to her. Piers Targett,
re-entering the conservatory with two topped-up
glasses of claret, witnessed the action.

'I see, Jude,' he said. 'Not content with having had
your one lesson from George, you're now booking up
more with the junior pro.'

'Something like that,' said Jude with a giggle.

Ned Jackson echoed her, but his giggle didn't sound
so comfortable.

OENONE PLAYFAIR WAS still maintaining her act when
Piers and Jude left. As the E-Type scrunched power-
fully off the gravel, Jude observed, 'So she'll never
find out what actually caused Reggie's death.'

'Well, I'm not about to tell her.' He then added,
quite sharply, 'And I hope you're not either.'

Jude was silent, faced by something of a moral di-
lemma. She and Carole had been specifically asked
by Oenone Playfair to find out the reason for Reggie's
presence at the tennis court on the night of his death.
Now, thanks to Piers' nocturnal revelations, she did
have some of that information. But would it help Oenone's peace of mind to know that her husband had
jumped instantly at a summons from Jonquil Targett?
That she'd asked him to meet her at the court 'like we
used to'? Wouldn't that knowledge be very hurtful to
the recently widowed Oenone Playfair?

She decided to mull the decision over for a while
and moved the conversation on to the subject of Wally
Edgington-Bewley's book. Had Piers read it?

'Well, not exactly "read". I've flicked through and looked at the photographs. We're talking a long time ago, though. When he first published it. It's a very Wally kind of book.'

'Do you mean it's a thumping good read?' asked Jude wryly.

He chuckled. 'I wouldn't quite go that far. It's a book for the real tennis completist. One man's journey, accompanied by various friends, to virtually all the active tennis courts in the world. Written by a man whose literary style was honed by writing reports on stock-market movements and long-term trends. I don't believe that anyone at the club has actually read every word of it—we've all got copies, mind. Wouldn't dream of not giving Wally our full support.' Another chuckle. 'Actually, I think you might find *Courts in the Act* a more effective soporific even than me trying to explain chases to you.'

'So are you saying I shouldn't read it?'

Piers Targett shrugged. 'Jude, I wouldn't dream of telling you what you should or shouldn't do. You're clearly too much your own woman to be told to do anything by anyone.'

'Thank you. Silver tongue in action again, I see.'

'No, it's just that when I'm with a beautiful woman, I cannot help myself from speaking the truth.'

'You oleaginous smoothie,' said Jude, but couldn't help smiling. She found it very difficult to get angry with Piers Targett. And even more difficult to stay angry with him.

He dropped her at Woodside Cottage about four. He was driving on up to London, where he had an early evening meeting with a business acquaintance, and would then be staying the night in Bayswater, before more meetings on the Thursday and Friday. He had at first suggested that Jude should join him, but she demurred. She wanted a little time on her own to think things through.

ONE THING SHE didn't want to put off, though, was talking to Ned Jackson. The junior professional had looked fairly spooked at Winnows and she wanted to contact him before he got too realistic about the level of threat she might pose to him.

For a moment she regretted that Carole wasn't doing this part of the investigation. Jude knew herself to be better at the empathetic 'Good Cop' kind of interview, but her neighbour's manner had a steeliness she lacked. And she had a feeling the conversation with Ned Jackson might need more of a 'Bad Cop' quality. Still, there wasn't time to brief Carole for the job. It had to be done straight away.

So, as soon as she was settled back into Woodside Cottage with a cup of herbal tea, Jude took out the card the young man had given her. It featured Ned Jackson's name, describing him as a 'Real Tennis Professional' and offering his services for lessons in the game. The address was given as Lockleigh House tennis court. Beneath that was a mobile number, which she rang.

'Ned Jackson.' On the few occasions she'd heard his voice before, there had been a brashness in it. Now he sounded cautious. Jude hoped that might be because he was worried that the call might be from her.

'Hi, it's Jude.'

'Yes, I wondered if you were going to ring.' He

now sounded a lot younger, a schoolboy who'd been caught in some misdemeanour. 'Look, I know what you overheard sounded bad, but it really isn't anything that important.'

Jude had to choose her words carefully. She didn't want to give away how little of Ned's conversation with George Hazlitt she'd actually heard. She wanted to lure the young pro into confirming her conjectures about his actual offence.

'Listen,' she said. 'I know you're worried that the committee's going to hear about this. As I promised, they won't hear it from me...so long as you tell me the details.'

'There aren't that many details,' said the boy petulantly. 'It's just that we haven't got anywhere else to go.'

'Oh?' said Jude, hoping that she sounded more knowing than she was.

'Look, the fact is, I've got a steady girlfriend, Kelly. We've got a flat together, so there's no way I'm going to take Tonya back there, is there? More than my life's worth, I'd be well in the shit. And Tonya's in an even worse position than me, you know, about having a place to go. She lives with her grandparents and they're so old fashioned that...well, there's absolutely no chance we could go there.'

Yesss! You've confirmed exactly what I suspected, thought Jude. 'So you're saying you've been conducting your relationship with Tonya Grace at the tennis court.'

'It's not a relationship. That sounds really heavy. It's just a bit of fun.'

'Does she know that?'

'Of course she does.' But at least Ned Jackson had the decency to sound embarrassed as he said the words.

'How do you explain to your girlfriend Kelly about your late hours at the court?'

'Oh, professionals often play out of hours. With other professionals. Part of the way we train. When the courts are heavily booked, it's the only chance we get…you know, and no distractions with phones ringing and that kind of stuff.'

'And your girlfriend's never questioned what you're doing?'

'Oh no. I've got Kelly well trained.'

The glibness of his reply grated on Jude. Once or twice in her own life she'd been involved with married or otherwise cohabiting men, and she remembered the instinctive lies with which they had regularly fobbed off their unsuspecting wives. Even the recollection of it made her feel shabby.

'So you and Tonya meet once the court bookings have finished? After nine thirty?'

'Yes. Or quite often the eight fifteen court doesn't get booked, particularly during the summer.'

'So you both have your electronic cards to get into the place?'

''Course we do. But I don't bring my car back in. That might draw attention from someone at Lockleigh House. So we just use the keypad entry to the court.'

'And you don't turn on the main lights, just the ones in the club room?'

'That's right. If the court lights are on they can be seen from Lockleigh House because of the glass roof. But the club room windows face off down the garden, so there's no danger of anyone knowing we're there, particularly if we've got the curtains drawn.' A cockiness was creeping back into his voice, pride at his own cleverness.

'So you stay there till...?'

'Well...'

'Till you've had sex?'

'Yeah, all right.'

'And how long might that be?'

'Depends.' There was a hint of a chuckle in his voice. Now he was definitely bragging.

'Have you ever stayed there all night?'

'No. Well, once or twice we've gone to sleep and, like, woken up in the small hours, but we've never been there when anyone might catch us in the morning.'

'So, if you've been covering your tracks so well, how did George Hazlitt find out what you'd been doing?'

Ned Jackson's voice was full of grievance as he said, 'Mate of mine, guy I often play with, told him.'

'Nice kind of mate.'

'Yeah, well, he's like that. Bad loser. Just 'cause I always beat him, even on handicap. And my handicap's going down, and his isn't. I'm now at plus six.' The junior pro's full self-assurance was returning.

'Does George know that it's Tonya you've been spending out-of-hours time at the court with?'

'God, no! My mate may be a shit, but he wouldn't want to lose me my job.'

'Would it be that serious?'

'If George found out I'd been messing around with

a junior member and that was passed on to the committee, I don't think it'd go down very well.'

'So it sounds like you won't be able to continue
these assignations with Tonya?'

'No, well, there you go.' He didn't sound too upset
about the situation. 'I think her and me were probably
getting to the end of the road, anyway.'

'Does she know that?' Jude asked again.

'She'll work it out.'

The callousness of his response made her angry, but
Jude didn't say anything. Her mind was buzzing with
possibilities…like, for instance, was Ned Jackson the
only person to have thought of using Lockleigh House
tennis court for carnal encounters?

But there was another question uppermost in her
mind, one that had to be asked out loud. 'Had you
and Tonya been at the court the night Reggie Playfair died?'

TWENTY-SEVEN

On the Friday morning Carole found that she had run out of Gulliver's dog biscuits. This was most unusual. Her shopping was normally planned with military efficiency, a monthly run to Sainsbury's at Rustington for the big stuff, and shorter weekly visits for perishables. For running out of dog biscuits she awarded herself a very serious black mark. It offended her image of her own efficiency. She hadn't been concentrating, thinking too much about the Lady in the Lake case.

As a result she had to make one of her rare visits to Allinstore, Fethering's famously inefficient supermarket. And while she was passing the shelves of newspapers in there, she saw a familiar face looking out of one of the front pages.

It was in *The Argus*, Brighton's daily newspaper, and the photograph was of Iain Holland. The headline read: 'COUNCILLOR SLAMS SOCIAL SERVICES.'

Back at High Tor over a coffee, to the sound of Gulliver demolishing a dog biscuit on the floor, Carole read the article. Iain Holland's outburst had been prompted by the disappearance of a teenage girl in care. Bolstering his credentials as a crusading local politician, he lambasted the inefficiencies of Brighton's Children's Services. He also mentioned how much he empathized with the family of the missing girl, because his own daughter from a previous marriage had disappeared and never been found.

Carole checked out the time-line. The report had been published the previous day. So when she'd met Iain Holland in the Two Ducks on the Wednesday he must have known it was about to appear. No wonder he had been so ready to see her. If there was anyone out there who knew that Marina was still alive he'd obviously wanted to keep them quiet rather than reveal how he had used her disappearance for his own political ends.

Carole thought back to how their Wednesday meeting had ended. Of course she had refused his offer to buy her silence, but the fact that he had made it seemed to confirm that Iain Holland knew Marina to be still alive. Where, though? Why hadn't she contacted her mother in all these years? Was she being imprisoned in some way? Abroad? In Russia? Or had her father bought her silence in the same way he tried to buy Carole's?

But more important than all these questions was the big one: how was Carole Seddon going to find out where Marina Holland was?

GULLIVER GOT THE bonus of another walk on Fethering Beach as his mistress tried to work out her options. There weren't many. The big advance she had made was in deducing from Iain Holland's behaviour the certainty that his daughter was alive. Otherwise, the only clue she had to Marina's whereabouts was still just the name. Vladimir.

Carole decided the only thing she could do was to put through another call to Donna Grodsky. Having made that decision halfway through their customary circuit of the beach she turned and headed straight back to High Tor. Gulliver was extremely disgruntled by this disruption to his routine.

The baby was gurgling happily in the background when Carole got through. Once she'd identified herself, she said, 'Kyle sounds happy.'

'Yes,' Donna Grodsky agreed. 'I've been piling up his beakers for him and knocking them down. He loves that. So then I do it again. And again. Terrific job for a grown woman, isn't it?'

'I think it's something most mothers have to go through.'

'Yes. Are you calling about Marina again?'

'I am. You remember you talked about this boy called Vladimir…?'

'Uh-huh.'

'…and you couldn't remember his second name. Well, I know it's a long shot, but I was just wondering whether, by any chance, something's jogged your memory…?'

'And I've suddenly remembered what it was?'

'Yes.'

'Wouldn't that be wonderfully neat?'

'It would,' Carole agreed, feeling a little foolish.

'Well, as it happens, you're in luck.'

'Really?'

'That night, the night after we met at the George's Head, Kyle woke me about two, like he usually does—and suddenly I remembered.'

'Oh, that's brilliant!'

'It came back to me, because I remembered Marina talking to me about this guy she really fancied who she'd met down the Russian club and she said it was a coincidence that his name started with the same letter as mine.'

'So what was it?'

'Gretchenko. Vladimir Gretchenko,' said Donna Grodsky.

TWENTY-EIGHT

THE DAY AFTER Reggie Playfair's funeral, Jude felt rest-less. She was beginning to realize that this would be a feature of any relationship she had with Piers Targett. While they were together she believed and trusted him. It was only when they were apart that the doubts crept in.

She also felt she should be catching up on some overdue healing sessions, but knew she was too distracted to summon up the necessary concentration to make them effective. And that made her guilty and unsatisfied.

She'd seen Carole Seddon go past Woodside Cottage a couple of times. Gulliver was doing well for walks that day. But Carole had made no attempt to contact her and Jude was quite relieved about that. There was still a slight awkwardness between the neighbours about her new lover. At some point Jude knew she must introduce Piers to Carole properly, but it was not an occasion she looked forward to with much relish. Of course they'd be perfectly polite to each other, but Jude would be aware of her friend's customary spikiness and overreaction. She couldn't somehow see them doing many social events as a threesome. And Carole would resent that.

Jude was also relieved—and at the same time guilty—about the fact that she hadn't brought Carole up to date on the advances she had made on the Reggie Playfair investigation. And that again was tied in with her closeness to Piers Targett. It wouldn't be easy to pass on what he had told her about his unstable wife's antics at Lockleigh House tennis court. Or to explain why she didn't want to spread the news of what Jonquil had been doing there.

And until she'd communicated that discovery to Carole, Jude didn't feel she could tell her about Ned Jackson using the court for his assignations with Tonya Grace. Which made her feel even more guilty.

There was no doubt about it, being in love always had this effect on Jude. The experience was exhilarating, but also distracting. Her life didn't run as efficiently when she had a lover. To use a tennis metaphor, it made her take her eye off the ball.

SHE TRIED TO counter her restlessness by yoga, she went for a walk on Fethering Beach, picking up fish and chips to eat on the way, but neither of these resources brought Jude the calm they usually did. Both just seemed to increase the number of questions she wanted to put to Piers when she next saw him.

Eventually, with something close to desperation, willing to find anything that would stop the same thoughts circling round in her head, she picked up the book that Wally Edgington-Bewley had given her. *Courts in the Act*.

The introduction made it clear that this was 'just the reminiscences of an old fogey of playing most of the real tennis courts of the world, recollections of amusing incidents and the great chums I have made in them.' The book had been expensively produced and

was illustrated by black-and-white photographs of the
insides and outsides of courts, as well as a younger
Wally Edgington-Bewley with some of his 'great
chums' in their tennis whites. As a frontispiece to the
book was a picture of the younger Wally in white shirt
and long white trousers, holding a racket and leaning
nonchalantly against a Rolls-Royce Silver Shadow.
The caption read: 'The Author with the Road-Eater'.

Courts in the Act had been a labour of love, which
was never going to trouble the best-sellers' charts.
Wally's style was dilatory and full of non-sequiturs.
He was obsessed by recording the scores of every
game he played, and on very few of the courts he
played on did he think the quality of the balls were
up to scratch.

Flicking through, Jude was surprised to see the
unlikely places where there were real tennis courts.
Hampton Court she knew about, and she would have
expected them to exist at Lord's, Queen's Club, Oxford and Cambridge Universities. Paris and Bordeaux
were perhaps predictable, but she would not have anticipated finding them in Philadelphia or Boston. And
she would never in a million years have guessed there
was one in Hobart, Tasmania.

It was Wally Edgington-Bewley's estimate that
there were forty-five active real tennis courts in the
world, and of those twenty-seven were in the British Isles.

As Jude idly turned the pages, she found *Courts in
the Act* had a certain charm. The author was clearly
obsessed, but it was a harmless obsession. She wondered whether Wally Edgington-Bewley had ever married. She couldn't see any mention of a wife, and she

rather doubted whether the woman existed who could match his passion for real tennis. Or maybe his love of the game had left no room for other passions in his life.

Her eye was arrested by yet another photograph of men in whites holding tennis rackets. The younger Wally was clearly recognizable, but it took Jude a moment to identify the younger Reggie Playfair and the younger Piers Targett. With the passage of the years Piers had changed less. His body shape in the photograph was much the same as it was now. And though his hair was black back then, he still wore it long, flopping down from a centre parting.

Time had been less kind to the Reggie Playfair of the photograph. His younger version already had a substantial paunch, but his arms and legs were well muscled and he looked fit. The three of them would have had a very vigorous game.

But with whom? Who was the fourth who made up their doubles?

There was a partial explanation in the photo's caption. It read: 'Paris Court, Rue Lauriston—The Old One, The Thin One and The Fat One (The Fair One had gone off to slip into something elegant)'.

A woman, it had to be a woman. 'The Fair One'. Was that a literal description of her colouring or just Wally's old-fashioned gallantry?

Jude read the accompanying text with interest.

'Paris was to be our next jaunt. The Road-Eater was hungry for the road and I was fortunate that my good chums, The Thin One, The Fat One and The Fair One had managed to persuade their better halves that nothing could be more helpful to the future of their marriages than accompanying The Old One on another jaunt, this time to Paris.

'Now for lovers of real tennis, which they call *jeu de paume*, France is in many ways a bit of a disappointment. The French used to love the game, it was a favourite sport of many of their kings as evidenced in William Shakespeare's great play *Henry V,* but then of course they had a bit of a hoo-ha known as the French Revolution. And suddenly being a toff was not so popular. In fact, if I might venture a pleasantry, it was a case of "Toff with his head!" And the same thing happened to the popularity of toffs' games. And of course tennis (which is believed to come from the French word "*tenez*") was one of those. And lots of the courts in Paris and the surrounding countryside were either demolished or used for other purposes, industrial or farming. It almost makes one weep to think of it.

'But thank the Lord, there are a few courts still in use, and the Paris court in Rue Lauriston is one of them, very near the Arc de Triomphe. Also very handily just opposite the court is the Cimarosa Hotel, into which I and my three chums booked, planning to have two days of tennis without missing out on the Parisian gastronomic delights and fine wines for which Paris is so famous. Is there anything better on the earth after a game of tennis than to sit down with a bottle of Bordeaux Premier Cru?

'We caught an early ferry to Dieppe, stopped for a *menu gastronomique* in Rouen and were ensconced in the Hotel Cimarosa in good time for our seven o'clock doubles. A close affair (on handicap) with The Old One and The Fat One finally overcoming The Thin One and The Fair One 6-4/5-6/6-3. And still time for an excellent dinner at a little bistro The Fair One knew from a time when she had been a Paris resident. No problem sleeping like tops that night!

'However, the next day all did not go according to plan as it should have done, due to crossed wires or some kind of communication snafu. After a good lunchtime *menu gastronomique* at a brasserie The Fair One knew, she, as ladies will, said that she needed to do a bit of shopping. After all, if you're a lady you don't come to the home of *haute couture* without checking out the wares on offer, do you? And since we were all gentleman one of our number suggested he should accompany her as a bodyguard to protect her from any surviving element of *sans-culottism* on the *rues de Paris*. Well, this was where the wires got crossed, as we discovered the next morning. While I was sure we'd agreed to another seven o'clock doubles that evening, somehow The Fair One and her escort got the idea that they were meant to be dining *à deux*, so we ended up playing a singles that evening (at level), which I won 6-5/4-6/6-2 (and got three in the winning gallery!).

'All confusions cleared up in the morning when we set off back in the Road-Eater to Blighty, stopping only for a *menu gastronomique* in an excellent restaurant in Beauvais. The pig's trotters were especially good and an excellent 1955 Chateau Palmer was imbibed.

'So, another jolly jaunt jaunted. Spouses reunited, God's in his heaven and all's right with the world! *Merci beaucoup*, gay Paree.'

JUDE FLICKED THROUGH the rest of *Courts in the Act*, but there appeared to be no further references to Reggie

Playfair. Was it conceivable that he and The Fair One had not played their evening doubles all that time ago because they were starting an affair, possibly even in bed together at the time of the court booking? Oenone Playfair, she remembered, suspected that her husband's illicit relationship had started in Paris.

So who, then, was The Fair One? Well, there weren't many candidates. It had to be Jonquil Targett. Piers had said she had been blonde before she was blonded. Also that she used to play a lot of real tennis. And he'd suspected that she and Reggie might have had a relationship. What was more, from what he'd said of her character, she was the kind of woman who'd glory in starting an affair with another man under her husband's nose.

Jude felt she had to contact Jonquil, but she didn't know how to go about it. On the one occasion the woman had contacted she had done so using Piers' iPhone. So her number wouldn't be on Jude's mobile. And Piers was so protective—or afraid—of his estranged wife that he wasn't likely to give his current lover a contact for her.

Then Jude had a brainwave. Of course, the last message on Reggie Playfair's phone had been from Jonquil setting up their encounter in Lockleigh House tennis court. And before Piers had interrupted her in the small hours of the Wednesday night, Jude had written down the number from which the fatal text had been sent.

Jude rootled about in the untidy pile of papers on her sitting-room floor, and triumphantly produced the Allinstore receipt on the back of which she had scribbled.

No procrastination now. Jude knew that her restlessness had two causes. One, frustration at not being able to find out the exact circumstances of Reggie Playfair's death. And two, uncertainty about Piers Targett's honesty. Ringing Jonquil promised to bring a resolution in both cases.

She keyed in the number and got a recorded voice. The speaker did not identify herself, but asked the caller to leave a message.

Jude didn't leave one. She was too shocked to work out what might be the right thing to say. Because, though she recognized the recorded voice, it wasn't Jonquil Targett's.

TWENTY-NINE

CAROLE SEDDON DID not allow herself to feel over-whelmed by the nature of her task. She was so excited by the progress she was making in her search for Marina Holland that she would not allow in any negative thoughts. She was trying to track down a young man called Vladimir Gretchenko, who had possibly lived in Brighton eight years previously. He could now be anywhere in the entire world. He might not even still be alive. And the idea that he was still in touch with Marina Holland—if indeed he ever had been in touch with Marina Holland—might well be fanciful.

Carole sat in front of her laptop in its permanent position in her spare room. She started by googling 'Vladimir Gretchenko'. To her surprise, a couple of entries came up, but they didn't seem very helpful. For one thing, the details were in Russian. And then again the means of contact was through Facebook.

Was Carole Seddon about to abandon the principles of a lifetime and register with a social network?

Not quite yet. She found that, without actually signing up to anything, she could access a page that offered to 'Find people with your last name on Facebook.'

The Vladimir Gretchenko whose photo appeared there was bespectacled and grey-haired. Far too old to have been a boy in a Brighton Russian Club eight years before.

So Carole Seddon concluded with some relief—though possibly not accuracy—that Facebook and Twitter would not be of any use to her investigation.

On the other hand, there was always good old directory enquiries, now of course a completely online service. She accessed 192.com.

The free people search came up with nothing in Brighton for 'Vladimir Gretchenko'. Now too caught up in her quest to exercise her usual parsimony, Carole paid for an advanced search. But that again produced no results.

Since she had bought six credits she next searched for Vladimir Gretchenko in East Sussex. Nothing. West Sussex—the same result.

She tried Hampshire, by now so hyper that she was prepared to go through every county in the British Isles. And maybe then she'd embark on the ones in Russia (assuming, that is, Russia had counties).

But Hampshire proved fruitful. There was a Vladimir Gretchenko listed in Southampton.

RATHER THAN CLARET-SOAKED, Jude now thought of Wally Edgington-Bewley's voice as marinated in 1955 Chateau Palmer as he expressed his delight at hearing from her.

'I was just ringing to say how much I enjoyed *Courts in the Act*.'

He was obviously chuffed to bits by her reaction, but his British instinct for self-depreciation came to the fore. 'Oh, it's a load of tosh, really. A poor thing, but mine own. I am quite pleased with the title, though, I must confess—a little bit clever, don't you think?'

'Very,' Jude lied.

'I just thought it'd be rather jolly to have a record of all that stuff, you know. It has been a kind of life-long obsession for me. I mean, I've really no pretensions to being a writer.'

Jude was far too gracious to agree with this last statement. 'I really enjoyed it,' she said. 'I was particularly interested in your visit to Paris.'

'Ah, *la belle Rue Lauriston, mais oui*. Well, of course you would be interested in that, because your Piers was on the jaunt with us.'

'"The Thin One"?'

'Exactly. Bit rotten of me to call the other young reprobate "The Fat One", but Reggie took it in good part. Always did have a bit of a pot, though. Still, he never minded a joke against himself, Reggie...poor old bugger.'

'And then of course there was "The Fair One"...'

'Yes, always nice to have a filly on board for one of those jaunts. Raises the tone, don't you know—not to mention the level of the conversation. The chatter of chaps on their own always has a tendency to sink to the lowest common denominator, eh? Doesn't take long to get back to prep school smut.'

Jude knew she would have to be circumspect in any enquiries she made about Jonquil Targett's role in the 'jaunt', so she started, 'It must have been nice for her to have her husband there too.'

'What?' Wally Edgington-Bewley sounded bewildered. 'Her husband wasn't in Paris. He was off on one of his foreign postings. Felicity had just settled one of their children into boarding school and she had a few days free. That's why she was able to come with us.'

After the shock it had just received, Jude's brain was reeling, realigning its assumptions, recasting The Fair One not as Jonquil Targett, but as Felicity Budgen.

She managed to come up with a formula of words that didn't make her sound too stupid. 'Yes, of course, I'm sorry, I get confused with all the relationships. You know, it's only been a few weeks since I met anyone at Lockleigh House tennis court.'

'Of course, of course.' Wally Edgington-Bewley didn't seem to have any problem accepting her explanation.

'I was rather amused,' Jude went on, 'by the confusion that happened your last night in Paris on that jaunt.'

'What was that?' asked Wally. 'Sorry, a while since I wrote the book and the memory's not what it was.'

'Oh, there was that business of you expecting to play a doubles and the other two not turning up and you ending up having a singles.'

'Oh yes, of course, remember now,' he said, and there was a new caution in his voice.

'Did you ever get an explanation for what happened?'

'Just crossed wires, you know. Cock-up on the communication front.'

'And did you hear what they actually did that evening?'

'No,' said Wally Edgington-Bewley firmly. 'Listen, Jude, I've never married myself, but one thing I've learned over a great many years is never to meddle in the marriages of others.'

Obviously he did know something. But equally obviously he was not going to say any more on the subject. Accepting this, Jude just showered him with more much-appreciated compliments on *Courts in the Act* and their conversation ended.

Then she redialled the number from which the last text message on Reggie Playfair's phone had been sent. And this time Felicity Budgen answered.

CAROLE DITHERED. She made herself a cup of tea. She tried to get her mind engaged in *The Times* crossword. She even contemplated taking Gulliver out for another walk.

But she knew she was fooling herself. She was going to give in sooner or later. And she did—sooner. Nothing—not wild horses nor her own perverse personality—could have stopped Carole Seddon from dialling that Southampton number.

A young female voice answered.

'Hello,' said Carole, thinking on her feet. 'Is that Marina Gretchenko?'

'Yes,' said the girl.

THIRTY

THE BUDGENS' HOUSE, called The Old Manor and situated just North of Fedborough, was even more luxuriously appointed than the Playfairs'. Felicity told Jude that they had bought it before her husband's final ambassadorial posting with a view to spending their retirement there. Its splendour suggested there must have been family money around as well as a Foreign Office income and pension.

When Jude had got through on the phone and said what she wanted to discuss, Felicity Budgen had not hesitated about asking her over. 'Don's out playing golf. By the time he's had a couple at the nineteenth hole, he won't be back till eight at the earliest.'

This was yet another part of the investigation in which Jude could not involve Carole. She felt bad about it, but there was no way she could introduce a stranger into the kind of conversation she was shortly to have.

Though she had expected Lady Budgen to be at best glacially polite, the woman's manner came across as warmer than that. But presumably that, too, was part of her diplomatic training. If you spend your entire life expressing interest in things that are not intrinsically interesting, you must get very good at faking quite a range of emotions.

Jude was ushered into a sitting room twice the size

of the one at Winnows, which had received the same level of attention from interior designers. She accepted the offer of coffee. Felicity said she would get it herself. 'I've given Inez the afternoon off.'

While her hostess was in the kitchen, Jude took in the room. On the mantelpiece stood an array of photographs of Sir Donald in the company of Her Majesty the Queen, as well as a lot of other recognizable foreign dignitaries. The display on the piano featured pictures of three unfeasibly good-looking children at various stages of development, usually on yachts or ponies.

Jude didn't exactly feel nervous, but she felt tense. There had been a strange quality in Felicity Budgen's manner both on the phone and now at the Old Manor House. A kind of resignation, as if she had been long expecting an encounter of this kind. As soon as Jude had mentioned 'what happened in Paris', Felicity seemed to recognize that the moment had come.

She brought the coffee on a lace-covered silver tray and poured it. There was not the slightest tremor in her hand as she did so. Then when they had both taken elegant sips, she said, 'Who told you about Paris?'

'I read about it in Wally Edgington-Bewley's book.'

'Ah.' Lady Budgen let out a light laugh. 'I had completely forgotten the mention of it in there. I remembered when he first published the book, we were a bit worried. But gradually, as nobody said anything, we realized that we couldn't be safer.'

'Oh?'

'Well, although almost everyone at the club bought a copy from Wally, none of them did more than look at the photographs. I'm sure there's not a person in the world who's actually read *Courts in the Act*.'

'Well, I read enough to be intrigued…particularly in the light of Reggie Playfair's death.'

'Yes.' Felicity Budgen looked elegantly thoughtful. 'Reggie Playfair's death has been a game-changer in many ways.'

'Was it in Paris that the relationship started?'

'Mm. The attraction had always been there, we admitted that to ourselves afterwards. But we never saw each other alone. Always a spouse on the scene. And of course we were preoccupied with our own lives, and in my case with the children. Anyway, I was abroad most of the time, supporting Donald as he climbed the greasy pole of the Foreign Office.'

'Until Paris.'

'Yes.' She sighed. 'I had come over to settle our youngest into Eton, you know, his first term. I'd done that with all of them when they'd started boarding school. Donald thought I was mollycoddling them. He kept saying that he'd just been sent off to board from India by his parents from the age of seven, and it'd never done him any harm.'

'And do you agree with that?'

Felicity Budgen smiled. 'How very perceptive of you, Jude. Donald always said that boarding school had made him the man he was…and I'm rather afraid that may have been true.' Not wishing to dwell on what was tantamount to a criticism of her husband, she went on, 'Anyway, I was in a rather vulnerable state at that time, round the Paris trip…you know, my age for one thing. Feeling that I was entering a distinctly less glamorous stage of my life. Also I tended to stay with my mother when I was in England, and that was never easy. She didn't belong to the generation who thought you should bolster your children's confidence. Rather the reverse.

'And with the youngest child off at school…was there any role left for me in life? Except for being frightfully loyal to Donald and smiling at a lot of people for whom I had no feelings at all? Many women perhaps would have been very happy with that situation. Maybe I should have been. But I can't pretend. I wasn't.'

'And then you have the offer of a jaunt to Paris in Wally Edgington-Bewley's Road-Eater?'

'Yes. And the dates just worked for me. And we'd both be there without our spouses. I think we both knew something was going to happen. There was a degree of calculation on both sides.'

'So his offer to accompany you shopping was pre-planned?'

'We hadn't actually talked about it, but we knew it was going to happen.'

'Did you go back to the Cimarosa Hotel?'

'God, no. He always had more style than that. He booked us into the Georges V.'

'And the affair continued after Paris?'

'Yes. When I was in England. Which wasn't very often.'

'And when you were back in England the two of you met at the Lockleigh House tennis court?'

Felicity Budgen arched a perfectly sculpted eyebrow. 'You have been doing your research. Yes, we tried hotels at first. But then I nearly bumped into a colleague of Donald's at The Dorchester and I realized it was just too risky. The one thing I could not allow to happen was for Donald to find out. My husband is an incredibly straight, uncomplicated man, who thinks the world is equally straight and uncomplicated. If he found out that his wife was having an affair, well, it would destroy him.

'So my lover and I were like two randy adolescents, desperate to find somewhere we could be alone to-gether. And his place was out of the question because of his wife. So yes…we ended up with squalid encoun-ters in the club room of Lockleigh House tennis court.'

'You won't have been the last couple to do that,' Jude observed.

'Oh?'

'Apparently Ned Jackson has been known to take his conquests there.'

As soon as she'd said it, she realized she shouldn't have done. She was, after all, speaking to the wife of the Lockleigh House club chairman. And she knew from George Hazlitt that Felicity Budgen had a par-ticular concern for the welfare of Tonya Grace. All in all, what Jude had just said was very stupid. Angry though she was at Ned Jackson's treatment of Tonya Grace, she didn't actually want to be the cause of his losing his job.

But fortunately Felicity Budgen seemed too caught up in a reverie of the past to have registered what she said. 'Yes, I suppose to an outsider our encounters would have appeared squalid. Squalid, but marvel-lous.'

'And,' asked Jude, 'was it for another squalid but marvellous encounter that you asked Reggie to meet you at the court in the early hours of the Wednesday before last?'

For the first time in their encounter Felicity Budgen's perfect demeanour cracked. Her jaw dropped and she looked totally flabbergasted as she said, 'Reggie? What's he got to do with it? It wasn't Reggie I went off with in Paris. It was Piers.'

THIRTY-ONE

THERE WERE SO many questions that Jude wanted to ask that for a moment she was too shocked to ask any of them. Finally she managed to blurt out, 'But why did you text Reggie to meet you at the court?'

'Ah, the reason for that…' Felicity began. Then she seemed to hear something and rose to look out of the front window. 'It's Donald. What on earth's he doing back at this time? Oh dear, he looks as if he's injured himself. I think you'd better go, Jude.'

The mistress of The Old Manor led her guest to the front door where they met the master of The Old Manor, entering in some discomfort.

'Ricked my back doing a wedge shot out of a bunker on the eighth, darling,' he said to his wife. 'Hurts like buggery. Only just managed to drive back.'

'You should have called me, darling. I'd have come and picked you up.'

'No, I was all right,' he said, though he patently wasn't.

'Jude just dropped by for some recipes I promised I'd give her.' Felicity Budgen dropped effortlessly into lying mode.

For a moment Jude worried that she wasn't carrying any recipes, but Sir Donald Budgen had no interest in her at all. 'Look, darling,' he was saying, 'could you help me upstairs? If I can get into bed, maybe the

pain'll be better. And then if you can get me some
paracetamol…and probably one of your toddies for
me to take it with… Ooh, God, this hurts. And I was
two up in the game when it happened. It's an abso-
lute bugger.'

Felicity Budgen made polite goodbyeing noises as
she helped her crippled husband across the hallway
towards the stairs. Jude let herself out, thinking that
the ex-ambassador was behaving like a small child.
And that perhaps in that dependency lay the secret of
the Budgens' enduring marriage.

Jude walked down the long drive and found herself on another country road miles from anywhere.
She'd have to ring for a taxi. If she was going to continue mixing with people from Lockleigh House tennis court she'd have to buy a car.

But at that moment it seemed extremely unlikely
that she would continue mixing with people from
Lockleigh House tennis court.

There were so many challenging questions with
which she needed to confront Piers Targett.

IT WAS WHEN Carole Seddon had said, with unsubstantiated certainty, the she knew Marina Gretchenko to be
the daughter of Iain Holland that the girl had started to
sound frightened, prompting fears she might just click
on a button and end the call. But rather than breaking
the connection, she seemed anxious to keep talking.
Trying to find out how much Carole actually knew,
perhaps. It was Marina who suggested they ought to
meet.

The girl certainly didn't want to let Carole know
where she lived. She also rejected the idea of a café

or pub. The only place she would agree to meet was in a children's playground.

Carole didn't know Southampton well, but as the Renault nosed through the traffic following Marina's instructions it was clear that the girl did not live in one of the more salubrious areas of the city. The playground she had specified was set in an urban wasteland of shabby high rises and low industrial units. Some of the swings were broken, the slide and climbing frame were disfigured by graffiti. The wooden slats of the benches had been burnt. Only the cement uprights remained like forlorn bookends.

Carole had again given the girl her grey hair, rimless glasses and Burberry raincoat as means of identification, but as she approached from the Renault she saw there wasn't going to be much of a problem about that. The other women present were all a good twenty-five years younger than her, and had about them an air of faded, drab hopelessness.

The one who must be Marina Gretchenko had been looking out for her. As soon as Carole pushed open the rusted wire-netted gate to the playground, she left the child she was pushing on a spring-based wooden horse and walked towards her. 'Carole?' she asked.

'Yes. You must be Marina.'

It was amazing that she was the same age as Donna Grodsky. The girl in the George's Head at Moulse-coomb may have been overweight, but she had been full of life and vigour. Whereas Marina Gretchenko looked as if all youth and energy had been drained out of her. Carole would never have recognized her from the photographs of the cocky, combative schoolgirl that had been all over the media at the time of her disappearance. Her cheekbones didn't look fine, merely prominent and the dark hair had no lustre. Marina wore a faded blue raincoat with a scarf wound high around her neck. And in spite of the overcast October day, she had on dark glasses.

A child came running up to her and wrapped itself around her legs. She snapped something at him in Russian and he returned to pushing round the elliptical paint-defaced roundabout.

'Yours?' asked Carole.

'Yes.' The girl's voice was hesitant and tentative, as if she hadn't spoken English for a long time. 'Four of them are mine. The little one's over there in the buggy.'

In her drive over to Southampton Carole had been trying to plan how she would get into the forthcoming interview, but she needn't have worried. Marina Gretchenko immediately asked, 'Does my father know you're meeting me?'

'Good heavens, no.'

'He doesn't even know you've found me?'

'No.'

The girl seemed considerably relieved by that news. 'Then why've you got in touch?' she asked.

'Well, your disappearance was quite a big story.'

'Was it?' She sounded genuinely unaware of the media storm she had unleashed.

'You must have seen the papers, the television reports.'

She shook her head. 'My husband doesn't like me reading papers.'

'You mean you're completely cut off from outside media?'

'We are happy together as a family. We do not need interference from the outside world.' The words were spoken doggedly, like an article of faith.

'When did you get married?' asked Carole.

'Soon after I left home. I moved in with Vladimir for a while, but he said that was not good. We should be married. So we got married.'

'What, when you were sixteen?'

'Yes.'

'And you never thought to tell your mother?'

'Vladimir said I should cut loose from my family. They were not Russian. We did not need them. My job was to be Vladimir's wife.'

'But you got in touch with your father?'

The girl blushed. 'I did not want to, but...we were going through a bad patch financially. This was two or three years ago. Vladimir had lost another job, the third baby was on the way, it wasn't a good time. I thought maybe I could ask my father for a loan, so I contacted him.'

'How did he react?'

'He was very surprised at first. He told me he had remarried and had two children. But he agreed to give us money.'

'Does he still give you money?'

The girl nodded. 'It is difficult,' she said defensively, 'for Vladimir. His English is not so good, it is hard for him to keep a job.'

In Carole's mind a pattern was beginning to take shape, and it wasn't a pretty one. 'Does your father attach any conditions to the money he gives you?'

'That I should not contact him. Which is why I was

so worried when I heard from you. If he finds out you know who I am he will stop paying the money.'

'Don't worry. I'm not about to tell him.'

'You mustn't ever do it. If Vladimir finds out we have lost the money from my father, he will…I don't know what he will do.'

'Beat you up?' suggested Carole coolly.

'No,' said Marina Gretchenko immediately. 'No, of course not.' But the nervous way the girl pulled her scarf higher on her neck made Carole sure her conjecture had been accurate.

She felt an unreasoning fury mounting inside her. A fury towards Vladimir Gretchenko that she would feel for any man who beat up his wife. But an even stronger fury whose object was Iain Holland.

The cynicism of the man's actions appalled her. Safe in the cosy world of his new squeaky-clean family, his thriving business, his promising political career, out of the blue he'd been contacted by the daughter he thought was dead. Having discovered Marina's circumstances, locked into an abusive marriage with a husband jealous to the point of paranoia about any contacts she had outside the family, Iain Holland had realized that that situation suited him very well. Marina was as safely out of his new life as if she actually had been dead. And he could easily afford the small regular payments that would maintain that *status quo*.

'There are,' said Carole gently, 'places you can get in touch with, people you can ring who can help in your situation. There are women's refuges and—'

'No,' she said. 'Vladimir would find out. It would make things worse. When the telephone bill comes, he checks through the calls I have made and asks me to explain every one. And he will not let me have a mobile.'

'You could make the call from a public phone box.'

'No! If Vladimir found out… No.' She repeated her mantra. 'We are happy together as a family.'

'Will your husband find out about my calling you?'

'No. Fortunately when you rang he was out. There is a Russian club he goes to.'

'But if I rang again?'

'You must not ring again. All I needed to find out from you is that you will not tell my father what you know about me. If I have your solemn promise on that, there is nothing more that needs to be said.' There was a desolation about the finality with which those words were said.

'Marina, isn't there anyone you can talk to? Don't you have any friends? I met Donna Grodsky who you were at school with—'

'Vladimir did not like Donna. He did not want me to see her.'

'So is there no one else?'

'Well…' Marina Gretchenko looked across to where one of her children was crying. She barked out something in Russian. The child wiped its nose miserably and moved away. 'There are not so many people in Southampton who Vladimir approves of. A lot of Poles, but very few Russians.'

'So you do have a friend?' prompted Carole.

'There is a young girl Vladimir does not mind me talking to. He knows her grandparents from Brighton. They are relatives of his and she lives with them. But the old man is suffering from Alzheimer's, so life is tough for her. Vladimir encourages me to talk to her. He thinks I can perhaps help her.'

'What's she called?'

'Tonya Grace.' The name meant nothing to Carole.

'Why does she live with her grandparents? Are her own parents dead?'

'Might as well be. God knows what happened to her father, he just went off. But her mother got into the Brighton drug scene. I think she's still living round there somewhere, but certainly in no state to be of any use to her daughter.'

'Marina, can't you talk to this Tonya? About the troubles in your marriage?'

'There are no troubles in my marriage. We are happy together as—'

'If that's true,' said Carole sharply, 'take off your dark glasses and let me see your eyes.'

But the girl wouldn't do that. Which was tantamount to an admission that her husband beat her up.

'Marina, are you sure you couldn't talk to Tonya about…?'

'No, I can't. Certainly not at the moment. She doesn't let me get a word in edgeways because she's got so many troubles of her own.'

'Oh?'

'Usual stuff. Some boy she's keen on's been messing her around. Don't know who he is, she met him through some sporting thing, I think. She's always been keen on sport. Anyway, if I ring Tonya at the moment, I just get a whole lot of crying about this boy and then she was going on about something terrible she saw, someone getting killed, I don't know. Anyway, basically, I'm not going to get any sympathy from Tonya at the moment.' She checked herself. 'Not of course that I need any sympathy. I only talk to Tonya because Vladimir thinks I can help her, and because she's a relative, a Russian.'

It seemed pretty clear to Carole that Marina Gretchenko had no resources of potential sympathy. There was no one she could turn to. And yet at that very moment in Brighton there was a woman whose only dream in life was to be reunited with her daughter.

'Marina,' said Carole, 'you got in touch with your father...'

'Yes?'

'Didn't you ever try to get in touch with your mother?'

'No.'

'Didn't you ever think of it?'

'Yes, I did. When I ran away from home I was very angry with her. I didn't think she understood me. And when I started living with Vladimir, he said I should shut myself off from her. It was what I wanted to do too, so I did. But then when I got in touch with Daddy...' It was the first time she had used the word. Carole remembered Susan Holland talking about the enduring bond between daughters and fathers.

'Did you ask him about your mother?'

'Yes, I thought maybe enough time had passed. So I knew Daddy was still in contact with her, and I asked him to ask her if she'd like me to give her a call.'

Carole was bewildered. If that conversation had ever taken place, there would never have been any cause for her to contact Susan Holland about the Lady in the Lake. 'But he never asked her, did he?'

'Yes, he did. Daddy told me he'd asked her. But

she'd replied that I'd hurt her so much, she never wanted to hear from me again.'

Carole Seddon's fury knew no bounds. In the annals of divorce she knew how vindictive ex-partners could be towards each other, but she'd never before heard of callousness to match that of Iain Holland.

THIRTY-TWO

Now she knew about Piers Targett's ongoing affair with Felicity Budgen, Jude could no longer keep out the flood of other suspicions about him that had been building up inside her. Had anything he had told her over the last few weeks been true?

She thought back to her first acquaintance with Lockleigh House tennis court, at the Sec's Cup a couple of Sundays back. And very clearly she remembered what Reggie Playfair had said after his collapse on the court, which in retrospect seemed like a dress rehearsal for the more serious one he was to suffer three days later. When he had interpreted Henry the doctor's suggestion that he might be about to 'pop his clogs', Reggie had announced, 'I'm not the kind of person who believes in the idea of carrying secrets to the grave. No, my instinct has always been to come clean and confront people.'

At the time it had just sounded like bluster. But, given events that had happened since, Jude could see that his words could have been heard by a guilty person as a threat. What secrets was Reggie Playfair ready to reveal? Might one of them be about the affair between Piers Targett and Felicity Budgen?

If that were the case, then someone might have felt the need for Reggie to be silenced before he made his revelation. Piers' account of Jonquil setting up the scenario of herself dressed as Agnes Wardock's ghost was so bizarre that Jude thought it could be true. And she felt pretty certain that the sight of that filmy white figure had caused Reggie Playfair's fatal heart attack.

Jonquil Targett was sufficiently weird to have thought up the charade for herself. But she was also suggestible enough to have someone plant the idea in her head. And who was more likely to have planted it than her estranged husband?

Jude felt profoundly miserable.

CAROLE, ON the other hand, as she drove back from Southampton, felt very nearly smug. She hadn't found out the solution to the mission on which she had first embarked—she had no idea who Fedborough's Lady in the Lake was—but she had solved the problem set by Susan Holland. She now had some wonderful news to impart to that desperate woman. She just had to decide on the best way to break it to her.

The other achievement that made her glow with pride was that she had conducted the investigation on her own. She had set out to unravel a mystery completely independent of Jude, and she had solved it. While her neighbour had been preoccupied with what might have been—but probably wasn't—a murder at Lockleigh House tennis court. And also preoccupied—not to say distracted—by her new lover, Piers Targett.

Carole Seddon decided she would keep her successful investigation secret a little longer. When she'd actually contacted Susan Holland, when mother and daughter were finally reunited, that would be the time to tell Jude what she'd been doing.

JUDE WAS NOT a woman without resources. She had a wide circle of friends, particularly from the alternative-therapy world, but none of them did she want to speak to that afternoon.

Nor, despite her customary enthusiasm for direct confrontation and getting things out in the open, did she want to speak to Piers Targett. Their next encounter was not going to be an easy one, and Jude also had the sick feeling that it would probably be their last. She wished she could go back to the airy, confident Piers she had first met, before his image became sullied with doubt and suspicion. But she knew such hopes were pointless and vain.

She wanted to talk to somebody, though. And it was with some surprise that she realized only one person would fit the bill. Someone who wouldn't offer too much easy sympathy, or alternative therapies to ease her pain. Someone who would talk to her directly and without sentiment.

For possibly the first time in their friendship, Jude really needed the company of Carole Seddon.

So she was relieved that Friday afternoon when she saw the neat Renault come back to the garage next door, and within five minutes of her neighbour's return Jude was ringing at the front door of High Tor.

As Jude knew she wouldn't, Carole didn't mention the emotional dimension in her suspicions of Piers Targett. None of that 'Ooh, it must be making you feel awful to have someone you love involved in...' that she would have got from her friends in the healing world. Instead, Carole first made a pot of strong coffee. Then, as she listened to Jude spell out the prog-

ress her investigation had made, she just treated Piers
as another suspect in a list of suspects.

And there was quite a lot to spell out. The two
women hadn't spoken about the case for nearly a week.
In fact they hadn't spoken at all since Carole had
brought Jude back from their visit to Cecil Wardock
in Lockleigh House the previous Saturday.

Jude gave her neighbour the edited version of what
she had found out, not detailing every cul-de-sac and
double-back that her suspicions had followed. Nor did
she describe each member of the Lockleigh House
tennis court she had encountered, merely the princi-
ple players in the mystery of Reggie Playfair's death.

'So...' said Carole after the silence that followed
Jude's exposition, 'at the moment the thinking is that
he was killed deliberately. The Agnes Wardock ghost
scenario was set up on the confident assumption that
seeing it would cause Reggie Playfair to have a fatal
heart attack?'

'Yes.'

Carole grimaced ruefully. 'Good luck to the bar-
rister who stands up in court and tries to get a conviction on that.'

'I'm not so concerned about a conviction in court.
I just want to know who set Reggie up for that rather
macabre death and why.'

'Well, the information you have is that he went to
the court following a text-message summons from
Felicity Budgen?'

'Yes.'

'So did he actually meet her there?'

'I can only assume so.'

'This tennis court,' Carole observed, 'is getting

rather full, isn't it, on the night in question? Felicity Budgen, Piers, the demented Jonquil in a wedding dress, and then poor Reggie Playfair.'

'Yes. I don't know whether they were all there at the same time.'

'Well, Jonquil and Reggie certainly were, otherwise she couldn't have killed him...if one can use such a transitive verb as "killed" in this context.' Carole was thoughtful for a moment. 'And you say Piers and Felicity Budgen had regular liaisons at the tennis court over the years?'

'Yes,' Jude confirmed, trying to keep her voice as neutral as possible.

'And do you know if that relationship was still ongoing...I mean, obviously until Piers took up with you?'

Jude was forced to admit that she didn't know. It was one of the many questions that would have to be asked when she and Piers Targett next met.

'It's funny,' said Carole. 'I would never have suspected that a real tennis court could be used as a venue for illicit assignations.'

'Well, I'm not sure that they all are, but over the years the Lockleigh House one has been. And it's a tradition that still continues.'

'Oh?'

'Ned Jackson, the junior professional, sees himself as a bit of a Lothario. He's been two-timing his girlfriend at the court with one of the younger members. Poor kid, he's treating her very badly. And she can't be much more than sixteen. Pretty girl called Tonya Grace.'

Carole Seddon looked thunderstruck. 'Do you

know, Jude,' she said, 'that's the second time I've heard that name today.'

It was a matter of moments to tell her neighbour the context in which Tonya Grace's name had come up.

'"Seeing someone killed"?' Jude echoed. 'My God, maybe Tonya was there the night of Reggie's death! Ned Jackson swore she wasn't, but he'd lie about anything to save his skin.'

'We need to talk to the girl,' said Carole. 'Have you any means of getting in touch with her?'

'Apparently Felicity Budgen's rather taken her under her wing, but I'm not sure that I want to contact Felicity right now. Simplest way would be through the court. I've got the number. I'll see if there's anyone there.'

George Hazlitt answered. 'Oh, hello, Jude. Booking your follow-up lesson, are you?'

'Not right now, actually. I was wondering if you had a number for Tonya Grace.'

'Thinking of setting up a game with her? Good idea. Though you'll have to be on your toes. She's getting very good these days. Still, with the handicap you should be OK.' He gave the mobile number. 'Actually, she's coming up to the court this afternoon, after school. Rang this morning and I'd just had a cancellation of the five forty-five court, so she booked it for a lesson with Ned. But now Ned's had to rush off for some family emergency. I've tried to ring Tonya to put her off, but her mobile seems to be off, so I'll have to hang around and give her the lesson myself. Which is a bit of a bugger, because I was hoping to get home early, what with it being a Friday. Still, the hazards of being a tennis pro, eh?'

As soon as the call was over, Jude tried the mobile number George had given her. It was still switched off.

Jude looked across at Carole, her eyes sparkling. 'Tonya's going to be at the court at five forty-five. We can see her there.'

THEY GOT THERE at five thirty to find a very disgruntled George Hazlitt in the pros' office packing up his bag.

'Is Tonya here?' asked Jude urgently.

'Yes. Except now she doesn't want her lesson. I've been waiting around all afternoon for her, she arrives, gets into her kit, then comes back here and asks where Ned is. I say he's gone off for this family emergency and I'm going to stand in for him. Whereupon she bursts into tears and says she doesn't want to have a lesson, after all. Then rushes back to the changing rooms.' He raised his eyes to heaven. 'Teenage girls! I've got a couple at home. I thought I came to work to get away from them.'

'I think I know what might be wrong with Tonya,' said Jude. 'Do you mind if I go and have a word with her?'

George Hazlitt shrugged. 'Do what you like. The door'll lock itself when you go out. Anyway, there'll be a doubles lot coming for the seven o'clock court.' He picked up his bag grumpily and made for the door. 'Have a good weekend,' he called out in a tone that didn't imply he was going to.

Not really aware that Carole had never been on a real tennis court before, Jude led the way down the walkway to the club room. The neighbour looked curiously at the large empty area on their left but made no comment.

Tonya Grace hadn't got as far as the ladies' changing room. She was crumpled on a leather sofa in front of the bare fireplace, sobbing her little heart out.

'Tonya,' said Jude gently, 'I'm Jude. You may have seen me round the court.'

The girl was too distressed to make any attempt to wipe her tears. She just went on crying.

'And this is my friend, Carole. Look, I think I know why you're so upset.'

'I doubt it,' said Tonya Grace, an edge of adolescent petulance showing through her tears.

'You wanted to see Ned, didn't you? To try and sort things out with him.'

'What if I did?'

'Listen, Tonya, I know about you meeting Ned here, you know, when the court's closed.'

'Do you?' The girl looked alarmed now. 'You mustn't tell my grandparents! My *babushka* thinks I've been having sleepovers with friends. She must never find out!'

'Don't worry, she won't,' Jude soothed. 'Look, I want to talk about a night you and Ned were here. I think it was probably the last time. It was the night Reggie Playfair died.'

Again alarm showed through the girl's tears. 'What do you know about it?'

'I know that you didn't do anything wrong, Tonya. But I know you saw things that upset you.'

'How do you know this? You weren't here too, were you?'

'No. I wasn't here. Ned Jackson said you didn't come here that night.'

'Well, he would say that, wouldn't he? He'd say any

lie that got him off the hook. Like today—this "family emergency". I bet he didn't have any family emergency until George said I'd booked a lesson with him.'

Sensing that a new tsunami of tears threatened, Jude said quickly, 'Tell me exactly what happened that night. You'll feel better if you do.'

Tonya Grace looked doubtful, unwilling to share her secrets with strangers.

Carole, who had so far not spoken, said, 'You didn't mind telling Marina Gretchenko about it, did you?'

Bewilderment flooded the girl's face. But the fact that this woman she'd never seen before knew her friend seemed to reassure her, to make her feel she could get the burden of painful recollection off her chest.

'Ned fixed up that we should meet that night. The usual time, the usual place, it was getting to be a habit. I didn't like it. I kept asking why we couldn't go out like normal couples, you know, down the pub, see a movie, have a meal. But he said he'd got this ex-girlfriend who was very jealous. And it was all over between them, but they still both lived in this flat which they were having trouble selling. You know, it really was all over, they had separate rooms and that, but… So I agreed to meet him here.'

'How do you normally travel here?' asked Jude.

'I get the train from Brighton to Clincham. I've got a friend there whose parents let me leave my bike in their garden. So I cycle the last bit.'

'All right, that night…'

'Well, it was like usual. Ned would bring a bottle of wine. We'd have a couple of glasses and then…well…'

'You had sex.'

The girl nodded, embarrassed. 'And then Ned had to go. He always had to go. He never stayed. And that made me feel miserable. It had started to rain outside and that made me feel even more miserable. I was going to sleep over with my friend in Clincham, but it was still going to be a nasty wet bike ride there. Anyway, Ned and I'd had this towel on the sofa…'

'This sofa?'

'Yes. And I wrapped the towel round me and sort of sat on the floor…and I was very miserable.'

'Why?'

'Well, I knew what I was doing with Ned wasn't right. 'Cause I really loved him, but I knew for him it was just sex. So I cried a bit and I finished up the wine that was left in the bottle and…then I must've gone to sleep. Next thing I know there's this woman here in the club room.'

'What time would that have been?'

'I don't know. It was still dark outside. Anyway, she hadn't seen me, because I was lying on the floor in front of the sofa and I sort of froze. And my only thought was that I must get out of the place as soon as I could.'

'Which would have meant going up along the side of the court?' asked Carole. 'The way we came in?'

'Not necessarily,' said Tonya Grace. 'The latch on that window over there's loose. You can get out into the Lockleigh House gardens that way. But obviously I couldn't move till the woman had gone. So I'm lying there, trying not to breathe—or not to make any noise breathing—and I can hear this woman and it sounds like she's changing into a dress or something…not in the changing rooms, right here in the club room…

'Then I hear a car approaching and, like, parking by the court, you know, where people park when they're coming to play here. The woman must have heard it too, because—it's really scary—because she starts giggling, and her giggles sound sort of, like, hysterical. And then she actually talks. I'm sure there's nobody else there, but she says, like, to herself, "If he's so desperate to see Agnes Wardock, then Agnes Wardock he will see." And she giggles again, and it's really horrible, like, you know, she's really lost it, like she's mad.'

'Did she say anything else?' asked Carole.

'Yes. After she's stopped giggling, she says, "It's the idea of a mad woman, but I like mad women's ideas", which is like saying she was mad. And she giggles again.

'Anyway, then the woman goes off into the court. And I thought maybe she was going outside, which would have meant if I waited a bit I could have got out the normal way, because going through the window you end up in a bed of shrubs which aren't very nice if it's been raining.

'So I went and looked out at the court through the crack in the door. The only light was coming from the club room, so I couldn't see much. And then I saw the beam of a torch coming from the main entrance. And whoever was holding the torch went on to the court, and he stood there, pointing the beam of his torch all around, up at the roof of the court at first. I couldn't think why he was doing that.'

Carole and Jude knew why. Agnes Wardock had hanged herself from one of the high walkways up there.

'Then he brought the torch beam down and ran it

along the galleries, starting at the hazard end with the winning gallery. And just as the beam was getting close to the dedans, I saw the woman step forward there. She was wearing a white dress and she had this long blonde hair. And when the torch beam reached her, suddenly there was this horrible noise from the man who was holding it. A sort of gasping, which I keep hearing. I wake up in the night and I've been hearing it in a dream, and it's horrible. Then there's a thump as the man falls on the court and the torch goes flying away. And I hear the voice of the woman say, "Surprise, surprise!" And then she gets hysterical and I can't tell whether she's laughing or crying.'

'So what did you do?' asked Carole.

'I got the hell out of the window in the club room as fast as I could. I grabbed my bike and rushed to the little gate out on to the road. But then, just as I was leaving, I looked back up at Lockleigh House. And there was a light at the window in the front, and there was an old man looking at me.'

Again Tonya Grace started to weep, big, ungainly tears pouring down her cheeks. 'He saw me! He knew that I'd been there!'

THIRTY-THREE

CAROLE OFFERED TO take the traumatized girl back to Brighton, but Tonya said it was all right, she'd cycle to Clincham and get the train from there. The girl was embarrassed now at having spilled out so much emotion to two virtual strangers.

'You say you mentioned what you'd seen on the court that night to Marina Gretchenko?' said Carole.

'Yes, but she wasn't very interested. Busy with all those children, and I think Vladimir was there when I rang.' The way she mentioned his name showed that she was aware of the domestic violence in the Gretchenko household.

'Did you tell anyone else?' asked Carole. 'About what you saw on the court?'

'No. Oh well, yes. Just one person.'

'And who was that?'

'There's this lady who plays tennis here—or at least she used to—and she's been very kind to me since I joined the club and—'

'Felicity Budgen,' Jude surmised.

'Yes.' Tonya was too emotionally drained to wonder how Jude knew that. 'Anyway, I did tell her about what happened, you know, me being here that night.'

'How did she react?'

'Oh. Well. She's a very kind woman, Felicity. She didn't bawl me out about being with Ned. She said

she'd never breathe a word to her husband about it…
though she might talk to George Hazlitt and get him
to have a quiet word with Ned.'

Maybe it was that 'quiet word' Jude had overheard
in Oenone Playfair's conservatory. 'When did you
have this conversation with Felicity, Tonya?'

'Oh, just this afternoon, before I left to come over
here.'

'And did you tell her you were coming here?'

'Yes.'

'And,' asked Carole, 'did you tell her about everything you'd witnessed on the court that night?'

'Yes, I did. Felicity's the only person I can really
talk to. My *babushka*'s always too busy looking after
my grandfather and Marina's caught up in her own
problems. Felicity's always been a good listener.'

Carole and Jude were both wondering how the
chairman's wife would have reacted to what she had
listened to from Tonya that afternoon. That depended,
really, on how much of it she already knew.

'And you told Felicity about the man in the window
at Lockleigh House?'

'Yes, I did.'

Both Carole and Jude were kicking themselves for
not having thought of Cecil Wardock earlier. Tom
Ruthven had described him as 'the eyes and ears of
Lockleigh House'. Insomniac, sitting at his window rereading the books that he had published, he could easily have witnessed all the comings and goings through
the little gate on the night in question. Cecil Wardock
could well be the perfect witness. Why on earth hadn't
they thought to question him before?

'Well, we're on the spot,' Carole concluded. 'We

must go and see him. No time like the present.' She rose from the sofa, then looked down to see why Jude wasn't doing the same.

'What's up?

'There's a call I have to make,' said Jude miserably.

'Ah.' Carole knew who it would be to. 'Shall I wait here for you?'

'If you wouldn't mind.'

THE BIT OF the pros' office with the computers and phones in it was locked, but there was a kind of ante-room whose door was always open. On its walls were lists of match results, members' handicaps and so on. From wooden pegs hung hire rackets and others that the pros had just restrung or repaired. There was also a glass-fronted cabinet, displaying new rackets and a variety of kit items marked with the distinctive Lock-leigh House tennis court insignia. Crossed rackets underneath a fish.

It was from the relative security of this room, with its door closed, that Jude rang Piers.

'Hello, light of my life,' he answered cheerily. 'I'm missing you like mad. When are we going to meet?'

'Piers,' said Jude evenly. 'I've found out more about what happened at the court the night Reggie Playfair died.'

'Oh.'

'Including the fact that you were having an ongoing affair with Felicity Budgen.'

To give him his due, he didn't come back with blustering denials. He just said, in a dull voice, 'I was going to tell you about that, in time. About Felicity. And you have to believe me—that's over.'

How many men over the years, thought Jude, have used that line to a new lover about a previous one. But at that moment she did actually believe Piers.

She heard the main entrance to the court click open, then the sound of footsteps walking softly down past the court towards the club room. Presumably one of the doubles players for the seven o'clock court.

'Listen, that's what caused it all,' Piers protested.

'Caused what?'

'This whole mess. It was me saying to Felicity that things were over between us that set the whole thing in motion.'

'And when did you tell her?'

'Obviously—' he sounded exasperated now— 'I told her when I met you.'

'So it had been going on up until three weeks ago.'

'To some extent. We didn't see each other very often. I think the relationship was on the way out before I met you. But, anyway, Felicity got into a very bad state when I told her. And somehow once it was over, she seemed to get even more worried that Don would get to hear about it.'

'And you understood what Reggie said about "secrets" during the Sec's Cup to be a threat that he was going to spill the beans?'

'I didn't hear it that way. But Felicity did. She was desperately worried that Reggie was going to tell Don. She said we had to silence him.'

'And so between you you came up with a rather elaborate plan to eliminate Reggie?'

'No.'

'And fortunately you had on hand a conveniently loopy estranged wife whom you could persuade to—'

'I didn't persuade—'

'You know you've committed murder, Piers,' said Jude solemnly.

'No, I haven't. You've got it all wrong.'

'I don't think so. You set up Jonquil to kill Reggie.'

Suddenly Jude heard Carole's voice calling from the far end of the court. 'Excuse me—can I help you?' Then there was a sound of footsteps hurrying past and the clicks of the court door opening and closing.

And through all this, Jude could hear Piers Targett saying, 'It wasn't me who set Jonquil up. It was Felicity!'

Then Carole was at the door. 'There's this strange woman just come in, looking for Tonya. She said she was going to kill her!'

Jude looked out of the office window. Immaculately dressed as ever in a pale grey trouser suit, Felicity Budgen was walking sedately across the garden toward Lockleigh House.

In one hand was a handbag.

In the other was the metal crank used for adjusting the height of the real tennis net.

THIRTY-FOUR

BY THE TIME Carole and Jude got outside the court Felicity Budgen had disappeared inside Lockleigh House Nursing Home for the Elderly. They didn't have to talk, they both knew where she was going. She had failed to kill one witness of her crimes, Tonya Grace. She was hoping to have better luck with Cecil Wardock.

The woman on reception in the great hall of Lockleigh House called after them as they rushed to the stairs. 'Hey, you can't go up there!' But Carole and Jude took no notice.

They dashed along the landing and burst in through Cecil Wardock's door.

The tableau that greeted them there might have been comical in different circumstances. Cecil Wardock, his chair facing away from the window on this occasion, was looking up at them in bewilderment. Behind him, in front of his precious bookshelves, stood the elegant Felicity Budgen, the crank handle in her hand upraised to be brought down on his thin skull.

At Carole and Jude's entrance she froze, then slowly lowered her arm.

'Well,' said Cecil Wardock, 'aren't I the popular one this afternoon? Delighted to see you again, ladies. To what do I owe this pleasure?'

'Oh,' said Jude, inadequately in the circumstances, 'we were just passing.'

'Well, what a nice surprise. Felicity was just getting a book down for me.'

'Yes,' she agreed. Placing the crank handle on a table, she reached into the bookshelves. '*Katherine Mansfield: A Biography*—that was the one, wasn't it, Cecil?'

'Yes, thank you, Felicity dear. Very stylishly written. Author's sadly dead now.' He stroked the book lovingly. 'Beautiful artefact, isn't it? Any book is, but this one more than most.' He let out a dry chuckle. 'Can't see anything as beautiful as this ever being replaced by a Kindle, can you?'

Once again Cecil Wardock stroked his book, then opened it at the title page. 'So much still to read,' he said. 'So much still to read.'

THIRTY-FIVE

AFTER HER MURDER threat and her attempt to commit the real thing, Felicity Budgen had become remarkably docile. She made no demur about accompanying Jude and Carole back to the tennis court's club room and, once there, agreed that a strong cup of coffee might be a good idea.

While the coffee was brewing, the four young men about to play the seven o'clock doubles emerged from the men's changing room. They recognized Felicity, who greeted them with effortless politeness and said she looked forward to encountering them for a game sometime soon. The rest of their conversation was played out against a background of cheery shouts from the court and the sound of balls thundering on penthouses.

'I think we know most of what happened,' said Jude.

'Did Piers tell you?'

'Not really. He told me some things, but I'm not sure that they were all true.'

'He would have been lying to protect me,' said Felicity. 'He's a very honourable man, Piers.'

Jude was not sure that she would have fully endorsed that description, but this wasn't the time to take issue.

'Look, I do want to say,' the former ambassador's

wife went on, 'that I hold nothing against you, Jude. Yes, I still love Piers, but I've known for a long time that I was not in a position to offer him the full-time support and attention that he needs. Whereas with you I think there's probably a strong chance he'll be able to find that.'

Though that was another statement from which Jude's opinion might now diverge, again she said nothing.

'But I can't deny that Piers' announcement that he'd fallen in love with you was a profound shock to me. I don't think I'd ever realized how much his presence in my life meant. Because I knew he could never be central to my everyday doings, perhaps I underestimated his importance. The knowledge that Piers was somewhere there in the background gave me the strength to get through times that were fairly tough for me emotionally. And when he said it was over between us…I think I went a little mad.'

There was a silence. For a moment Jude felt tempted to apologize for the unwitting disruption she had caused to Felicity Budgen's life, but she curbed the instinct.

'When did you decide you'd have to kill Reggie Playfair?' asked Carole, practical as ever.

'Well, it was strange…' Felicity's manner, as it had been from the start of their conversation, remained politely matter-of-fact, as if she were hosting a charity tea party rather than confessing to a murder. 'I suppose I had been suppressing it all the years since I started the relationship with Piers Targett but once it ended, all the guilt and paranoia I should perhaps have felt earlier came flooding in. I suppose, standing back from the situation for the first time, I realized the size of the risk I had been taking…you know, the threat I had been posing to my marriage to Donald.

'And I became more than ever afraid that the news of what had happened might get out from someone who knew about it.'

'Someone like Reggie Playfair?' Carole suggested.

'Yes.'

'You had some history with Reggie, didn't you?' asked Jude.

'How do you mean?'

'Well, the speed with which he answered your texted summons to come down here to the court. Your message also included the words "like we used to do".'

'Ah. I understand. Yes, Reggie and I had met on the court a few times—and at night because he didn't want Oenone to know. Those meetings also started around that period when I had abandoned my youngest to the joys of Eton. Reggie was in a bad way around that time too.'

'Oh?'

'He never really got over the grief of losing their baby. Reggie wasn't the sort to share emotional pressures—I don't think he and Oenone ever talked about what happened—but somehow he seemed able to discuss it with me. Donald and I also lost a baby— a late miscarriage before we had Harry—so maybe Reggie found me empathetic about his suffering.

'Also he had this strange fantasy about seeing the ghost of his dead daughter. And I had experienced similar hallucinations about the child Donald and I lost. So Reggie and I talked about that too.'

'Do you believe in ghosts?' asked Jude gently.

'I don't see why they shouldn't exist. Everything else in life is so untidy and unfinished. It doesn't seem to me totally beyond the realms of possibility that some part of a dead person lingers in the world they are meant to have left behind.'

'So you knew the story about Agnes Wardock's ghost?'

'Of course. Cecil Wardock told me.' She spoke of him without any reference to—or perhaps memory of—the fact that she had only recently been trying to brain him with a blunt instrument.

There was a silence. Then Carole asked, 'So how many times did you and Reggie meet here?'

'Oh, maybe a dozen over the years.'

'And there wasn't any sexual element in your relationship?'

'On my side, certainly not. I'd known Reggie for years. Very fond of him, but I'd never felt about him in that way. Besides, I do have standards. Oenone's a friend. I would never do that to a friend.'

Jude couldn't help saying, 'It didn't stop you with Piers.'

'The situation was entirely different. Jonquil had effectively walked out of that marriage. And she continually put Piers through the kind of purgatory that… Well, let's just say, I didn't feel any guilt about Jonquil.'

'Do you think,' asked Jude, 'that Jonquil ever had an affair with Reggie?'

'No,' Felicity Budgen replied firmly. 'He wouldn't have done that. I think even with me, though it was a sexual thing he felt for me, he wouldn't have…I mean, if I'd been more accommodating, if I'd offered him any encouragement... No, he was devoted to Oenone.'

Carole picked up the interrogation. 'You said there was no sexual element on your side between you and Reggie. But for him you've just said it was "a sexual thing".'

Felicity Budgen grimaced. 'Yes, sexual at some level, but...not real. I think in some strange way he did live in hope of my changing my mind about him at some point. But no, he was just infatuated with me.' She spoke as if infatuation was a tiresome inconvenience that she had had to go through more than once during her life. Maybe it was an occupational hazard for women who went through life being as beautiful as Felicity Budgen, thought Carole.

'And that infatuation continued right through to his death,' she suggested.

'Maybe. It wasn't something I encouraged.'

'I think you knew it was still there, though,' Carole persisted. 'You knew he would immediately respond when you texted him to join you here "like we used to".'

'Perhaps.'

'So,' said Jude, 'could we go back to what Reggie said after he'd had that fall at the Sec's Cup?'

'Very well.'

'You thought he was threatening to spill the beans?'

'Exactly. And it was at that moment that I knew I had to kill him.'

'But why,' asked Carole, 'did you set up that elaborate way of doing it?'

'Well, would you believe that in my previous life I have very rarely been faced with the challenge of how to kill someone.' A half-smile played around Felicity Budgen's lips as she said this. 'I have many competences—most of which have been necessary to my life as the wife of an ambassador—but murder is not one of them.

'Also I was looking for a method that could look like an accident, and I knew from Oenone about Reggie's history of heart trouble. As I say, he'd talked to me about his interest in ghosts…we'd even discussed the story of Agnes Wardock. And then when I mentioned the idea of dressing up as a ghost to Jonquil, she absolutely leapt on the idea.'

'Oh, it was you who mentioned it to Jonquil?' said Jude, relieved that at least one thing Piers had told her hadn't been a lie.

'Yes.'

'But you didn't tell her the aim of the exercise was to kill Reggie?' asked Carole.

'Good heavens, no. I just said it was a bit of fun. You know, Reggie Playfair had been going on about the supposed ghost of Lockleigh House tennis court… wouldn't it be jolly to set up a special viewing for him? Jonquil thought it was a hysterically funny idea.'

Felicity Budgen smoothed a delicate hand across her fine brow. 'I think I've been in a rather strange state recently. There are things I've done that I can't really believe. I mean, what I've just said I did to Reggie… was that really me? Did I do that?'

'I don't think there's much doubt about it,' said Carole firmly. 'Within the last hour you were also about to brain Cecil Wardock—and you threatened to kill Tonya Grace.'

'Yes. Yes.' She nodded as if reminding herself. 'It all seemed terribly important then. It doesn't seem so important now. I must have had a lot bottled up inside me. I think the reason that murder appealed was that I was *so sick of being nice to people!*' The venom with which these last words were spat out seemed to surprise the speaker as much as anyone. 'Yes,' she repeated more calmly, 'I have been in a very strange state.'

'You're not well,' said Jude. 'You need help, psychiatric help.'

'What, a one-way ticket to the funny farm? Donald wouldn't like that. Donald doesn't believe in mental illness. He thinks all problems can be sorted out by a strong drink or a game of golf.'

'Then Donald needs to change his ideas,' said Jude. 'Felicity, you definitely need help.'

'Yes,' she said, almost gratefully. 'I think I do.'

SIR DONALD BUDGEN was extremely put out when Carole Seddon rang and said he should come and collect his wife from Lockleigh House tennis court.

'She's got her car there,' he protested. 'And I've got a dodgy back.'

'She's in no state to drive.'

'Then she can organize a bloody taxi.'

'You should come and collect her,' insisted Carole. With bad grace he gave in.

Carole, Jude and Lady Budgen didn't talk a lot more. They just sat together in the club room, in a silence that seemed perversely companionable. When the doubles players came off the court at eight fifteen, Felicity joshed with them about their game and agreed it was a pity that nobody had taken the last booking of the day. Given the small number of real tennis courts in the country, it was a shame that any time-slot should go unfilled.

The doubles players had changed and gone by the time Sir Donald Budgen arrived. 'What is this non-sense, Felicity?' he demanded. 'You "in a state"—what on earth does that mean?'

'She's had a shock,' said Jude gently. 'She's not well.'

The ex-ambassador looked at his wife and something he saw in her face seemed to unnerve him. 'What's all this about, darling?' he asked in a milder tone. 'You can't be ill, can you, old sausage?'

And the idea that she might be really frightened him.

THIRTY-SIX

CAROLE AND JUDE might have known that Cecil Wardock would have been very neat in his record keeping. He had always been an efficient man in his professional life and he brought that efficiency to the log he kept of nocturnal comings and goings at Lockleigh House.

They had gone straight back to the nursing home after the Budgens had left. In the interim since they had last been there the residents had had their evening meal. The woman on reception was of the view that it was rather late for another visit, and rang through to check Cecil Wardock's own views on the subject. It was only with his enthusiastic say-so that Carole and Jude were allowed upstairs.

Jude felt pretty stupid as they approached the old man's room. She should have made the connection. After all, hadn't Tom Ruthven described his distant relative as 'the eyes and ears of Lockleigh House'? Jude herself had seen from his window how perfectly placed an insomniac Cecil Wardock would be to witness the arrivals and departures at the main gates of Lockleigh House. If they'd asked him earlier, they could have saved themselves a great deal of trouble.

'It was when I first arrived here at Lockleigh House that I started it,' the old man explained. 'I was not in a very good state of mind at the time. My wife had not died long before and the step of moving into a nursing home seemed to me a huge one, an acknowledgement that, to all intents and purposes, my life was over. My sleeping patterns were completely destroyed and it was then that I embarked on my career as a nocturnal chronicler.

'I was also at that time suspicious that certain of my possessions seemed to have disappeared in the course of the move from my own house. So initially my vigilance was directed towards the tracking down of thieves. In retrospect, I think that too was just a symptom of my general malaise. I don't probably think anyone was stealing from me. It was my overriding misery that made me paranoid.

'Anyway, as I settled down into the routine of my new life I came to terms with accepting that some things had gone forever, and I got into the pattern of reading—' he gestured to the bookshelves— 'which has provided me with such intellectual sustenance.' He chuckled. 'Do you know, I have only three more books to read before I reach the end of my entire publishing *oeuvre*.'

'And then of course you start again at the beginning,' said Jude.

'That indeed has been my invariable practice, so there is no reason why the cycle should not be repeated one more time.' But as he spoke the old man sounded distant and thoughtful.

Then with an effort he brought his concentration back to the present. 'I did not, however, break the habit of making entries in my log.' He tapped a black-covered notebook on the table beside him. 'An old man's idle diversion, you may say, but I derived some harmless satisfaction from the record keeping.'

'You only did it during the night time?' asked Carole.

'Oh yes, just while I was wakeful in the small hours. Frequently there was nothing to record. Weeks would go by with no after-hours visitors to the tennis court.'

'And you never mentioned to anyone at the tennis court what you were doing?'

Cecil Wardock spread his thin hands wide in a gesture of ignorance. 'I don't know anyone at the tennis court. Well, except for Tom Ruthven and I certainly didn't mention what I was doing to him. No, I don't know the names of any of them...though I did make up names for some of the ones who appeared regularly.'

'Oh?'

'There's a young man—I think he might work at the court, he's certainly around there a lot...and he's certainly around a lot after hours...him I nicknamed "Lothario".'

'Very appositely,' said Jude.

'As I say, I don't know him, but I can't think of another reason for his regular late-night visits to the court. Particularly because his arrival is always quickly followed by that of a young lady.'

'Always the same young lady?'

'Over the years there have been a few different ones. But recently it has been the same girl, the one with the bicycle. She I nickname "The Damsel in Distress".'

'Why?' asked Carole.

'Because she always looks a little frightened, as

if she doesn't really think she should be doing what she is doing.'

'Your nicknames are very accurate,' observed Jude.

'Any other regulars there?' asked Carole.

'There's an older couple. I don't know whether they meet at the court for the same purpose as "Lothario", but appearances make that unlikely, in her case at least. She is a very *soignée* lady, who looks as though in her mouth the temperature of butter would not change by the tiniest subdivision of a degree. My nickname for her is "Lady Muck".'

'And who does she meet?' asked Jude miserably.

'A tall man with long white hair. Whatever time of night, he always strolls through the gate as if he hasn't a care in the world. I call him "The Smoothie".'

Jude nodded, avoiding her neighbour's eye.

Carole didn't notice; she was too concerned with getting Cecil Wardock on to one specific date. 'Could we go back to the night of the Tuesday before last…?'

The old publisher flicked back through the pages of his black notebook. 'Ah, that was quite a night, wasn't it? Like Piccadilly Circus it was here then.'

Cecil Wardock showed them the relevant page of fountain-pen-written entries and arranged with the girl at reception to have a photocopy made of it. When they were back at Woodside Cottage, over a bottle of Chilean Chardonnay, Carole and Jude once again read through the neat italic record of that night's events.

10.17 p.m.	*The Damsel in Distress arrives (with her bicycle).*
10.32 p.m.	*Lothario arrives.*
11.08 p.m.	*Lothario leaves.*

2.33 a.m.	*A tall (unknown) woman with long blonde hair arrives.*
3.19 a.m.	*A man driving a BMW enters through the main gates (for which he has an electronic entry card).*
3.47 a.m.	*The Damsel in Distress leaves hurriedly on her bicycle.*
4.41 a.m.	*The Smoothie arrives.*
4.53 a.m.	*The Smoothie leaves with the (unknown) tall blonde woman.*
7.22 a.m.	*The Smoothie returns through the main gates in his red E-Type Jaguar.*
7.29 a.m.	*A plump, blonde-haired lady arrives.*

THERE WASN'T MUCH there that needed explanation. When he'd received the summons from Felicity Budgen, Reggie Playfair must have taken a taxi from London to Pulborough to pick up his car. Otherwise Carole and Jude could piece together the complete sequence of events.

'Funny,' said Carole. 'The one person who wasn't actually at the court that night was the person who committed the crime. Felicity Budgen. She set the whole thing in motion.'

Jude nodded listlessly.

The nearest approximation Carole Seddon could do to a teasing grin appeared on her face. '"A plump, blonde-haired lady". Hm. I wonder what nickname Cecil Wardock would have given you if he had the chance…?'

'"The Sucker"?' suggested Jude.

THIRTY-SEVEN

OF COURSE THE police never heard about Reggie Play-fair's murder. Just as well, probably. As Carole had observed, it would have been a difficult case to bring to court.

And, except for a select few, none of the members of Lockleigh House tennis court had ever thought it was murder, anyway. Reggie Playfair had had a heart attack. 'Poor old bugger.' Only Jonty Westmacott still occasionally muttered darkly about 'foul play'.

So there was never any question of Felicity Budgen being prosecuted. But her husband did finally, un-willingly admit that she needed psychiatric help. She spent four months in an exclusive private clinic. The Budgens' acquaintances were told this was for 'a little gynie op', which was acceptable in a way that treatment for mental illness wouldn't have been.

Then Lady Budgen returned to The Old Manor and to her extensive good works. She went back to doing what she'd done all her adult life—being frightfully loyal to Sir Donald while smiling at a lot of people for whom she had no feelings at all. And their marriage was as happy as it had ever been.

Cecil Wardock died within a few weeks of his last meeting with Carole and Jude. He had just finished rereading the final, bottom-right book on his shelves, but never got round to starting the cycle again at the top left. Which he would have regarded as a very neat, satisfactory death.

The activities of Lockleigh House tennis court continued much as before. George Hazlitt still tried to recruit new members who would broaden the club's demographic. Ned Jackson received a talking-to so severe that he never again used the court premises for anything other than real tennis. In time he married his long-term girlfriend, Kelly, and got his handicap down to plus three. Then he lost interest in real tennis at the professional level and took a job in marketing.

And at eleven o'clock every Wednesday morning, the Old Boys' doubles was played by Wally Edgington-Bewley, Tom Ruthven, Rod Farrar and Jonty Westmacott, the last-named of whom always had some physical reason to explain the age-related decline in his real tennis skills.

Tonya Grace's tennis, by contrast, improved by leaps and bounds. So much so that she was awarded the annual Potter Plate for Most Improved Player. She also found a boyfriend who was nice to her.

And nobody ever did more than look at the pictures of Wally Edgington-Bewley's *magnum opus, Courts in the Act*.

Oenone Playfair remained as bright-eyed and cheery as ever when she was in company, and nobody ever knew what pain she suffered when she was on her own. She was, however, deeply relieved when Carole and Jude reassured her that her husband had never had an affair with any female member of the club.

Carole Seddon had her own moment of triumph when she rang Susan Holland and was able to give the desolate mother her daughter's phone number. At first, meetings between the two were difficult because of the paranoid jealousy of Vladimir Gretchenko, but very slowly the situation improved. Marina made contact with the local authorities about domestic violence, and even managed to get her husband along to some joint counselling meetings. The marriage was never going to be ideal, but maybe some progress could be achieved.

And Susan Holland did get to know the four grandchildren of whose existence she had been unaware.

The situation for Marina's father was less happy. The story of his paying the daughter of his first marriage to keep out of his life and letting her mother believe her to be dead was leaked to the Brighton press and spread from there to the nationals. There was no secret about who had done the leaking. Susan Holland's fury, when she knew that her ex-husband had been responsible for her eight years of anguish, knew no bounds. Destroying his career was the very least she could do by way of revenge.

Very quickly the name of Iain Holland was no longer being mentioned by the 'high-ups in the Conservative Party' and his name vanished from their shortlists. The residents of his ward also took their first opportunity to elect another councillor in his place. And his new squeaky-clean marriage broke up.

None of which, in Carole Seddon's view, was sufficient punishment for what he had done.

She, however, was much cheered by the return of her grandchild from Anaheim, Orange County, California. Lily, with her parents, came down to Fethering to see her grandmother on the very first weekend they were back. Carole thought Lily looked absolutely beautiful (though she did secretly feel that the souvenir cuddly Donald Duck they had bought for her in Disneyland was 'rather vulgar').

And Fedborough's Lady in the Lake remained forever unidentified.

Returning to normal life in Fethering was harder for Jude. She and Piers Targett did see each other a few more times, but his lies—or perhaps, more accurately, the truths he had chosen not to reveal—lay between them. She did however believe him when he assured her he had had no idea that Felicity Budgen had set up Jonquil's charade as the ghost of Agnes Wardock.

Though Piers protested that he loved her, Jude could not forget the fact that his love for her had precipitated the events that led to Reggie Playfair's death. She also knew that he would never be entirely free of the capricious demands of the woman who was still his wife, Jonquil.

Jude loved Piers too, but increasingly she knew that their futures did not lie together. She was unlikely ever to go back on to a real tennis court. On the plus side, however, she would never have to face that awkward moment when she had to introduce Piers Targett to Carole Seddon.

So Jude did the inevitable thing and told Piers that their relationship was at an end.

But it hurt.

* * * * *